After the Voyage

An Irish American Story

Brenda Murphy

BRICKTOP
2016

This book is a work of fiction. References to historical events, real people, or real locales are used fictitiously.

Bricktop Hill Books
PO Box 1016
Willimantic, CT 06226

Library of Congress Control Number: 2016903531

ISBN 10: 0-9973669-0-7

ISBN 13: 978-0-9973669-0-7

For Edna McGlynn and Priscilla McGlynn Murphy

Contents

Part One: *Maggie Qualter Terrett* 9

Part Two: *Richard Terrett* 53

Part Three: *Tom Terrett* 123

Part Four: *Josie Terrett* 203

Part Five: *Mary Terrett McGlynn* 255

Afterword 304

Acknowledgements 307

Further Reading 308

Maggie Qualter Terrett, about 1923

Part One

Maggie Qualter Terrett

Chapter 1

1881

Maggie Qualter picked up the mail from the floor under the door slot and went out to check the front stoop to see if it would need sweeping before she went upstairs. She looked down the street to the capitol building. It was a windy day, and the dust from the line of horses and buggies and omnibuses that stretched in front of her filled the air. But the stoop looked all right, for now. She stood for a moment with the mail in her hands, a neat, compact little figure in her dark blue dress and gingham apron, just enjoying the cool breeze on her flushed face and looking at the chaotic Albany scene in front of her.

It had been a busy morning. With all the dust, it had taken longer than usual to sweep the steps and entry hall, and she'd had to hurry with the dining room and parlor before the Reeds' breakfast. Then Mrs. Reed had told her to get the lighter blankets from the cedar chests in the attic before she made up the bedrooms. While she was washing the breakfast dishes, Jane kept needing her help with this or that preparation for luncheon. Then, because of the dust that was tracked in, she'd had to roll up the hall rugs and take them out back to beat them in addition to the regular morning jobs.

Now it was nearly noon, and time to go up to her room to wash and change into her afternoon uniform so she could answer the door and serve the tea for the afternoon callers.

Giving a little sigh, she went back inside and was quickly sorting through the mail when she had a start. The sight of her sister Bridget's handwriting gave her a moment of pleasure, then an anxious feeling. She placed the Reeds' mail in the basket on the hall table, and ran up the back stairs to her room on the third floor to read the letter.

"Dear Maggie,

I hope you are well. Pat and little Martin are in the pink. I'm feeling a little better now that spring is here, and I get outside for a while each day."

Maggie let out a quick breath. It was not a turn for the worse.

"I'm writing with some good news from Pat. He's found a suitor for you, he thinks."

Maggie laughed. A suitor indeed. What was this Pat Nolan had stirred up for her now? The sisters had been joking for a few months about finding suitors for each of them now that Nelly was here and there was no need to bring anyone else over from Athenry. Kate had surprised them all last year by taking up with John Kirker, a young man in his early thirties, when Kate was nearing forty, but Maggie had to admit that now they were married, they seemed very happy together.

"The young man is Richard Terrett. Pat knows him from the Hibernians in Woburn. He's from Portarlington in Queen's County. He's a widower with two wee children, one just a year old. A very steady man with a good job at Squire's tannery. He even owns a house. And Pat says to tell you he's never seen him take a drink."

Maggie smiled. Pat's nod to her teetotaling ways.

"He thinks he's about thirty years of age, and he's a handsome man to look at."

Maggie doubted Pat's judgment on that. But it was an intriguing thought. If Kate could find a husband, and one she was devoted to, why couldn't she?

"We would like to have you come and visit soon so you can meet him. Pat has mentioned you to him, and he would like it too."

Maggie could only imagine what Pat had told Richard Terrett about her.

"So write and say when you can come, Maggie, for I think this is a good chance for you, and I am lonesome to see you.

Your loving sister,

Bridget Nolan."

Maggie brought the letter with her when she went to meet her other sisters at Kate's house on Sunday. They had a good laugh over the idea of Pat Nolan picking out a husband for Maggie. But as they talked it over, the sisters urged her to meet him. What did she have to lose? When you're in your late thirties, suitors do not grow on trees. If she wanted to marry at all, she would have to do it soon.

On Monday morning, Maggie found Mrs. Reed in the parlor checking the responses to the invitations for her Friday tea. She stood quietly, her hands folded in front of her, until her mistress looked up. "Yes, Margaret."

"I've collected the wash to send out, Ma'am. Did you have anything special you want to have done?"

"No, Margaret, just the linens and whatever was in the clothes hampers."

"Yes, Ma'am." She waited.

Mrs. Reed looked up. "Was there something else, Margaret?"

"Yes, Ma'am. I've had a letter from my sister Bridget in Woburn, near Boston. She's not well, you know, and she asked me to come and visit her. I was wondering if I could swap my Thursday for Saturday. That way I could go down on the afternoon train and come back Sunday evening."

Maggie could see that Mrs. Reed's first instinct was, as always, to say no to the help. But she thought better of it, realizing that she could use Maggie on Thursday, getting ready for the tea. "All right, Margaret. But you must realize this is a special favor. I can't run the household properly if I can't count on the servants to be here on schedule. And you'll have to be all finished cleaning up after the tea on Friday night."

"Yes, Ma'am. Thank you very much, Ma'am. I appreciate it."

"You're welcome, Margaret. I hope your sister is not too ill?"

"No, Ma'am, the doctor says it's chronic bronchitis." She knew better than to say the word consumption. "We have to watch to make sure it doesn't turn into pneumonia. I'll go down and do the housework and make her some nourishing food."

"That's good, Margaret. You're a good sister. If there's any food left after the tea you can take some of it to her."

"Thank you, Ma'am." The way Mrs. Reed calculated to the penny, she knew there would be precious little food left after the tea.

Maggie made sure her letter to Bridget got into the morning mail. Then she spent the rest of the week wondering what Richard Terrett would think of her and devising ways to smarten up her plain blue Sunday dress, which was not the newest. "At least he won't think I waste all my money on clothes," she decided.

When the train pulled into Woburn station, there was Pat Nolan waiting for her, with a grin on his freckled face as wide as a barn door. "Hello, Pat," she said.

"Hello, Maggie. You're looking well after your trip." He took her little bag and they began walking toward the Nolans' flat.

"Are you ready to meet your suitor, then?"

"Slow down, Pat Nolan. He's hardly my suitor. I've not even met the man."

"Oh, but he will be. He's that eager to meet you."

"Go on with you, Pat. What did you tell him about me?"

"Nothing but the truth, Maggie. I told him you were a kind and a generous woman who loves children and would take good care of his babies for him. I also told him you were a fine looking woman, which you are, and that you never walk when you can run."

"Oh, whisht, now. How old did you say I am?"

"I told him you were about thirty years of age, about the same as him."

"But Pat, I'm six or seven years older than that, at least."

"You look younger. Anyone would take you for a girl in her twenties."

"But if we go on with this, he's bound to find out."

"Well, if he does, what does it matter, really?"

"He might want a bigger family, for one thing."

"And so. Here's your sister Kate nearly forty years of age and having her first child."

"Yes, and probably her last, but John knows it. It isn't fair to lie."

"Well, I've told him now, so just go along with it unless he asks. If he asks, you'll know it's a point with him, but if not, he probably doesn't care."

When they all met for Mass at St. Charles's the next day, Bridget had to admit to herself that Pat was right about Richard Terrett. He was a handsome man, with a dignified, powerful bearing, regular features, dark brown hair, and strikingly deep blue eyes. He was tall for her, but then practically any man would be. She felt small and plain beside him, and tried to make up for it with laughter and lively chatter on the walk home. She showed off her skill at cookery by making a nice Sunday dinner for them all. Richard stayed for the afternoon, and they talked of their families and the old times in Ireland. Pat and Richard talked a bit about the Hibernians and the tanneries. She could see that he was a figure among the men, and his view of things mattered.

When it was time for her to go, Richard escorted her to the train station, and they talked more personally. He told her about the children and his hopes for making a good life for them. She thought he was a bit stiff at first. But she soon saw that he was just shy with her, and a little embarrassed by his position as a potential suitor. He was well-spoken and polite, and a straightforward, honest person. And he was devoted to his children, Tom and Josie. Anyone could see that.

Two weeks later, Maggie told Mrs. Reed that the situation in Woburn was urgent, and she needed to go and attend to things again.

"Well, if you feel you must, Margaret. If your sister is greatly in need of you. But you can't make this a habit.

Family is important, but you have a responsibility to our family too. Your job must be your first priority."

"Yes, Ma'am. I understand. It's just that this is a critical time. It looks like things will be much better if we come through this week all right."

Maggie made dinner for the family and Richard again this time, but afterwards he took her over to his sister Ann's house, next door to his own, where they had tea with Ann's and his sister Margaret's families, and Maggie finally got to meet the children. She got on well with three-year-old Tom, and baby Josie took to her. She was a dear little thing with big eyes in a cheerful round face, and Maggie felt motherly to her immediately. Richard showed her the house, a two-story with seven rooms, which was nearly brand new.

"The house is lovely, Richard. Your wife knew how to make a place comfortable," she told him. The house indeed showed that a talented hand had been at work creating quilts and braided rugs and covers for the furniture, but Maggie's expert eye could see that it needed attention, especially a good cleaning. Of course that was understandable with only a man to keep house. "Do you own the house? It belongs to you?"

He colored a bit. "Well, not exactly, Margaret. I have a mortgage on it. But I'm making the payments regularly. It will be mine when the principal payment is made, ten years from now."

"And all this land. Is that your cowshed on top of the little hill?"

"Yes, we used to have a cow, but I sold it. It got to be too much for me." He looked at the ground and cleared his throat. "The land between the houses is partly mine and partly the Connollys'. We had a garden in the past. I just didn't get to it this year." He looked down again, and she felt a pang of sympathy for him. Pat had said that he was very broken up when his wife died.

When they got back to the Connollys', Maggie asked Ann about the garden, which had been shared between the two houses. "There seems to be plenty of room for a cow and some chickens as well," said Maggie.

"Yes," said Ann. "I've never had time for them myself. I'm the nurse-midwife of the neighborhood, as well as taking care of my own brood here. Richard's wife Kate was a farmer's daughter, and she kept a cow in the shed there and sold milk to the neighbors. They were planning to build a chicken coop, but they hadn't gotten to it yet."

"Ah, yes, I can see it's a perfect place for it. It's just what I would have done."

Richard never made any reference to Maggie's age, or to any desire for a big family, so she followed Pat's advice and did not bring the subject up. She went back to Albany thinking that she might just marry this man. He was a good man by all accounts, and a dependable one with money. And he didn't drink. She knew she could make a comfortable home for the family and do the things she had loved growing up on the farm, gardening and taking care of the animals, as well as the housekeeping she had learned in the big houses.

After conferring with the sisters in Albany, Maggie wrote to Richard, inviting him to come to tea at her sister Kate's house in Albany, and two weeks later, he spent a Sunday afternoon with Kate and John and the other Albany sisters, Mary and Annie and little Mary and Nelly. He was a bit stiff again in the company of her family, but by now Maggie understood it was his shyness, and thought it endearing. Even on their best company behavior, her family could be overwhelming for anyone, as John would often tell them. He at least was happy for a male ally. After Richard left to catch the train, the sisters agreed he was handsome and well-spoken, and Nelly said she knew they could warm him up a bit once he was part of the family. With all his good qualities, it would be foolish to turn down a proposal if it came.

Two weeks later, Richard came to Albany and met Maggie for Mass. Afterwards, he took her to eat dinner in a fancy restaurant, something she had done only three times before in her life. They had a nice, quiet conversation together, and as they walked in the park afterwards, he asked her if she would consider being his wife. In his earnest way, he explained what he hoped their life could be together, and laid out his plans for the future.

"I know it's a lot to ask, Margaret, to take on two little children, but I'd like to think I'm offering you my family as well as my home. I could see you took to Tom and Josie, and they to you."

"Oh, yes," she said. "They're dear little ones that I could care for as my own, and I think I can make a home for you all."

When Maggie gave her notice to the Reeds, Mrs. Reed was none too happy. She told Maggie she had thought she was not being honest about her reasons for going to Woburn. Maggie didn't answer. It was true. But, considering Mrs. Reed's behavior to her over the years, she didn't care. She was grateful when Mr. Reed quietly gave her ten dollars as a wedding gift, and she used it to make a dress.

Maggie and Richard were married at St. Charles's in Woburn on September 18, 1881. They chose a Thursday so that her Albany sisters could come, except for Kate, who was expecting her baby soon. They were able to get the Thursday morning off as well as the afternoon, so they came down on Wednesday evening and stayed with Bridget and Pat.

The subject of Maggie's age still had not come up when it came time to fill out the marriage certificate. Since she did not know her actual birth date, she thought she might as well keep to Pat Nolan's plan. She gave her birth year as 1851, making her a year younger than Richard. She knew this was much too late, for it would have made her nineteen years of age when she came to America, and she knew she had been well into her twenties. But as Pat had said, what did it matter really?

After a nice wedding breakfast for the family, the sisters caught the train back to Albany. Ann took care of the children while Maggie and Richard took the train to Boston, where they spent their first three days together, and then they went home to his house at 19 Arlington Street near the southeast edge of Woburn.

The three days were an eye-opener for Maggie. She was amazed at the things Richard knew, like just how big the Public Gardens were, and what the Common had been used for through the years. He knew who the architects were for many of the buildings, and when they were built. He knew the different historical sites of the American Revolution, and where Benjamin Franklin's father was buried. It wasn't as if he had stored up these things to impress her. All of it seemed to just be in his head and come out when it was wanted. When they visited the Natural History Museum in the Back Bay, he seemed to know a little something about each of the exhibits. He worked at entertaining her, and she appreciated it. Never in her life had she been the focus of such attention. Each time they stopped for something to eat, he consulted her taste and tried to get her something she considered a treat. She had a wonderful time, and it rubbed off on him too. It was already obvious to her that she was going to have to be the source of fun and good cheer in the family, but she thought she had enough for all of them.

The only disappointment for Maggie on their wedding trip was sex. It was not that she had unrealistic expectations. She was a farm girl who had grown up in a one-room cabin. She knew perfectly well how sex worked, and she had sometimes heard the stifled sounds of her parents' pleasure from the bed in the corner of the room. She didn't expect the kind of thing that Kate described between her and John. They were in love, as they would tell you. But she had hoped for a special joy, something theirs alone that they could share. So far, they hadn't found it. Richard was considerate and patient, but he seemed distant, only partly there. Maggie was beginning to get used to his body, and she liked it, but she wasn't sure he felt the same way about hers. Maybe it was too soon after his first wife's death. She hoped that love would grow with their marriage.

When they got back to Woburn, the good beginning they had made was threatened by something Maggie had never thought of. Richard asked if she would like to deposit her savings in the Winchester Savings Bank in her new name. When she told him she hadn't enough to bother with, only her last wages and what was left of the ten dollars from Mr. Reed, he looked surprised. "But I thought you had a nest egg. Didn't you give Bridget and Pat the fare for their trip to Ireland?"

She tried to carry it off lightly, while explaining the truth to him. "That's why I've only a few dollars. Bridget and Pat have gone twice to Ireland. We thought it would help poor Bridget's health, and I was happy to pay for the trips, but it was all I'd saved." She could see that he felt he'd been deceived, but whether by her or by Pat, she didn't know. "I don't know what Pat's told you, Richard, but I've never had much money. Since I came over, I was always saving for passage for my sisters, and then when I did get a little ahead after Nelly came, poor Bridget needed it."

He said that of course she had done right to help her family, but she could see it was a shock to him. "I mean to be a help to you, Richard," she said, "not a burden. Before long I will have a cow and some chickens, and I can sell milk and eggs to the neighbors, and of course I'll plant the kitchen garden in the spring."

He was agreeable to this, and said he would help her by building the chicken coop and getting the shed ready for the cow, but she could see that a deep distrust had been planted where money was concerned. When he came home the next Saturday with his wages, she asked him how he wanted to handle the household accounts. Her brother-in-law Jim Connolly, like most of the men, just handed his pay over to his wife and took a small amount for his pocket money, but some of the men, Ann had told Maggie, kept the money and gave their wives a household allowance. Given what she knew of his ways already, Maggie expected that Richard would be one of them.

"I would prefer to handle the household accounts myself, Margaret. I'm used to it now, and I just pay Jim Haney's bill at the grocery each week on my way home from work." Maggie was stunned. Did he mean this as the insult she took it for?

"Is it because you don't trust me with the money, Richard?"

"Why no, Margaret. I just prefer to keep the figures so I know where the money is going. We're going to have to be careful to save enough for the mortgage." Another reference to her lack of savings? "Your egg and milk money will be yours to spend as you think fit."

"If that's how you want it, Richard, but it's not how the other houses are run. What will the other women think?"

His square jaw set firm. "I don't care, Margaret, and you shouldn't either. It's no concern of theirs." Well, perhaps it wasn't, but that would not keep them from gossiping about it when they found out, as of course they would. Maggie decided to leave it for another day when she and Richard had gotten to know each other better. But every time she brought it up, he seemed to get more stubborn, not less. He would not put the money in her hands. In the end, it turned out not to be a hardship. He was very careful with money, but he didn't skimp on food or when she or the children needed something. She charged almost everything they needed at the store, and the milk and egg money was enough to save her face with the neighbors. But still this issue lay between them, and try as she might, Maggie could not let it go.

The lie about her age also continued to bother her. She'd gone along with it, but she would never have done it if Pat hadn't put her in that position. After a while, of course, Richard began to suspect that she was older than she had said, and he questioned her about her age. She was always able to get around it somehow, but she knew he didn't believe her. It rankled that he thought her dishonest, but there it was. She had gone along with Pat to begin with, and there was no end to it that she could see.

Chapter 2

1916

Edna sat up in bed and listened to the sound of the Ford touring car as it headed down Summer Street toward Cabot. When the noise had faded, she crept out of the room where her baby sister Doris was fast asleep. On the other side of the hall, her brothers tore out of their room and made for the stairs, seven-year-old Georgie followed by Andrew and little Evvie. Their grandmother Maggie was in the kitchen waiting for them, a neat little white-haired figure in her rocking chair by the stove, her warm smile lighting her blue eyes. As Evvie climbed into her lap and the others crowded around, she told them, as she always did, that they would have to go back to bed soon. No one protested. They knew they wouldn't be heading to bed until their parents came back from the movies, a good two hours from now, and the Ford would give them plenty of warning.

"Tell us about the time you all had to chase the pig down the road," said Andrew, grabbing her hand.

"Tell us about the banshee," said Georgie.

"No, tell us about when you were as big as me," said Evvie, his wide brown eyes looking eagerly into hers.

Maggie smiled at him. "Well, I can't remember that so well, Evvie."

Edna looked speculatively at her grandmother. "What's the first thing you remember, Marmsie?"

"Well, that's something to think about," she said. "When I was little, before we moved to the farm, we lived in a nice house on the grounds of the manor."

"What's 'the manor'?" Andrew asked.

"It was the house where the landlord lived. The man who owned all the land around. The farmers rented the land from him."

"And wasn't your father a farmer?" asked Edna.

"Ah, not at first," said Maggie. "Your great-grandfather, Martin Qualter, was a very well-educated man. He studied at the Irish seminary in Paris, France."

Edna was skeptical. "How did he ever get to France from Ireland? I thought you were poor. And if he was in the seminary, wasn't he a priest? How could he have a family?"

"Well, Dearie, when your great-grandfather was a boy, a hundred years ago, there were hardly any schools in Ireland for Catholics. It was just a few years after it was against the law for Catholics to learn to read and write."

Georgie, sprawled on the rag rug, perked up at this. "Why don't we have that law here?"

Maggie laughed. "Well, the people in Ireland didn't think as you do, Georgie. They did what they could to make up for it. They had what they called 'hedge schools.' The priests, or other people who had some education, gathered the children where they could, in houses or stables, or outside—next to the hedges sometimes, you see—and they would teach them the old Irish poems and songs, and to read and write English, and figuring—arithmetic. Your great-grandfather was quick at his books, like your mother, and our Edna here, and soon the priest was teaching him Latin as well, and Greek. He said that the priest didn't know much more Greek than he did, but they worked at it together.

"It was the priest, Father Burke, who fixed it so that your great-grandfather could go to France. He convinced the Bishop that it would be worth sending him because he was such a bright student. They named him a 'poor scholar,' meaning his way was to be paid, and the school would cost him nothing. He used to say it was the hardest thing he ever did, leaving his family to go off to France, knowing nothing of what he would find there. And well I know how he felt, for it was the same when I left my family to come here to America. But at least I was going to your Aunt Kate in Albany. He knew nothing of the seminary or anyone in it."

"Did he like it when he got there?" asked Edna.

"Well, he learned a great deal. He was the most educated man I ever saw. Always did be reading when he had a chance, and sometimes in Latin and Greek. But it seems he wasn't cut out for the priesthood. He was never one to be told what to do, and he didn't take to the vow of obedience." She smiled. "They sent him back to Ireland before he was ordained. I don't know if it was his idea or theirs. He never said. So he had an education, but there was nothing for him to do in Ireland outside of the Church, because at that time they wouldn't hire Catholics to do any kind of brain work. Well, he came home to Athenry, and he got a job as an estate agent, which meant that he was in charge of the farm owned by a rich English landlord. He leased the land to the tenants and collected the rents and managed everything about the landlord's own farm that wasn't leased to tenants."

"So he was the boss." said Georgie.

"He was, except for the landlord. But it was very hard on him at times. And those are some of my earliest memories. It was the time of *an Gorta Mór*, the great hunger—or the famine, they call it. At the beginning, we didn't really feel it at home. We knew the potato crop had failed, and that was what the farmers lived on. They raised grain and pigs, but they had to give all that to the landlord to pay the rent and to the tax collector. They all kept a small patch to raise potatoes on. Potatoes, you know, are very nourishing, and you could grow enough to feed a family for the year in a small field. If a farmer had a cow and a few chickens and a potato patch, the family would be all right. But the potatoes did be getting these blights, diseases, some years, and the crop would fail."

"What did they eat then?" asked Georgie.

"Well that was just it, you see. They couldn't eat the grain they'd raised, because if they did, they wouldn't be able to pay the rent, and they would be thrown out on the road. Most years, if there was a blight, they would get by on their milk and eggs, and what flour and oats they were able to buy with any little savings they had. But in the great hunger, the blight came for five years, one after another, and they ran out of savings, and they sold everything they had, and many ate the grain and livestock they'd raised and got thrown out on the road. Many just starved for want of food." The children watched her with solemn faces as she closed her eyes and slowly shook her head.

"Our family didn't feel it at first because our house was on the manor farm, and my father had a salary to live on. My first memory of it was when I was not much bigger than Evvie here, three or four years of age. We were eating our dinner, which wasn't anything fancy, but there was enough for all of us. One of the tenants knocked on the door. I will never forget the look of him. He was so very thin, like a skeleton. His eyes just burned. He stood with his hand on the door jamb like he would fall over if you touched him. I was just a wee girl, but I felt ashamed to be eating in front of him. He'd come to ask my father for permission to go into the fields of the manor farm and dig up the roots of the cabbages that had already been harvested. He was hoping they could make some kind of soup out of them."

"Did he let him?" asked Georgie.

"He did, for all the good it would do him, and my mother gave him some of our dinner to take home to his family, but there was too much hunger for anyone to stop it. And it was not long before we felt it ourselves." She went silent, her arms around Evvie.

"What happened?" asked Edna.

"Well," she said, slowly, "it had been months and months, and people were desperate. They did be making soup from nettles, and even grass, just to stave off the hunger pangs. You knew when people were in a very bad way because their mouths were stained green. The landlord's sheep began to go missing. It was a terrible thing to steal a sheep. You could hang for it. But people were doing it to feed their families. The landlord was an Englishman who cared nothing for his tenants. You would not dare have as much as a geranium in front of the door, for fear the landlord would think you were too prosperous and raise your rent. He told my father to find out who was stealing the sheep and turn them in. Well, he knew who stole the latest one. He told us that later. One night, he was walking the land and he smelled lamb cooking in a poor cottage where, for many a day, they had been eating nothing but nettle soup or a bit of oats that the neighbors had been able to spare. He knew they had no money, and had long since sold everything but the clothes on their backs."

"Who was it?" asked Georgie.

"He never told us. He never told anyone. He told the landlord he could not find the thief. The landlord didn't believe him, of course, and hauled him into court to get him to tell on his neighbor, but he would not. Then the landlord fired him off his job and threw us out of our house onto the road."

Everyone went wide-eyed at this. "Did he really throw you out onto the road?" asked Edna.

"Not himself. He wouldn't lower himself to such dirty doings as that. They sent the soldiers with some lackeys who were so desperate for food they'd take any work, and they came to the house and put our belongings out on the road. Then they tumbled the house."

"How could they tumble a house?" asked Andrew, looking at the walls around him.

"That's what we called it. The landlords did it all the time, so that the people who were thrown out didn't come back there to live, and as a sign there would be no more people on that land. They were trying to get the people off the land so they could turn to sheep and cattle farming. It took a lot less people, so they didn't have to pay so much to the poor tax. That day, the men took crowbars and climbed up on the roof and collapsed it into the house. The roof was made from thatch, you know, big bundles of reeds tied together. Then they took the crowbars and sledge hammers to the walls. They were stones, held together with mortar made from lime, and covered with lime. So the walls just tumbled in. And then they set it on fire. We stood on the road and watched it burn."

Edna looked at her grandmother. "Why didn't your father tell who stole the sheep? It would have saved his family from that, and it was a crime."

"He didn't think it was a crime for a man to steal a sheep to feed his starving family, especially if he stole it from a man who had more than enough. Or at least not a hanging crime. He felt it would be making him guilty of the man's death to inform on him. And then the family would certainly have starved. My father could not go against his conscience on a thing like that."

"He was right," said Georgie. "I would never tell."

"But what happened to the family after you were put out on the road?" asked Edna.

"We survived by kindness. The tenants liked your great-grandfather, even if he was the landlord's agent, for he was just and fair to them, and he never cheated on the rents for his own profit, as many did. And he hadn't told about the sheep. The neighbors stored our furniture, what little we had, in their houses. We had no cart or horse, and we walked to Gortaleva. A long walk it was, too. Ten miles is a long distance for a wee girl, you know, like walking from Beverly to Lynn.

The children had been to Lynn in the car, and they agreed that it was a long way.

"All along the road we saw people who had been turned out from the land their families had farmed for generations, with nowhere to go." She look down and shook her head slowly. "The sights we saw on that road. I still see them in my dreams. Families in rags, starving and sick, sitting by the side of the road or walking to nowhere with the hope that someone would give them something to eat. Some of them built skelps—holes dug into the sides of ditches—so they could get a little shelter from the rain and the night, and they did be sleeping in the ditches until they died of hunger or the ship's fever. So you see we were better off than most. When we got to Gortaleva, my uncle Michael took us in, though he had little enough room for his own family. He was a blacksmith in Gortaleva, a village attached to a big estate, and my father was able to get enough work to get us through the winter."

"How did you get the farm then?" asked Georgie.

"Well, there was no landlord who would rent my father any land, but one of the tenants in Lackagh, back in Athenry, had an empty cabin on his land after his son died of the fever. He let us have it, and my father helped him work the farm. It was a poor little house, and we suffered as much from the hunger as our neighbors did then. The blight came again to the potatoes, and we had almost nothing to eat that winter. We all had 'the ship's fever,' typhoid they say it was. It was hardest on the babies. We lost my baby sister Bridget to the hunger. I remember now my mother sitting by the door, with the dead child in her lap, sobbing and sobbing, and the priest standing there, trying to console her.

"I'll tell you now, if it were not for the Americans, we would all have died. They were Protestants, too, the Quakers and the Congregationalists from New England. There was a soup kitchen set up near our village where they would give us cornmeal mush, a certain measure for each one in the family. It was terrible stuff, but it kept body and soul together for many a family through the winter." She looked down at the floor.

"I did something I've been forever sorry for then. Kate and I did be fetching the meal each day with the neighbor girls, and one day we were coming across the fields carrying our pitchers of mush. One of the girls tripped on a rock. She broke her pitcher and spilled all the mush. She cried and cried, because she knew her family would have nothing to eat that day. I didn't like the girl, so I laughed at her bad luck. It's one of the most mean-spirited things I ever have done."

Edna did not think this was so terrible, but she knew her grandmother too well to say so.

"But things got better afterwards, didn't they? Didn't you have fun living on the farm?" asked Georgie.

"Fun is it," said Marmsie. "I suppose we did have some fun, but it was very hard work. You know, we had no boys in the family after my little brother Martin died, God rest him, so Kate and I helped our father in the fields while the smaller girls helped my mother at home. You see my hands."

The children looked at the familiar bent fingers and swollen joints. "That's the mark of the plow. They've been like that since I was a young girl. My father was a very neat and careful farmer. He saw to it that we did everything right about the work. Every year, we painted the cabin with lime, inside and out, to make it sparkle and keep out the bugs. Every three years, the three of us, he and I and Kate, carried reeds from the bog and thatched the roof, and every month, we changed out the reeds that we used like a carpet on the floor. And we would go to the bog and cut the turf that we carried to the house and dried and stacked for the fire."

Georgie sat up at this. "Turf—you mean you burned grass?"

"Ah, no. We scraped the grass off the top of the turf in the bog, and it was a dark, heavy soil that you could cut into blocks. Peat, they call it here. When it's dry, it makes a lovely, even fire. It smells wonderful, and isn't so smoky and messy as a wood fire. We did all the cooking over the open hearth."

"What about the animals?" asked Andrew.

"We didn't have any at first, but after the great hunger was over, my father was able to make enough from his hard work to buy a cow and chickens and a few lambs, and a pig to raise each year. The little girls fed the animals and gathered the eggs, but it was Kate and I who milked the cow and helped our father with the shearing and butchering and curing. Butchering the pig each year was a big job but a very important one. It gave us food throughout the winter, even when the crops were not good, as happened sometimes even after the great hunger was over. The sheep we mostly did be turning over to the landlord for rent, but in good years we kept a few and sheared them in the spring. My mother taught us all to spin the wool from the sheep and make it into yarn for knitting or weave it into cloth. We had a loom in the corner of the kitchen that every one of us took our turn at, and my mother taught us all to sew, so it wasn't just the men's work that I learned to do."

"It was all so much work," said Georgie. "Didn't you have any fun at all? What did you do on Christmas?"

"Well, on Christmas, we did no work, except to take care of the animals. That made it special. Everyone burned a light in the window so that if anyone should come by on the road, whether the neighbors or poor travelers looking for shelter like Joseph and Mary on the way to Bethlehem, they would know there would be a welcome for them. We would walk across the fields to midnight Mass in Athenry, meeting up with the neighbors as we walked and having a fine time. I loved the Mass in the dark with the singing of the Christmas hymns."

"What about presents?" asked Andrew.

She laughed. "No, no presents, and no Santa Claus. He hadn't gotten to traveling to Ireland at that time. But we had a nice day of rest at home, and sometimes the neighbors would come in. We'd have some singing then, and maybe some dancing. My father would recite a poem for us. He knew many of the old Irish poems. Most everyone could speak English by then, especially the children. We did be going to the government school in the winter. But we preferred to speak in Irish."

"You and Aunt Nelly and Delia Gill still speak in Irish," said Edna.

"Yes, it's a comfort. I suppose we don't even know we're doing it. The old tongue takes us home to Athenry when we were girls."

"Would you ever want to go back and visit?"

"No, Lovie, I've no wish to take that voyage again."

Edna looked at her. "Why did you and Aunt Kate ever leave? It must have been so hard to leave your family behind."

"Ah, yes. But there was nothing else for it. Everyone at home was poor, and there was nothing for us to do but work on the farm. My father always said there was a big world beyond Galway Bay, and he didn't want us to wear out our lives on a pitiful scrap of land in Athenry. He had seen for himself, you know, when he was in France. So with his scrimping and saving, he finally put together the four pounds for the passage. That was about twenty dollars, a fortune for a small farmer in those days. He brought us all together—Mary, Kate, Annie, Bridget, little Mary, Nelly, and me—and he told us that the money would be enough to buy passage for one of us, and then that one could work to bring the next one, and then those two to bring the next one, and so on, the way all the families did be managing since the days of the great hunger. One of us would have to go first, and we all knew before she said so that Kate would be the one. She was always the boldest and bravest of us. And so Kate was the first to go. She sailed for New York, and through a neighbor from home, she got a job working as a housemaid in a big house in Albany. She was lucky that the house provided her with uniforms, and she spent none of her salary except for one decent dress to wear on the street and to Mass on Sundays. At the end of the year, she sent for me, and I was ready to come."

Georgie looked up at his grandmother as he lay stretched on the rug. "I'm hungry, Marmsie. Can we have some bread and butter and molasses?"

She smiled down at him. "You can. You know I'd never refuse you something to eat when you're hungry." She slid deftly out of her chair without disturbing the sleeping Evvie.

"Take out the things, Edna, while I take Evvie up to bed. Then I'll cut you all a nice slice of bread to eat before you go up." Edna took the bread from the bread box and the butter from the ice box and set them on the table, and Georgie lugged the heavy jug of molasses from the pantry to the table. When they were all sitting around the table near the stove with their mouths full of fresh bread and butter generously drizzled with molasses, Edna looked at Maggie thoughtfully.

"How old were you when you got on the ship to come over here?"

"Ah, I don't know exactly. We did not celebrate birthdays at home the way we do here. I don't know the day I was born. I remember once when we were out in the field, my father told me that I was then twenty years of age, but I don't know how long it was after that I came to America. I'll never forget the six weeks on that ship, an old sailing ship it was, not a steamer. That would have cost more."

"I wish I could go on a sailing ship for six weeks," said Georgie.

Marmsie laughed. "Well, you wouldn't have wanted to be on that ship for six weeks—at least not in steerage where I was. They had us down below in the hold of the ship, and there was no privacy at all, no beds, or anything. Just one big room for the women and one for the men. You found a space on the floor and made yourself up a bed from your belongings. There was no place to wash except a space at the end of the room where the sailors would set some buckets of water. What with so many suffering from the sea-sickness, the stench was something terrible. I was lucky not to get sea-sick unless it was very rough, so I spent as much time as I could up on deck, walking, or finding a sheltered spot to sit in. There was nothing to do and nothing to see except water for those six long weeks. I watched the sailors managing the ship, and talked with some of the other passengers who were girls like myself, going to make a new life in America, but they were long days and longer nights when I had to go below and try to sleep amidst the stench and the noise of babies crying and people snoring, and worse."

"Did they have good food on the ship?" asked Georgie, licking the molasses off his fingers.

"Well, some did, I suppose. There were passengers in first class and second class who had their dining room and their cook, but not those of us in steerage. You could buy your passage with or without food, so most of us had brought our own sea store. The sailors brought us hot water, and I had a box of tea and mostly ate what they called hard tack, a kind of biscuit made from flour and water that was true to its name. You could easily break a tooth on it. You had to dip it in the tea or hot water to eat it. I don't know which was worse, the cornmeal mush during the great hunger or the hard tack on the ship. I was very glad to say goodbye to that when I landed in New York."

"Did you go to work with Aunt Kate?" asked Edna.

"No, I went up to Albany, but there was no place for me in the house where she worked, so Kate paid for me to stay with some people until I could make a new dress and present a decent appearance, and then I found a job as a maid of all work. I worked in quite a few houses, always looking out for a better situation, you know. After a few years, I came to the Reeds' house, 221 State Street, in view of the state capitol, which I liked a good deal, and there I stayed. It was just Mr. and Mrs. Reed. They were an elderly couple, and had no children. He was a fine gentleman, a retired merchant, very considerate of the help. I didn't like her so well. She was suspicious of us, Jane the cook and me. She had these bowls of fruit placed around the house, and didn't she count the pieces of fruit to make sure we weren't eating it."

She bridled at the memory of this thirty-year-old insult. "Why, I would not touch as much of it as would blind your eye. But the work and the master were to my liking, so I put up with the mistress. I didn't have to cook, but just did the housework, and they supplied the uniforms. In the morning, I wore a dark cotton dress with a gingham apron while I did the cleaning. In the afternoon, I changed into a white or black dress, depending on the season, with a fancy apron, to answer the door and serve tea. Then I would set the table and serve the dinner and do the dishes. They gave me my own little room on the third floor, and I ate what they ate, so I was treated well. Together, Kate and I saved our money, and we were able to send for Mary, and then we all saved until we brought Annie and Bridget and little Mary and Nelly. "

"Why do you have two sisters named Mary?" asked Edna.

"Your Aunt Mary Nohelty is my half-sister. Little Mary, Mary Kern, that is, is my little sister. It wasn't unusual to have two children in a family with the same name in those days, especially if one had died. My sister Bridget was named for my baby sister who died in the great hunger.

"What about your mother and father?" asked Edna. "Why didn't they come to America?"

"Ah, my father died in 1874, God rest him, just before we brought our youngest sister Nelly to America. I don't know if he would have come or not. We tried to talk my mother into coming, but she was set on marrying someone from home and staying there. He was a waster, a worthless man. We knew she would come to rue it, but her mind was set on it. I don't think she had the heart to pull up and come to another country at her age. So Nelly came by herself and our mother married the waster and stood by him till they died in the workhouse."

"What's 'the workhouse'?" asked Andrew.

"It's what they have in Ireland for people who have no work and no more money and nothing to eat. They give them work to do and a cot to sleep on and some food. Many, many people went to the workhouses, especially during the great hunger, but very few of them came out again."

"Why?"

"They died. Most were starving and sick when they got there, and those that weren't got sick afterwards."

"Was your mother starving and sick?"

"I don't know. I hope not. We all sent her money, but I'm sure the waster took it and spent it on drink and such. It was a very sad thing not to be able to help her."

Georgie sat back and pulled his feet up on his chair. "Did you have any fun when you worked in Albany?"

"Fun again, is it. Well, there isn't much time for fun when you're in service. You only get Thursday afternoons and Sundays off, but we made the most of it. We'd all gather together after Mass. Mrs. Reed didn't like me to have visitors, but the family Kate worked for didn't mind if we used the kitchen on Sunday afternoons. So we'd have a fine tea party of our own. We went to socials and fairs at the church, and after all the sisters were here and we didn't have to be so careful with the money, we all made nice dresses and would go to the dances that were held by the Ancient Order of Hibernians and some of the other societies. There were hundreds and hundreds of Irish serving maids in Albany in those days, and plenty of young Irish men as well. We had a grand time on many a Sunday or Thursday night."

"Is that where you met our grandfather?" asked Edna.

Maggie went silent for a minute. "No," she said. "That was Pat Nolan's doing."

"Uncle Pat who's married to Aunt Julia?"

"Yes, but you know Julia's not really your aunt. Pat Nolan was married to my little sister Bridget, God rest her, before she died of consumption—tuberculosis they call it now. They were living in Woburn, and they knew your grandfather there."

Suddenly alert, Georgie jumped up from the table. "It's them," he said. And in a minute, everyone could make out the sound of the Ford coming down Summer Street. Georgie and Andrew ran for the stairs while Edna put the bread and butter away and Maggie set the jug of molasses in the pantry and wiped the crumbs off the table. When they heard the engine being cut off and the barn door behind the house slamming shut, Edna skipped up the stairs. Maggie slowly made her way across the kitchen, straightening things as she went.

"Oh, there you are," she said as her daughter and son-in-law came through the back door. "I was just going up to bed. Was it a good picture?"

"It was pretty good," said George, "but I think William Gillette is getting a little old to be playing Sherlock Holmes."

"He's no matinee idol," said Mary. "Not anymore. How were the children, Marm?"

"Oh, they're all snug in their beds. I'll be off myself now. Good night to you. Sleep well."

Chapter 3

1928

Edna reveled in the house's unaccustomed quiet. Not only were there no little brothers and sisters constantly interrupting her at the dining room table, there was no interminable monotone speech about her mother's current preoccupation, no socialist rant from Georgie. She was actually enjoying her work, planning the history course that she would be teaching in a few weeks, when she started her job at Keene Normal School. It was so quiet that she heard Marmsie's uncertain step on the stairs five minutes before she stepped into the dining room. "I'm feeling lonesome tonight, Edna," she said, "can you take a few minutes for a cup of tea?"

Edna smiled up at her. "I'd like that, Marmsie," she said. Their talks together had been a pleasure for both of them since Edna was a little girl, and Edna particularly liked it when Marmsie was in a mood like this because it promised talk of the days when her grandmother was young. Edna told her to rest in her rocking chair, and while she was brewing the tea, asked, "Do you miss my grandfather, Marmsie, is that what makes you feel lonesome sometimes?"

Marmsie looked a bit startled. "Well, no, to tell you the truth, Dearie. It's not Dick that I miss so much as my sisters and the family at home."

"Were you very much in love when you married him?"

Marmsie laughed a little at this. "Well, not in the way that you mean. We didn't think so much of that. It was a much more practical thing. It was your Uncle Pat arranged the match, and we hardly knew each other when we married." We got off on the wrong foot, so to say, as far as the marriage was concerned."

"Why?"

"Pat, you know, is a big talker, and he was eager to make the match for Bridget's sake, God rest her. He told Dick that I was thirty years of age when I was closer to forty, and he told Dick I had a lot of money saved when I had nothing."

This did not fit with Edna's view of courtship. "Well, what was it like when you met him? Did you like him? Was he handsome?"

"Oh, I thought he was very handsome. He had deep blue eyes like your mother's and Georgie's, and dark brown hair. He carried himself well."

"Did you grow to love each other after you were married?"

"I don't know. Your grandfather was a good man and an impressive man. He was a good provider who took care of his family. He loved his children. He was well respected in the parish and the city. I was proud to be his wife. But we didn't have the same—temperament. You know I love talking and laughing and music. You'd never know it from the way I hobble about now, but in my day, I loved to dance, and I was good at it. I used to love what we called 'kitchen rackets.' We would gather in someone's house where they would have a fiddler in, and we would sing and dance to the old songs.

"Your grandfather was a reserved, some said a dour man. Your cousin Helen used to call him 'the old grouch' when he was not in hearing. He was not a drinking man, thank heaven, and wasn't much on going out to have a good time. He had no more education than I had, but he loved to read, like you and your father. He read the newspaper from cover to cover and knew all about the events of the world. He was always going to the library downtown and bringing books home. He loved learning and reciting poetry. I liked to listen to him, but this wasn't really my interest, you know. I don't think we would ever have married if we'd met in the general way of things, but we learned to get on, and we made a good life for our family. He was a good husband to me, and generous to my relatives. The family used to say they knew they would always find shelter with Maggie and Dick if they needed it."

"Did he find out about your age?"

"In a roundabout way, yes. When I had your mother, I had a hard time. That was 1883, two years after we married. I was a day and a night in labor, and Dick's sister Ann, who was the midwife, had to call in the doctor in the end. They were that worried about me. I can't remember much of it, but it was a terrible time. The doctor told Dick it was to be expected with someone having her first child at my age, which he took to be forty at least. I must have looked like death after all those hours of labor, so I'm sure I looked forty. What's more, I think he was about right. Anyway, after the birth, he told us I could have no more children. It was a relief after the time I'd had, but disappointing still. There was Kate, older than I was, and having Mary and Margaret and John, one after the other, like it was nothing." She sighed. "But that was Kate. She just did what she made up her mind to do. It was never that simple for me, somehow. I think Dick would have liked to have more children. He never said a word about it, but I know he held it against me that I wasn't truthful about my age."

"Did he get over the problem about the money?"

"In a way. He saw that I was a good housekeeper. I kept a big kitchen garden and supplied all the vegetables, and I made money for us by keeping the cow and chickens and selling eggs and milk to the neighbors. It was what carried us through the hard times when he was laid off from the tannery, and the months when he was on strike back in 1889. But he said I was flighty with money, and he insisted on keeping the household accounts himself." She bridled. "I had to ask him for money for everything that I couldn't pay for with the milk and egg money. It was an insult."

She thought for a minute. "It was the money that was always a sore point between us. That and the raising of the children. Part of that was his sister Ann's doing. She lived next door, and she had loved his first wife Kate as well as the two children, so when I came along, she watched like a hawk to see that I would not be a mean stepmother to them. And I wasn't. I cared for Tom and Josie as well as my own Mary. Better, in fact. I was so worried that Ann would point out any slighting of them that I always gave the best half to Josie, as your mother will tell you. I used to dress Mary and Josie alike so no one could say that Mary had the better clothes. But you couldn't do everything alike."

"What about Tom?"

"Well, Tom was a boy, so that was different. I made sure that he was clean and fed and had decent clothes to wear, but his father took charge of him from the beginning. It was the girls that were the problem. It was my place to bring them up, and teach them to keep house, but I worried about giving Josie any chores to do because Ann would say I was picking on her, and to tell you the truth, it was always quicker and easier to just do it myself."

"What about Mama?"

"Well, since Josie didn't have to do housework, I couldn't make Mary do it, could I? She would have run right to her father to complain. And rightly so, I suppose. So I just took care of the house myself, and they learned to sew and cook at school. But Dick insisted on attending to the children's education and their religious upbringing. He was a very religious man. Each night, you know, he led us in family prayers—not only the rosary, but prayers for the repose of the souls of many friends and relatives. It was three Hail Marys for this one and three Hail Marys for that one until you were a good half hour on your knees with it. We went to Mass every Sunday of course, and he insisted that the girls join the Young Ladies Sodality in the parish when they graduated from grammar school so they would be spending their free time in activities with other Catholic young girls."

"Was he a mean father?"

"No, not a *mean* father. He doted on his children. But he was strict with them, especially about morals. They'd not dare to tell a lie to him. And he was very strict about their school work. Every night that he wasn't out at a meeting of the Hibernians or the Knights of Labor or the Democrats, he did be sitting at home with the children. They would all be around the table with the kerosene lamp burning, he reading and they doing their lessons. And he would pay attention to what they were doing. He checked the Arithmetic, and he quizzed them on their lessons. That was the hard part for me, watching Tom and Josie suffer through that. Tom was a bit of a slacker about his lessons, and he always tried to get away with having the thing half-memorized, but Dick kept him at it till he had it. And poor Josie, she just had no head for the books. He would get more and more impatient, and she would get more and more flustered, and often it ended in tears."

"What about Mama?"

"Oh, Mary was always quick at her lessons. She had a wonderful memory, like Dick and like you. She went to school too young, at four, and it was a while before she learned to behave herself properly. So she spent some time in the corner with a dunce cap on her head, but she always got her lessons with no trouble, and memorized long passages of poems and the Bible. Her father was very proud of her, and always praising her. That didn't help poor Josie."

"Did Josie hold it against Mama?"

"Ah, no. I wouldn't say that she did. She loved her little sister, and would do anything for her. Josie was a cheerful and a generous soul, God rest her."

"She was always nice to me. The house was more cheerful when she was around."

"It was." Maggie looked down at the table in front of her. "I do wish she hadn't gone to Boston to live. It was a bad thing so."

"Why?"

Maggie looked up, but didn't meet Edna's eyes. "It's just a bad thing for a young woman to be by herself in the city. I wish I could have kept her with me, but there was no place for her when I came to live with your mother and father."

Edna looked at her grandmother. "You know, it sounds like you never had your way about anything. It's so different from Mama and Dad. Did my grandfather decide everything in the house?"

Maggie laughed. "Well, you know, I'm an easy-going person, and Dick was definitely not easy-going, so it usually worked out that way."

"Did you miss him when he died?"

"Well, I did, yes. But we were not as close as some couples. I was proud that he was such a leader in the city, but it took so much of his time. He was out at meetings two or three nights of most weeks, and more if there were problems at the tannery or an election. And I think that being so well known in the union hurt his chances to get better work at Beggs and Cobb. He could easily have been a foreman with his skills and the way the men looked up to him. But everyone knew his name at that time, and he stood for labor against the owners."

She stopped and thought a minute, remembering. "When he ran for mayor, he was giving speeches around the city every night, and sometimes I had to go too. Just to wear my Sunday best and put in an appearance on his arm, you know, but it was hard for me. I don't take to the limelight and meeting new people, especially if they're not Irish people. But he loved it. It's a curious thing that he was such a shy man in a personal conversation, but always comfortable addressing a crowd. He would have appreciated a wife who could do more for him in politics. Between worrying about the labor union and dealing with the politics and breathing the air of two tanneries just at the end of the street, I had a lot of sick headaches then. They got much better once I moved to Beverly."

Edna smiled. "But it must have been hard living here sometimes, with Mama and all of us around all the time and not having your own house if you were used to it."

"Well, you know your mother wasn't always so—complicated, as you say. Mary and I used to divide the work between us when you were young and it worked out well for us all."

She laughed a little. "It was almost like having my old job at the Reeds' back. I did the housemaid's work and Mary did the fancy cooking and the projects. In the morning I always have been the first to rise in the house, and I did be lighting the stove and cooking your father's breakfast for him so he could get to work at 7:00. Then in the old days, it was me making the beds and sweeping all the floors and putting things to rights in the morning after I washed the breakfast dishes, and I always had the potatoes on to boil in time for your father's dinner at noon. I kept my chickens, you remember, on Summer Street, but I gave them up before we moved to McKay Street because that neighbor, Mr. Wilson, complained. Of course I've always looked after you children. It's been a good life being a grandmother."

She smiled at her favorite granddaughter, and a look passed between them. "Well, enough of this now. I'll leave you to finish your work before they all come back to plague you. I'm not feeling so lonesome now, and we both of us will be wishing we were alone soon. Goodnight, Dearie."

"Goodnight, Marmsie. Pleasant dreams."

~~~

On a hot August day two weeks later, Edna, tired from packing, came out to sit in the shade on the front porch. Maggie had had the same idea. She stood at the railing,
~~~

looking out over the Shoe Pond, a faint breeze ruffling the wisps of hair around her face. It made Edna think of the young woman she had been when she crossed the ocean on a sailing ship in 1870 to make her home in America. "Marmsie," she said. "Have you ever thought of going back to Ireland?"

Maggie turned toward her. "No, Dearie," she said. "There's nobody there I would know now."

~~~

In 1928, Maggie, who was in her late eighties, at last began to take an interest in politics. Al Smith, the Irish Catholic Governor of New York, was the Democratic nominee for president. Maggie had heard him speak several times when she was visiting her sisters in Albany. She overlooked his anti-Prohibition stance in her enthusiasm for his candidacy, and told her daughter Mary that she wanted to register to vote for the first time.

*****

Boston *Globe*, August 30, 1928, page 11.

BEVERLY REGISTRATION 10,130
NEW HIGH MARK

BEVERLY, Aug. 29—Today, the last of the opportunities for registrations for the primaries, brought in 606 new names, making a total of 10,130 names on the voting list. This is the biggest ever. During the past three days 1220 names were added to the list.

The feature of the registration was the adding of Mrs. Margaret Terrett of McKay St. She is 88 years old and was brought in by friends. She declared herself as a Smith supporter.
~~~

*****

On November 6, 1928, Maggie left her daughter's home for the last time, to cast her first vote in a presidential election. She wore her Sunday best, an old-fashioned black silk bonnet held on by ribbons tied in a bow beneath her chin, and a black dress, stockings, and heavy shawl. George drove her and Mary to the polls. Maggie was so feeble that, when they came back, George and Mary had to take her arms and almost carry her tiny frame up the two sets of steps leading to the front door. Maggie's granddaughter Priscilla, six years old, stood inside the screen door and watched. Suddenly, Maggie looked up with a broad smile. "I voted for Al Smith!" she said, proudly. Priscilla never forgot it.

Edna McGlynn in 1928

Richard Terrett at work, about 1885

Part Two

Richard Terrett

Chapter 4

1898

Richard Terrett got home from work earlier than usual on this mild Saturday in March. He hadn't lingered to talk with the other men about conditions in the tannery or local politics, but had headed straight home. He called up the stairs, "Tom!"

"What is it, Pa? I'm just packing up my things so Mary can have my room when I'm gone."

"Come down a minute. I'd like a word."

As his son clambered down the stairs, Richard thought, "He's such a boy. Just a boy."

"Is something wrong, Pa?"

He looked into Tom's flushed, slightly anxious face. "No, lad. I just thought we might talk a bit. The women are planning a big dinner for tomorrow to see you off, so there won't be any quiet in this house. The traditional thing on this occasion would be for a father to buy his son a pint, but since we're teetotalers both, I thought we might take a walk instead."

Tom's handsome face relaxed into his good-natured grin, his clear blue eyes, so like his grandmother's, looking affectionately into Richard's. "All right, Pa. I'd like that."

"We could walk along the Mystic to Arlington and pay a visit to your Aunt Mag. I know she would want to see you if you're going to go."

"All right. I wouldn't mind a piece of Aunt Mag's mince pie."

"I'll just wash up and change out of my work clothes."

As they started down the road, Richard put his hand on Tom's shoulder. "I want you to know I'm not going to try to talk you out of it anymore, Tom. I've made all the arguments I have to muster. You're old enough to make your own decisions."

"Thanks, Pa. You know I didn't make the decision lightly. I know the war, if it comes, will not be all guts and glory. I do. But I just have to go. You know I've always wanted to join the Navy and go to sea. I may be sitting at a machinist's bench for the rest of my life, but I have to see what's beyond Woburn and Winchester first. This is my chance. Who knows when they'll be looking for machinists and firemen again."

"I see that, lad. I just wish it was otherwise. But it occurred to me today that I was two years younger than you are now when I took ship for America. Although it wasn't as if I was leaving anything behind. Mag and Ann were already here, and they helped me with the passage money. My aunt and uncle had been good to me, but it was time for me to be out on my own."

"You know, you never told us much about Ireland. It's so different with Marm. I feel like I know every chicken and pig they had as well as all the family. But you never tell stories the way she does."

"No, it was all so hard and sad, the life there. It's always just made me downhearted to think of it, so I've tried to forget about it and concentrate on the present and the future, and what we can be doing to get on in the world and make things better."

He walked in silence for a few minutes. "Of course there are some things you can't forget. My earliest memory of Ireland is my father's funeral. You know my father's family were Protestants. My grandfather came from England, and he was not happy that my father had married a Catholic girl. He had little to do with him after that. My mother's family, the Connorses, were very angry that the Terretts didn't come to the wake and the funeral. A while later, we were evicted, and we came to live with my aunt and uncle, just down the road. Of course everything was just down the road in Tirhogar.

"Why were you evicted?"

"I don't really know, to tell you the truth. The Connorses always said it was my grandfather—the Terretts were the landlords for the house, and also for the house the Connorses lived in. They said he threw my mother and us out onto the road because he was so angry that my father had married a Catholic. I'm sure that was part of it, but it was also economic. My mother couldn't have farmed even the small piece of land we had. I don't know how she could have paid the rent. Anyway, we ended up living with my aunt and uncle. A year or so later, my mother died. My aunt used to say it was from a broken heart. So Aunt Lizzie and Uncle Pat were left with Mag and Ann and me."

"Did they have enough money to take care of you?"

"They had very little. I'm sure it wasn't easy to have us on top of their own children."

An angry look crossed Richard's face, and he reddened. He shoved his hands into his pockets and looked down at the road as he walked.

After his father had told him all of this so calmly, the sudden change of mood surprised Tom. "What is it, Pa?"

Richard looked up. "I just thought of something I hadn't thought of in years. Once when I was about ten years old, I overheard my aunt and uncle talking at night, and they were worrying about where they would get clothes for all of us for the winter. 'I've patched them till there's nothing left to patch,' Aunt Lizzie said. 'You'd think those Terretts would do something for poor Mary's children. I see their cousins about in lovely new clothes.' I made up my mind that my grandfather would help us, as he ought. I was afraid of talking to him, but I felt I had to do something to take care of myself and my sisters. You might say it was the first speech I ever made. I planned what I would say. I felt I had justice on my side, and I meant to stand up and speak out as I did when I recited at school.

"The next day, I walked down the road to the house where my grandfather and my Uncle Michael's family lived, and I walked up the path and rapped on the door. A strange man opened the door and looked down at me. 'What is it you want?' he said.

"I spoke right up." Unconsciously, his head went back and his shoulders straightened. "'My name is Richard Terrett, and I've come to see my grandfather, Richard Terrett.' The man looked startled, and then laughed. 'So Richard Terrett is your grandfather, is he? Well, I'll just fetch him for you then.' He went off with a grin as if he was in for a good show. That made me angry, so I was determined to stand up to them. Before long, the old man himself stood in the doorway. To me he looked very tall and grim. Nervous as I was, I was curious about him. He looked a little like my father, except that my father was kind and he looked like an old grump.

"'What do you want?' he said.

"'I'm your grandson Richard, and I want to know if you will help me and your granddaughters, Margaret and Ann. We've no decent clothes to wear to school. I thought maybe you could help us, or our cousins might have some clothes that are too small for them now that they could pass on to us.'

"My grandfather looked down at me, pointed his finger in my face and said, 'Get out of here, you little beggar, and if you set a foot on this property again, I will get the authorities on you.' I turned and went. I wanted to cry. I wanted to shout at the old man, kick at him, but I did not. I could see the man who had answered the door, behind my grandfather, watching. I would not give him the satisfaction."

Tom stood still in the road and looked at his father. "What an awful thing for him to do. Your grandfather."

Richard faced him, the hint of a smile lighting his eyes. "Yes. But you know, Tom, it did something for me. Call it my grandfather's legacy. After that, I was determined that I would stand on my own two feet, but I would not grow up to be a mean, stingy old man, or refuse to help my family."

He put his hand on Tom's shoulder, and they walked along again. "I suppose that's why we have always had a steady stream of relatives staying in the house. Maggie feels the same way. That's something we've always agreed on."

"What about your education? I know that's something that was always important to you. You certainly saw to it that I got mine."

Tom grinned at his father, and Richard shook his head. "Well, we did get through those twelve years, didn't we? And I was very proud to watch you walk across the platform and receive your high school diploma. I didn't come near that. My uncle sent me to the Christian Brothers in Portarlington for a few years, but he couldn't afford it for long. After I was old enough to work, at eleven or twelve years of age, I was always working for him or for anyone who would take me on."

He looked off down the road for a minute. "I know this will sound crazy to you, lad, but I missed school, especially the poetry. I had a book of poems I'd won as a prize for recitation in my last year at school, and I read the poems over and over till I had many of them memorized. That's what started me on poetry. And I read everything else I could get my hands on. Of course that was mainly old newspapers. I worked hard, contributed to the household, and saved everything I could. Like my older sisters, I had my sights fixed on America. There was nothing for me in Tirhogar, or even Portarlington. In 1869, when I was eighteen years of age, I had saved enough money to book my passage to New York. My sisters had gone to Boston, and by then they were settled in Woburn and Arlington, but I wanted to see the big city and try my luck there, at least at first."

Tom looked at his father. "I didn't know you lived in New York. Was it exciting?"

Richard laughed. "Well it was not quite what I had imagined after listening to the stories of the immigrants who'd come back to Portarlington. It was just overwhelming to someone like me, who'd never even been to Dublin before I took ship. The noise, the stench, the enormous crowds of people and horses and the various horse cars and carts and wagons and buggies in constant motion everywhere. It was worth your life to get across the street. Two days after I arrived, I found myself in a tenement bedroom shared with a man who claimed to be an Indian and slept wrapped in a blanket on the floor with a knife under his head." He laughed. "I was glad to have the bed to myself, but the knife made me nervous. Then I woke on Sunday morning to hear what I thought was a sewing machine running downstairs in the landlady's room. When I questioned her, she assured me it was a mechanical eggbeater, but I did not quite believe her. I had very strict views in those days, and did not think it right to live in a house where sewing was done on the Sabbath. Anyway, I decided New York was not for me, and I took a train to Boston, and came out to Ann's. I decided I liked Woburn much better than New York, and I stayed. There were already more than twenty tanneries in town, and between the hides and the smokestacks and the tanning chemicals, parts of the town smelled almost as bad as New York, but I got used to it."

Tom grinned. "I suppose we could take anything in the way of smells after the tanneries. Anyway, I'm counting on that as I travel the world."

"I'm glad to hear that Woburn's given you some kind of advantage."

So they walked on companionably, father and son, Tom trying not to show how eager he was to get off and see the world, and Richard trying not to show that he was afraid for his son, and broken-hearted at his leaving.

When they returned that evening, Richard was tired. Maggie and the girls were still bustling around the kitchen and the dining room, preparing for Tom's farewell dinner. He put a dining room chair on the front stoop and sat down to enjoy the still mild evening. His talk with Tom had stirred memories and feelings that had been suspended for years. As he remembered the world he'd seen through his nineteen-year-old eyes, he marveled that he had gotten from there to here.

The Hibernians Hall the night Ann's husband Jim had taken him to his first meeting back in 1869. He could see the scene like it was yesterday. The men from home. They stood in groups with open faces, talking, laughing together, singing, like they had all the time in the world. Not like the Americans, always doing business, always in a hurry. That night, Richard had felt himself really relax for the first time since he had boarded the ship for America. There were even men from Queen's County who knew some people he knew and were happy to hear all the news of them he could muster. They welcomed him, and they helped him to find his first job and placed him in a boarding house. They made him believe he could actually live in this country. He would never forget the debt he owed to the Hibernians.

Richard had taken eagerly to his first job at Squire's as a currier, an earnest student learning to apply the color and other finishes to the tanned hides before they were shipped out. And he had marveled at the pay, enough for a comfortable room in a clean boarding house with good food and money enough left over not only to keep himself decently clothed but even to save toward a marriage and family. He had settled into the rhythm of the tannery worker's life that nearly every laboring man in Woburn lived, working fifty-nine hours a week with short days on Saturdays and Sundays off for church and leisure. He cherished his Sundays. Because of the connection to his mother, his religion meant a good deal to him, and he never missed a Sunday Mass at St. Charles's. In the afternoon, he often went to visit his sisters and their quickly expanding families. He discovered other young men who shared his interest in reading and poetry. There were lectures at the Lyceum Hall, and he went to meetings of the Irish Literary Association.

One of the things Richard liked most about living in Woburn was that ever-astonishing American institution, the public library. When he first came to Woburn, the library was in a downtown storefront. He didn't quite believe it when he walked by and saw the sign "public" library, since there was no such thing in Queen's County, or in Dublin, for all he knew. But when he went in and looked around, no one stopped him, and he saw other workingmen like himself sitting at the tables reading. He soon got himself a library card with borrowing privileges, and spent an hour or so after early closing at Squire's on Saturdays, carefully choosing the two books he was allowed each week. One was always literature, for enjoyment. The other had to have some educational purpose. He read widely in history and science and political theory as well as many volumes of speeches by great orators.

Leaning back in his chair, Richard allowed the memories to flood his mind. It was 1875 when he met Catherine Kernan, and his life changed. He could see her now as she had stood before him at St. Charles's church social, a tall, shapely girl of eighteen with curly brown hair a shade darker than his own and arresting green eyes. Her complexion was dark for an Irish girl, tanned by the sun as she worked on her family's farm, and her cheeks glowed with health. They soon found they had no shortage of things to talk about. She was more intellectual than the other girls he knew and had more patience for serious talk. They both loved to read, and wished they'd had more of an education. And he found her beautiful. Within a short time, the romantic poetry he so loved had a very particular subject in his imagination, and his saving for the future had a very particular goal. Richard fell passionately in love with Catherine, in a way that overwhelmed him, that he hadn't imagined happening to him, for all his poetry reading. He thought of her constantly, couldn't wait until the end of the week when he could visit her at the Kernans' farm out in Wilmington. And she loved him too. This beautiful, extraordinary girl. That was the astonishing thing. They would never say it to anyone else, but they felt that they were deeply, spiritually bonded. Richard never proposed to Catherine. They just started talking about "when we're married," as if the future were a charmed circle when their lives would be their own, and everything would be right.

Catherine's father was something else again. Since she was just turned nineteen, Richard knew he would have to get her father's approval for the marriage. Bernard Kernan was an old farmer from County Clare who didn't care for life in America at all. He wanted nothing to do with the Woburn tanneries or any factory, and insisted on farming as he had at home, keeping dairy cows and growing vegetables, which he brought to various markets in Woburn and Winchester, almost as if it were market day in Portarlington. He was stubborn and set in his ways, and worked his family hard to make the farm pay. Richard knew he would have a time convincing the old man to let him marry his eldest daughter.

Conferring with Kate, he chose the quiet hour after Sunday dinner as the time when the old man was most likely to be receptive, or at least less irascible than usual. Richard didn't beat about the bush. He sat down across from Bernard in the parlor and said, "Mr. Kernan, I would like to ask your permission to marry your daughter, Kate."

Kernan looked at him. Richard knew he'd been expecting this. "You would, would you? And can you tell me why I should give my first-born daughter to you?"

"Well, I have a good steady job as a currier at Squire's. I've worked there for seven years now, and I've saved almost four hundred dollars for us to get married on. I'm a good Catholic, and I don't drink or smoke or gamble. Kate is very dear to me, and I think I can make her a good husband."

"As for your being a good Catholic, that's neither here nor there to me, but I'm glad you don't waste your money on drink or tobacco or gambling. When did you come over here? What is your family? What did you do in the old country?"

"I came in 1869, at the age of eighteen, and I've been on my own since then. My sister, Ann Connolly, lives in Woburn. We have another sister, Margaret Cahill, who lives in Arlington. Our parents died when I was little, and we were raised by my mother's brother, who has a small farm in the townland of Tirhogar, in Portarlington, Queen's County." He was exaggerating this a bit. His uncle's three acres could hardly be called a farm.

Bernard perked up at this. "A farmer. And did you work on the farm?"

"Oh yes, from the time I was eleven years old, I worked on his farm and several others. I can do just about anything on a farm." Richard thought he was creating an advantage by hinting that he could help out a bit, but Bernard had another idea. The old man eyed him shrewdly.

"I'll tell you what, Dick. I'll give my blessing to this marriage, but only if you and Kate live on the farm here. I can't afford to spare her now. Her sisters are too young to do the work in the dairy. And the farm needs a young man. I'm getting older, and I can't see to things as I used to. If you settle here, you may take it over eventually."

Richard was stunned. This was not the future that he and Kate dreamed of. Certainly not their charmed circle. Not that he wanted to work as a currier all his life, but he saw the farm as a step backward. He wanted to be in town where there were people to talk to, people with forward-looking ideas and plans. He knew that Kate felt she had spent more than enough time milking cows and scouring milk pails. "That's a very generous offer, Mr. Kernan, and I appreciate it. But it's not what either of us want. We want to build a life in town. And it would be a long walk for me every day to get to Squire's. I don't know how much help I would be to you on the farm."

Bernard's jaw set. He was adamant. "Let me be the judge of that. If you want to marry my daughter, you must come out to the farm."

For Richard, there was no choice, and he knew Kate would say the same. "Well, we'll try it, Mr. Kernan."

So Richard married his Kate, and moved out to the Kernan farm. He was able to find work at a smaller currying shop, near the Wilmington line. Still it was not an easy life. In the summer, Bernard expected him to work until dark after he got home from his shift. But he didn't much mind the extra work. He was young and strong and it was good to be out in the fresh air after currying hides for eleven hours a day. And being with Kate, every morning and all night long, made up a hundred times for dealing with Bernard. The farm did well with them all working, and they were able to add some cows.

Richard took great joy in the birth of his son in August, 1877. He named him Thomas Augustine, after his father and his favorite saint. At twenty-nine, Richard was a happy man. He had a family he loved deeply and a steady, fairly well-paying job. But he and Kate longed for a home of their own where they could live and raise their children as they thought best, without interference from Bernard. They were determined to free themselves gradually from the farm. Kate was teaching her sisters about the dairy, and in a year or two, they would be old enough to handle everything about the milk on their own. One good thing about living on the farm was that Richard was able to save most of his pay, so they would have a good nest egg when they moved.

What really bothered Richard about living in Wilmington was that Bernard stubbornly refused to let them use the horse to drive to church on Sunday. The closest Catholic church was three miles away. It took them nearly an hour to walk when the weather was good. In the winter, it was sometimes impossible for Kate to go. When Kate was coming close to delivering her second baby, in the spring of 1879, enough was enough. He decided to have it out with Bernard.

Richard found his father-in-law in the barn, checking on one of the cows. "The dragon in his den," he thought. He meant to sound pleasant but businesslike. "Could I have a word with you, Bernard?"

Bernard turned his head and looked at him, and then his jaw set in its familiar way. He stood up, the light from the window framing his hulking body. The image of his grandfather so many years before came into Richard's mind. Only this time he was not a powerless little boy, but a man who was fully capable of taking care of himself and his family.

"Now that the baby is getting close, Kate will need her rest on Sunday. She can't be walking all that way to church and back. We'll need to take the horse and wagon."

"Kate's a strong girl. The horse needs its rest more than the two of you."

"It's light work for the horse to take us to town and back."

"I'll not give in on this, Dick. This farm depends on that horse. You can stay here and say your prayers if it's too much for you to walk to town."

"I'm afraid I'll not give in either. Kate and I try to be good Catholics. We go to Mass every Sunday. I know you don't share our conviction, but I ask you to respect it. And I will not have my wife walking six miles in the heat and the rain when she has a child coming. If we can't take the horse, we will have to move into town."

Bernard hesitated. Richard could see him calculating. Bernard knew Richard was stubborn. Almost as stubborn as he was. And he did not take his religion lightly. But the farm was Bernard's life, and the animals were the farm. "Well, you'll have to go then," he said.

So Richard and Kate moved into Woburn, and he went back to work at Squire's. In July of 1880, a daughter was born. They named her Bridget Veronica after Kate's mother, but Tommy, who had wanted a brother, insisted on calling the baby Joe. So Josie she became to everyone in the family ever after. Just a month later, a new house next door to his sister Ann's was put on the market. Richard and Kate decided the time had come for them to have their own home. On the strength of his job, he was able to invest his savings and take a mortgage on the house at 19 Arlington Street. It was a two-story with a parlor, dining room and kitchen downstairs, four rooms upstairs, a large attic, and a full cellar. In the first few weeks after they bought it, Richard would stand across the street and look at the house on the way home from work, thinking of how far he'd come from being thrown out of his home and sleeping in the loft of Aunt Lizzie and Uncle Pat's cabin in Tirhogar.

Having no money to spare after the down payment, they furnished the house with second-hand furniture and odds and ends that Richard's sisters and Kate's mother gave them. Kate soon had the house looking homey. Her handiwork showed in the quilt on the bed, the table cloths, and the braided rugs on the floor, and they spent a good deal of time selecting lithographs to put on the walls. Richard and Kate soon established a comfortable life in Woburn. He worked his fifty-nine hours a week and was tired at night, but it was still a great joy to come home to his wife and her good cooking and comfortable house, and to play with his children.

Freed from the farm work on Saturday afternoons, Richard was able to resume his old habit of going to the library and picking out his book, although it was usually one rather than two now, as he had other things to occupy his time. In 1879, an imposing new sandstone building had been built for the library on Pleasant Street. Richard always felt a little twinge of excitement, the promise of something new, when he climbed up the little hill, crossed the wide lawn, and entered the building. He never could get over the Woburn public library. He didn't go out at night much, but sitting and reading to Kate as she sewed or knitted in the evening was the best recreation he could imagine.

Then, in the fall, sickness came to the house. In November, the children both had sore throats, and Tommy came down with scarlet fever. After nursing him for a week, Kate got it too. As a girl, Richard's sister Ann had learned something about medicines from their father, whose avocation was collecting herbs and making medicinal preparations. With Ann's careful nursing, Kate and Tommy both got over the scarlet fever, but a couple of weeks later, Kate got sick again, and this time it was more serious. Ann said she was just run down from the earlier illness and taking care of the children, but Richard could see she was worried.

Ann did everything she could, but finally she told him to call the doctor, who diagnosed rheumatic fever, and said Kate's heart was affected. Between them, the doctor and Ann did their best for her, but on the fifth of December, she died, and Richard's world came to an end. He would never recover from the loss of Kate, try as he might to be a good Catholic, a good husband to Maggie, a good father to the children, an upstanding member of the community. He learned to deal with grief by staying in motion, by always having too much to do, by praying and by constant reading in the few hours he might have time to reflect, but the hollowness was always there.

And now he was losing his and Kate's first born and only son. He could feel the sadness descending on him. He sighed deeply, stood up, and took his chair inside. It was time for prayers and bed.

Chapter 5

1881

After a solemn high funeral Mass at St. Charles's, Catherine Terrett was buried in Calvary Cemetery, and Richard was left with two small children and his grief. The Connollys helped all they could. Ann and the two girls, Mary and Margaret, looked after Tom and Josie along with their own baby, and cooked for everyone. Richard went to work and came home and that was all. The charmed circle he had lived in with Kate had broken, and all he knew was darkness. He hardly looked at the children, trying to rid himself of the black thought that Kate would still be alive if they hadn't made her sick. Ann and Jim watched with growing unease as Richard seemed to drown in his grief.

When six months had gone by, Ann decided that something had to be done, and she attacked with characteristic bluntness what she knew would be a weak spot in the wall that Richard had built around him. "You have to think of marrying again, Dick," she said. "The children need a mother and a home. I've done the best I could for them, but you know I've five of my own to look after. We both know what it is to grow up without a mother or a home. Surely you don't want your children to go through that."

Richard had çertainly thought about it. It was one of the thoughts that had most plagued him throughout the misery of the last months. But he could not imagine courting a woman. Not after Kate.

Ann, however, was ready with a plan. “You know Pat Nolan. He thinks his sister-in-law might make a good match for you. She works as a maid for some rich people in Albany, and knows well how to keep house. He says she loves children and has plenty of money. She’s given the passage money for Pat and poor Bridget to go back to Ireland more than once since Bridget’s been stricken with consumption.”

“How old is she?”

“Pat says he thinks she’s about thirty, about your age. She’s a little bit of a thing, and never walks when she can run.”

That suited Richard. He wasn’t interested in a young girl or a love affair. A pleasant, mature woman who would keep a comfortable house and look after the children well was something he could imagine. And a little money wouldn’t hurt. The principal would be due on the mortgage in a few years, and he could use some help with that. “Well, I’ll talk to Pat, and we’ll see,” he said

Bridget Nolan seemed delighted to hear of Richard Terrett’s interest in her sister. She wrote to her immediately, and two weeks later, Margaret Qualter arranged to take the late train down from Albany on Saturday night and stay in Woburn through Sunday. Richard was invited to Sunday dinner after church, which Margaret cooked, an excellent meal. She was a bright, animated woman, with lively blue eyes, a pale complexion, and plain features, but pleasant to look at, especially when she smiled, which was often. She looked about thirty, as Pat had said. Richard thought she was a little high in animal spirits, but that could certainly be the strain of the occasion. He was aware of being more animated than usual himself.

As he walked her to the station, they talked more intimately. She was indeed tiny, probably not five feet tall or a hundred pounds. She hardly came up to Richard's shoulder. He liked that, since she was so different from Kate, who was tall and amply made. He wanted no reminders. They talked about their families, their homes in Ireland. She was from Athenry in County Galway, the Gaeltacht. Gaelic was her first language. He was pleased to hear that her father was an educated man who had been to school in France, although they'd fallen on hard times during the great hunger. Her father had been an estate agent who was discharged for being too easy on his tenants. His was a tax collector who sometimes paid the taxes himself to give his neighbors more time. Like his family, hers had been evicted from their house by a landlord, although it wasn't a relative. She was devoted to her family. She talked happily about working to bring each sister over to America in turn until they were all here. He liked her. He enjoyed her company. He felt no romantic sparks, which was fine with him.

Two weeks later, Margaret came down to stay with the Nolans again, and this time Richard brought her to Ann's house to meet the Connollys and his children. He was happy to see that she did indeed seem to take to the children, especially baby Josie. He showed her his house, and she expressed her admiration for its condition and the decorating that Kate had done. They did some more walking and talking, and he took her to the train. Ann and Jim seemed to like her, and Ann told him all sorts of ways in which she would be a good match, things he hadn't even thought of. Apparently, Ann had found out that she would happily keep a cow and some chickens and plant a kitchen garden.

Two weeks after that, Richard visited Margaret in Albany and met many of her relatives, not all of whom he was able to place. She seemed to have two sisters named Mary. They were a nice family, although more lively and talkative than he was used to. He spent two more weeks thinking about it, and then went to Albany and asked Margaret to marry him. She agreed, and they set the date. They were married at St. Charles's on the eighteenth of September, 1881.

The marriage did not start out well. Kate had always been an open book to Richard. As passionate young lovers, they could not get enough of sharing their thoughts and their secrets. But he had the sense that Margaret kept back a good deal, as indeed did he, and that she was not always truthful. The first big issue was money. Pat Nolan had given him to understand that Margaret would be bringing a good deal of savings to the marriage. Soon after the wedding, Richard asked if she wanted him to put her money in the Winchester Savings Bank. She told him that she only had a few dollars from her wages and a wedding gift from her employers, the Reeds. When she explained that she had spent all her savings on her sisters' passages to America and Bridget and Pat's trips back to Ireland, he did his best to mask his disappointment.

So much for the help with the mortgage. Richard respected Margaret's generous spirit, but he thought she showed a certain flightiness when it came to money. He decided to continue keeping the household accounts himself, rather than turning them over to her. He stopped into Jim Haney's grocery on pay day to scrutinize the account before he paid it, and gave Margaret money when she needed it. Margaret saw this as an insult to her. She felt it was humiliating to have her husband looking over her grocery account. Richard could see her point, but he did not give in.

They could not afford to have his pay frittered away as her savings had been.

Another thing that troubled Richard was the issue of Margaret's age. She had told the clerk that she was thirty years of age, a year younger than he, when they filled out the marriage certificate, but as time went by, he began to suspect that she was appreciably older. One day after they'd been married a few months, he decided to find out.

"You know, I don't know when your birthday is, Maggie."

"I don't know either, Dick. We never took notice of such things at home as they do over here, did you?"

"No, we didn't," he said, "but I know when I was born."

Margaret laughed. "Well I probably would too if I was born on Christmas day." She looked up at him, and he had to smile. They both knew the Christmas birthday was a fiction for the Americans, who were always looking for a birth date for their forms and papers. If all the Irish immigrants who gave December twenty-fifth, March seventeenth, or July fourth as their birthdays were actually born on those days it would be the subject of a scientific study.

"The records in my parish were destroyed by a fire. All I know is that my father told me once when we were working in the fields that I would be twenty years of age on my next birthday. He didn't say what day that was."

"What year was that?"

"Well, let's see, it must have been in 1870. It was just before I came over. I was nineteen then."

From stories that her relatives and she herself had told him, he doubted this. He reckoned that she was a good deal older than nineteen when she came. Not that he cared, really, except that he suspected she had lied to him. A lie was not a good thing, especially in a marriage. It made him distrustful of her, and he suspected that she deceived him in smaller ways as well.

As time went on, they got used to each other. Maggie was a good mother to the children, an excellent housekeeper, and a dutiful wife. As Ann had predicted, she contributed to their income by keeping a cow and chickens and a big vegetable garden. Not only did she supply most of their food, she sold milk and eggs to the neighbors. The money from this was hers to spend as she wished, and she more often spent it on the children or on small luxuries for the table than on herself. She made all the children's clothes as well as her own, and he had never lived in a cleaner house.

For his part, he tried to be a good husband and father. He took more notice of the children, and especially enjoyed reading to Tom now that he was old enough to understand. Maggie had had as much schooling as he, but she didn't care much for books or reading. She was a naturally busy person, and she said that sitting and reading made her nervous, but she did sit with her sewing and listen when he read stories to Tom. As his little son grew older, he made a point of choosing one book at the library each week that he thought Tom would enjoy as well as a book for himself. Tom loved adventure stories, especially those about sailing the seas. They read and re-read Stevenson's *Treasure Island* and *Kidnapped*, and Richard discovered Herman Melville's *Redburn* and *White-Jacket*, but Tom didn't care for them because there were "too many words and not enough adventures." They started *Moby-Dick*, but Tom couldn't follow it, so Richard finished it on his own, and thought it the best book about the sea he had ever read.

Richard spent more time in the library now. During the few hours when it was open and he wasn't working, he would often be found in the big, open reading room. He sometimes felt it was the place where he was most at home, surrounded by the quiet, the warm tones of pine and butternut wood, the alcoves of bookshelves, and the light streaming in the big, two-story windows with their gothic arches, a place so different from the dark, low building where he worked on endless piles of hides six days a week.

Bringing Maggie into his life helped to bring Richard back to reality. He began to think again about the plans he had had for his family's future and to feel more ambitious about getting on in the world. He wanted Tom and Josie to have an education. He would not have them going to work at ten years of age, as many local children did. There was no chance for him to rise from the job of currier at Squire's, so he began to think of switching to a shop where he could work his way up to a better-paying skilled job. Fortunately, in 1881, William Beggs and Elisha Cobb opened a brand new tannery in Winchester, not too far from Arlington Street, and Richard was taken on.

When he went to work there, Beggs and Cobb had the largest and most up-to-date plant among the twenty or so tanneries in Woburn and Winchester. There were separate spaces built for each stage of the complicated process of making leather. Richard was taken on as a leather setter, a job that appealed to him because it meant handling the hides after they had already gone through the tanning process. His work was to run the hides between two heavy drums to press the excess moisture out and to smooth and stretch them so they would be ready to hang up in the drying room, the final stage before the color and finishing was applied. It was steady, heavy work, but much cleaner than scraping the hair or flesh off the hides, and he didn't have to be around the tannin and lime and acids that were used earlier in the process. He quickly became known as a skillful, dependable worker, and his job paid ten dollars a week, two dollars more than he was getting at Squire's. He worried less about the mortgage now, and he found he liked working at Beggs and Cobb. There were many friends from St. Charles's and the Hibernians among the men, some of whom shared his interest in politics. Like most of the others, he had become a citizen as soon as he could, three years after his arrival. He voted, enthusiastically, in every election, but he hadn't been active in local politics. Now he started going to meetings of the Democratic Party.

Chapter 6

1883–1890

In May of 1883, after a long and difficult labor, Maggie Terrett gave birth to a daughter. Richard had been intensely worried. It had begun during the night, and in the morning, when the pains had taken her harder, he had brought the children over to the Connollys' for the girls to look after. Ann sent Richard to work, telling him he would be of no use there, and she and another midwife spelled each other with Maggie. But when he got home from work, she still had not given birth, and was exhausted. They called in the doctor. He said she was not in danger. It was just taking a long time.

"This is her first child, and she's not a young woman," he said. Richard sat downstairs and prayed. Finally, the baby came, and both she and Maggie were all right. Richard was surprised at the depth of his relief. He hadn't realized how worried he was, or perhaps how much he had come to care about Maggie. When the doctor told him that Maggie would probably not have any more children, he was disappointed, but so relieved that she was all right, and so taken with his little daughter, that he was able to make his peace with it.

They called the little girl Mary Angeline, and by the time she was a toddler, she did look like an angel, a pre-Raphaelite one, he thought, with her porcelain complexion, her golden blonde ringlets, her classic features, and her deep blue eyes, like his. Richard came to love this golden child above all else. Maggie noticed, and warned him about favoring her over the other children, especially Josie. It didn't help Josie that Mary was very bright and that Richard taught her to read and sent her to St. Charles's school at four years of age. At first she was a year behind Josie at school, but then Josie was kept back a year, and they were in the same class. Josie was constantly subjected to comparisons with her bright little sister, and Maggie felt they should balance it out at home by making much of Josie and a little less of Mary. To convince himself as much as Maggie, Richard insisted that he was not was favoring her.

"Of course I treat them all the same, Maggie," he would say. "Is there anything I've given to Mary that the others don't have?" Maggie couldn't point to anything like that, and she generally let the subject drop.

Richard was proud of his family, and for the most part enjoyed his comfortable home. Maggie was a good and cheerful helpmate. But having felt true intimacy with Kate, he knew a great deal was missing from their marriage. They had few tastes in common. Richard grew ever more informed about a number of subjects and ever more interested in learning more. He still delighted in reading and reciting poetry, and he tried to pass this interest on to his children. He was disappointed that Maggie cared nothing for literature or history or politics or intellectual conversation. Her idea of leisure, formed during her many years in domestic service, was visiting with friends and relatives over a pot of tea and talking about people and their doings. There was a steady stream of her relatives coming through the house, her sisters and nieces from Albany and New York, or cousins newly landed from Ireland who could always find a place to stay with them until they got themselves situated. Richard did not begrudge her this and considered it his duty to help the new immigrants as his relatives and others in the community had helped him, but the constant noise and activity and the disruption bothered him. He sought the peace and intellectual stimulation of the library.

One Saturday evening in the summer of 1883, Tim Malloy, one of the other leather setters, caught up with Richard as he left the tannery. Richard liked the small, quick-witted man. He was a reader too. At least he read the Boston *Globe*, and Richard enjoyed their conversations about the state of the world and what they referred to as "the future of the working man."

"There's a meeting tonight that I think you'd find interesting, Dick. It has to do with the future of the working man." Tim flashed his trademark grin.

"Oh, a trade union. You know what I think about strikes, Tim. The owners almost always win. Then they fire the men who led the strike, things go on as before or worse, and the rest of the workers are just out the pay they lost during the strike."

"This isn't a trade union, or it's much more than a trade union. I do think you'd find it interesting."

"Well if you think so, Tim. What is it then?"

"I can't tell you that, and I'll have to get your word that you won't tell about anything you hear there."

Richard smiled. "You know I'm a good Catholic, Tim. I can't be swearing any blood oaths."

"That's all right. Your word is good enough for me. And I hope you do come. You'll find a lot of agreement with your views on things. 7:30 tonight in the back room of the Hibernian Hall. You'll need to go in the back door."

Richard rolled his eyes and went on home, but Tim had piqued his interest, as he'd known he would. That evening Richard told Maggie he had a meeting at the Hibernian Hall and went to find out what it was all about.

Tim grinned when he saw Richard, and pointed to the seat he'd saved for him. "I thought you'd come."

The small meeting room was full, perhaps forty men in all. T. P Dolan, a tannery worker, got up to introduce the speaker as David F. Moreland of the Knights of Labor. Richard gave Tim a look, and he nodded. They had talked about the Knights, a group that seemed to be coming on in a number of industries, but it was such a secret thing that it was hard to find out anything about it. It seemed to be one of those trade unions like the Knights of St. Crispin, representing the shoemakers, that wanted to turn back the clock and become like the craft guilds that used to put on the Easter plays in medieval times.

David Moreland did not look like a tannery worker. He looked to be in his late twenties, a well-dressed, slight man of average height with a carefully groomed mustache. Rather elaborate pince-nez were perched on his nose. When he spoke, though, it was in a confident, resonant tone. "Good evening, Gentlemen," he said. "I'm proud to be addressing a group of fellow tannery workers in the town where I grew up."

The man behind Richard snorted and whispered to his neighbor, "The only work he ever did in a tannery was in the office when he was home from college."

He looked it. Richard was curious to find out why a college man was presenting himself as one of them, and what he wanted from them.

"There is a lot of misconception about the Knights of Labor," Moreland said, "so first I would like to explain who we are and where we came from. We are not a trade union, and we do not believe that strikes are a particularly effective weapon for workingmen to use."

Tim glanced at Richard. "The organization began in Philadelphia, on Thanksgiving evening, 1869, when our first Master Workman, Uriah Stephens, met with a few others and designed a secret Order that would be a brotherhood for all workingmen. Our first concern is with a man's character. When we're initiated, we all vow to live by a code of personal behavior that includes honesty, personal integrity, patriotism, chivalry, and mutual assistance, and anyone who violates it is ejected. Although we are not a temperance organization, drunkenness is not tolerated. We permit no man to become or to continue a member of the Order who engages in the sale of intoxicating liquor. The reason is that upholding the good of humanity is a principle of the Order, and we do not believe a liquor seller can be regarded as a benefactor of the human race. Otherwise, any male of eighteen years or any female of sixteen years is eligible for membership, except lawyers, bankers, professional gamblers, and stock brokers." Laughter among the men.

"Now, you've probably heard about us as a secret organization. Well, we were entirely secret at the beginning, for the protection of our members and because the founders believed that the deepest fraternity would be built on the privacy of our code and our ritual. Recently the Order has become more public, and our rituals are no longer as elaborate because we want to work harder at bringing more workingmen (and women) within the fraternity. We believe that mutual assistance should be the central value of this fraternity. When one workingman is attacked or oppressed, the others must stand by him. When one shop finds it necessary to strike, we must stand by it. As an organization, we do not believe in strikes. We believe in the principle of arbitration, and in working to put laws that require arbitration of labor issues into effect in every state. But we also believe that a man who is oppressed beyond a certain point and does not strike is a coward. And when he does, he deserves the assistance of his fellow workers." A general murmur among the group indicated the contentiousness of this issue.

"On the questions of the day, we believe in equal pay for equal work, whether the worker be a white man, a Negro, or a woman. We believe that a regular day's work should be reduced to eight hours." A general assent to this. "We also believe that children under the age of fourteen should be in school, and not in factories or mines. That's why we support an end to child labor. We do not endorse any political party, and we have members belonging to every party. I should point out that local assemblies are completely free to create their own agendas as long as they fall within the general principles and rules of the Order. And now, I would be pleased to answer questions, if you have them."

Richard listened to the questions and answers about starting a local assembly and the relationship of the assembly to the national organization and the Order's stand on various questions. Once he got over Moreland's appearance, he was impressed by his knowledge and enthusiasm, and he admired the principles of the organization. He had always believed that a man's good character was the essential thing, and he liked the idea of a fraternal order based on shared values rather than a trade union that treated workers as units of production.

Richard was interested enough to go to a second meeting, where Moreland gave a lecture on the history of labor which he thought very knowledgeable, though he disagreed on a few things, and there was some discussion of contemporary issues. The men who had returned for the second meeting were given the Order's constitution to study. Richard found that he agreed with almost everything in it, especially the principle of arbitration. At the next meeting, he joined with Tim and about twenty others in petitioning to found a new assembly of the Knights of Labor for Woburn's curriers and tanners. The next time they met, Moreland, as Grand Master Workman of the National Assembly of Leather Workers, enacted the ceremony to found and institute a local assembly with the men.

On this occasion, Moreland assumed a demeanor that to Richard seemed somewhere between that of a priest saying Mass and the President of the Ancient Order of Hibernians presiding over a meeting. The ceremony was not especially elaborate, but the men felt a little self-conscious and awkward performing in the unfamiliar ritual as Knights of Labor. Moreland, with his pince-nez in place and his most solemn air, read the constitution aloud, and then asked them, "Do you approve of those objects and all legitimate effort for the benefit of labor and the cause of humanity?" When they affirmed this, he asked, "Are you willing to take a pledge of secrecy, obedience and mutual assistance that will not interfere with any religious convictions you may entertain or your duty to your country?" When they affirmed this, he placed a drawing of the Great Seal of Knighthood in the center of the room, directing the men to form a circle around it, and said, "Thus do I imprint the Great Seal of Knighthood at the center, and thereby dedicate this new Assembly to the service of Humanity."

The men took the pledge of honor, in which they promised not to reveal any of the signs or secret workings of the Order, or to reveal to any employer or other person the name of any member without his permission, and to defend the life, interest, reputation and family of all the members and help all members to procure employment and secure just remuneration. They also affirmed that they would consider the pledge of secrecy binding until death. Like the other men, Richard took this pledge, made upon his word of honor, very seriously. He never broke it.

With a decisive motion, Moreland rapped the table once, then told the men to be seated, came to the center of the room and said, "Now by the authority vested in me, I declare this assemblage duly and legally organized and founded as a Local Assembly of the Order of the Knights of Labor." So was born Woburn's Local Assembly 2956, Tanners and Curriers.

Richard's career with the Knights of Labor paralleled the growth of the organization. When he joined in 1883, it was still largely confined to Pennsylvania and some areas in the South, and just beginning to have a presence in New England. Between 1883 and 1888, the growth of the organization was massive. The combination of the dropping of absolute secrecy and high-profile strikes against Western Union and several railroads brought the organization to public view. In 1885, a successful strike against Jay Gould's South West Railway conglomerate brought world recognition and a dramatic rise in membership. The organization had about one million members in 1885. At its peak in 1886, about one in five American workers was a Knight of Labor. During this tremendous expansion, the character of the organization changed. In 1880, it was primarily a fraternal order. In 1886, it was primarily a labor union.

In Massachusetts, the membership of the Knights reflected the national trend. In the early 1880s, it was concentrated in the more skilled trades, the furniture manufacturers in Gardner and the shoe and leather trades in manufacturing centers like Woburn and Winchester. As the movement caught on, local assemblies were started in the poorer cotton manufacturing towns. Two assemblies composed almost entirely of women were established by the shoe stitchers in Natick and Milford. Eventually, there were four local assemblies in Woburn and neighboring Winchester, two of curriers and tanners and two of mixed trades.

As he got to know David Moreland a little and listened to him deliver a number of speeches, Richard developed a great admiration for his knowledge and his ability to call on a seemingly bottomless store of rhetoric to meet any occasion. While he felt his own lack of training and limited education, Richard hoped to emulate Moreland in some ways. His fellow workers had always respected his knowledge and opinions, and he thought he had ideas on a number of issues that were worth sharing. Although he had never made a public speech before, he had never been shy in an argument, and had enjoyed reciting for an audience since his school days. With Tim's encouragement, he asked the program chairman of the assembly if he would like him to speak on the topic of "the history and purpose of fraternal orders in America." Only too glad to have another speaker, the chair assigned him to speak at a meeting two weeks later.

Richard prepared very carefully. He had read not only the Order's publications on the topic, but some other things he had found in the library when he was deciding whether or not to join. He had found that, although there were significant differences among such groups as the Freemasons, the Odd Fellows, the Knights of Honor, the Knights of the Golden Eagle, the Ancient Order of Hibernians, they all shared the ideal of fraternity and mutual assistance that he thought was most valuable in the Knights of Labor. He wanted to emphasize to the members that this should always be their ideal, whether in fraternal activities or in labor actions. He spent some extra time in the library that week, outlining the points he would make and noting particular facts he wanted to emphasize.

The lecture turned out to be a bit short, because he got through his points more quickly than he had expected, but the men listened respectfully and applauded him sincerely. Moreland shook his hand at the end of the meeting, and said, "Nice work, Terrett. That was a thought-provoking lecture."

Richard had never experienced anything like this. Here he was, a tannery hand with five years' education, addressing an audience about his own ideas and being congratulated on his speech by an eloquent college graduate. He became a regular speaker on a variety of topics, and his advice was often asked on issues before the assembly. As he rose in its ranks throughout the 1880s, he gave more and more of his time to the Knights of Labor, and he earned a reputation among the tanners and curriers as an inspiring and effective leader. Richard worked his way through the hierarchy of the Order, finally assuming the highest local office of Master Workman of the Knights' Local Assembly 2956, Curriers and Tanners.

When a mass meeting was called in August of 1889 to protest a wage cut at Eustace Cummings & Company, Richard naturally was elected to chair it. In accepting the chair, he reminded the men that they had compromised on wages three years earlier in the spirit of arbitration and that the manufacturers had cut wages several times since. His statement that "the workingmen of Woburn had suffered altogether too long, and had been ground down beyond endurance" was quoted in the Boston *Journal*.

Richard introduced David Moreland to give the major speech. Moreland, who had always counseled arbitration in the past, surprised him by calling on the men to unite in opposition to the wage cut, saying, "I feel it is time to stand up and protest. It is a well-known fact that in many shops the men's condition is not much better than a mere slave. Men have been discharged simply because they have opened their mouths in complaint, and we can stand this petty tyranny no longer. They make only a machine of a man, and he is looked at in the same light as a stoning or a blackening machine. If you have any manhood, you will demand a recognition of our rights." He urged them to appoint a committee to go to Cummings and protest the wage cut, saying that the General Assembly of the Knights would back them if they struck, and he personally would raise the money from the other assemblies for the strike fund. The meeting voted to send Moreland and two other men to "wait upon Mr. Cummings and in behalf of the workingmen of Woburn protest against the reduction." The action was successful in staving off the wage cut, at least for the time being.

A natural outgrowth of his work in the Knights was Richard's increasing interest in local politics. Although the Knights of Labor resolutely refrained from endorsing any candidate or party and made it clear that no member would be compelled to vote with the majority on anything, their statement of principles stressed that their agenda could only be realized through legislation. It was the duty of all to assist in nominating and supporting with their votes only those candidates who would pledge their support to the pro-labor agenda.

Richard looked to Grand Master Workman Terence Powderly as his example. After assuming leadership of his local assembly, he had been elected mayor of Scranton, Pennsylvania, and had held that office until his position as national leader of the Knights had made it too much for him. Locally, David Moreland was active in Democratic politics and had recently been made City Clerk. Richard believed that the only way to get the interests of labor represented in the local government, which was largely controlled by tannery owners and other wealthy men, was to get workingmen elected. He worked for the Democrats, and in 1886 they nominated him for Constable, although the ticket wasn't elected.

In 1888, Woburn, which had been a town, had just ratified its new city charter and was about to elect its first mayor. Richard attended the city nominating convention of the Democrats and watched the election carefully with an eye to seeing what the possibilities were. He was not surprised to find Republican Edward Johnson, a ninth-generation descendent of the first settler of Woburn and the son of a prominent banker, elected the first mayor of Woburn. Johnson promptly announced that reducing taxes would be the signature aim of his administration and declared that the number of police and fireman should be cut to save money. Richard knew that the same people who had always run the town—the bankers and tannery owners and lawyers, the closed circle of wealthy families—would continue to run the city, unless the labor vote exercised its strength, which was in sheer numbers. So without injecting politics directly into any of the Knights of Labor's official activities, he took every chance he got to talk to fellow Knights about the importance of forming a solid labor majority that could really influence what happened in the city.

As he had hoped, there were a number of tannery workers present at Woburn's Democratic nominating convention in 1889. They were incensed when the meeting voted to endorse Mayor Edward Johnson as the Democrats' candidate as well as the Republicans', but they didn't know what to do about it. Tim Malloy took Richard aside and talked to him with uncharacteristic earnestness. He showed him the nomination form he had gotten from the City Clerk's office, expecting just this outcome from the meeting. "This form requires fifty signatures from eligible voters, Dick. If you will run for mayor, I will have the signatures for you tomorrow."

Richard's jaw dropped. "Me? Why wouldn't we ask David Moreland? He's the Knight with the best political connections in the city, and he's an educated man."

"I knew you'd say that," said Tim, "but Moreland's not going to run for us. He has a cushy job as City Clerk where he's connected to both political parties. Why would he jeopardize that? I know you admire him, Dick, but to be frank, I've never been sure whether he was one of us among them, or one of them among us."

Much as he respected Moreland and his talents, Richard knew what Tim meant, but he still couldn't see himself as a candidate for mayor. "You know as much about the city as I do, Tim. Why don't you run?"

Tim grinned. "I know a lot, but these Yankees take one look at my mug and my red hair and see 'Mick.' You can talk like they do, and when you're dressed in a nice dark suit, you look like them. It's not only our men who listen to you, but some of the other people in town as well. You could get elected, Dick. I couldn't. It's what we need for labor to really have our say in how things are run. Why shouldn't you be the mayor?"

Richard knew that Maggie wouldn't like this. She never said anything directly, but had already made it clear that she thought he spent too much time with all the activity for the

Knights, leaving her to cope with the children, the house, the vegetable garden, and the animals by herself. A campaign would require that she make some public appearances with him, which he knew she would dread. But he also knew that Tim was right. Anyway, there was no chance he would be elected. It was just a first step. It was the symbolism of the thing for the other men that was important—a workingman, a Knight of Labor, running for mayor.

"All right, Tim. You can try. We might as well see what happens."

The next day was Saturday, the short day at the tanneries. Tim started quietly collecting signatures there and finished after work. True to his word, when he showed up at Richard's house that afternoon, he had collected fifty-three signatures. They quickly filled out the rest of the forms and headed for City Hall. But when Richard tried to file the petition at the City Clerk's Office, he was told he was too late, that the last day to file had been the day before, the day of the Democratic convention. They appealed to David Moreland, who, as City Clerk, was empowered to make the judgment about this. Although they were not expecting him to embrace their cause with enthusiasm, they were surprised at the brusqueness of his reply when they explained the problem.

"I'm sorry, gentlemen, but it's too late. You had to file yesterday."

Tim flushed. "But the convention was only held yesterday. How is a man supposed to know whether he wants to run independently or not?"

"I'm sorry, that's the rule. But I will consult the City Solicitor for his opinion."

Tim and Richard knew very well that the City Solicitor was a political appointee of the mayor's, an insider who would do whatever the mayor wanted. Tim grew a little insistent. "You have the power to make this decision, Moreland. This is a chance to use it to help workingmen. It's just what the Knights are always talking about."

Moreland became annoyed. He removed his pince-nez from his nose, leaned back in his chair, and looked coldly at Tim over his desk. "My office requires that I be impartial," he said. "I've spent a long time building the trust of both the Republican and Democratic officials in this city. Given my affiliation with the Knights, that trust would be completely undermined if there were even the appearance of favoritism to the labor constituency."

Richard saw that it was time to intervene. "That's completely understandable," he said. "We'll wait for the City Solicitor's ruling."

When they left the office, Tim said, "I hope you see now what I mean about Moreland. He makes grand public speeches, but we can't count on him to be on our side in anything. The City Solicitor's going to rule against us, so we need to have a plan to fight back. I'll check with a few Democratic lawyers to get their opinion on the rule about filing, and you scour today's and tomorrow's newspapers to see if any other towns have allowed candidates to file after Friday."

It was no surprise when the City Solicitor agreed with Moreland's decision, and he refused to hear any more appeals. But Tim was by no means ready to give up. He organized support in every ward of the city, and he encouraged Richard to write a letter to the newspapers explaining the situation.

*****

"Mr. Terrett Objects," Boston *Globe*, November 29, 1889, page 7.

" . . . To Whom It May Concern: Be it known to the citizens of Woburn, irrespective of past party affiliations. We believe that an injustice has been done us on account of the action of the city clerk and city solicitor of Woburn, by not allowing the name Richard Terrett, as a candidate for mayor, to be printed on the tickets.

Richard Terrett received the names of 53 qualified voters inside of three hours on Saturday, Nov. 23. The paper was certified by a justice of the peace, and by the registrars of voters, and yet David F. Moreland, city clerk, and Francis P. Curran, city solicitor, stood on their dignity and said that nomination papers filed on Saturday, Nov. 23, were too late, notwithstanding the opinion of such counsellors as M. T. Allen, J. W. Johnson, J. G. Maguire and others to the contrary, and also notwithstanding the fact that Brockton, Holyoke, Taunton, Holbrook and other places received nominations the same day.

Now, we have not one harsh word to say against Edward F. Johnson, the Republican candidate for mayor, but, on the contrary, would say that he has been very friendly with us. However, we can get there, provided all lovers of liberty and fair play do their duty Dec. 3.

In each compartment will be a pencil with which to write the name of Richard Terrett X under the name of Edward F. Johnson.

Very respectfully,
Richard Terrett."

*****

With his name not even on the ballot, Richard didn't expect much from the election, but he campaigned whole-heartedly for the next two weeks, making speeches around the city that promoted a pro-labor platform and explaining exactly why the policies that Johnson's administration pursued were not good for the majority of citizens. The biggest problem they faced was trying to run a write-in campaign when probably half of Richard's supporters couldn't read or write. Tim came up with the idea of having stickers with Richard's name printed up so that the voters could just stick them on the ballot under Johnson's name and mark them with an X.

When the election was held on December third, of course Johnson won, but Richard made a surprisingly good showing for a write-in candidate. He received more than eight hundred votes to Johnson's 1,385, although four hundred of them were thrown out because the stickers were put in the wrong place or not marked with an X in the right place on the ballot. Overall, the election returned a heavy Republican majority of Aldermen and City Council members, many of them connected with the tannery owners. Among those elected to the City Council was William Beggs, the owner of the tannery where Richard worked.

On December eighth, just five days after the mayoral election, the owners of the tanneries and currying shops in Woburn and Winchester announced that they had formed a Leather Manufacturer's Association and issued a new price list, or list of wages, that would be in effect throughout the industry. They insisted it was only a list of minimum wages below which no manufacturer could go, undercutting the others by saving on labor. The list of wages, they said, would not prevent any manufacturer from paying more. The men found this laughable. The wages listed in the newspaper were lower than the current ones that had been in effect since the last arbitration of 1886, which were lower than the wages of the previous two years.

The published compact of the Leather Manufacturers' Association also provided that, if a difference arose between one employer and his employees which they could not settle, all of the other manufacturers would cease work, thus establishing a lockout throughout the industry. As they probably expected, the first lockout went into effect just three days later, when one of the manufacturers shut down in anticipation of a strike after the price list was posted, and the others prepared to shut down in accordance with their agreement. The Knights reacted immediately, calling a general strike in the whole industry. Beggs and Cobb, where Richard worked, was among the four shops that issued lockouts. The rest of the twenty-four manufacturers were struck by the men.

On December eleventh, a mass meeting of nearly two thousand tanners and curriers was held in the roller-skating rink owned by Carter's Skating Academy. Several speakers from the Divisional Assembly of the Knights of Labor reviewed the history of strikes, counseled moderation, and expressed the opinion that the fight would be a short one. Richard offered a resolution to the meeting that was in keeping with the pro-arbitration principles of the Knights.

*****

"Deserted Woburn," Boston *Globe*, December 12, 1889, page 8.

" . . . Whereas, we the workingmen of the city of Woburn feel aggrieved at the strife now existing in our midst between labor and capital, where unity and harmony should prevail, the cause of which is attributed to a price list recently issued by the manufacturers of this city;

Resolved, That we, the Knights of Labor, firmly protest, in a friendly spirit, and in the name of humanity, against said price list, as being unfit to be received by Christian men, who are to maintain their families in respect and honesty, be it further

Resolved, That we submit a copy of our price list, together with a copy of the manufacturers' list to the State Board of Arbitration for settlement, hoping that we may receive equality of rights and equality of privileges before the constitutional laws of Massachusetts."

*****

Richard's resolution was adopted unanimously by the meeting. By the evening of December twelfth, there was only one Woburn tannery in operation, the one owned by Captain John P. Crane, who had refused to join the manufacturers' cartel and had not cut his wages. Crane, a vociferously independent and liberal-minded man, instead raised the wages for several classes of his laborers. In keeping with his modern views, Crane had done away with his factory whistle some time earlier, but as a way of demonstrating their enthusiastic support for Crane, the men went out and acquired a whistle, set it up, and took it on themselves to blow it in order to show that there was one tannery in town where they were proud to work. The J. P. Crane tannery, at the end of Belmont Street, was just down the hill from Richard's land. Every time he heard the whistle, he regretted his choice of employers.

The manufacturers were in no hurry to settle the strike. There were many people in the city who believed that the tannery owners had precipitated it because the shoe industry was paying low prices for leather, and they were overstocked. In fact, the strike did raise the price of leather, as customers bought what they could in anticipation of a shortage if the strike went on. Throughout the next month, the manufacturers managed to sell off their accumulated stock and got good prices for it.

The month of December was a bleak one for the striking families. The Knights' strike fund paid them just enough for essential food and coal. If they had nothing extra put by, they suffered. Still, no one broke ranks, and the workers from Boston who were hired by Skinner & True to unload their hides refused to work once they understood there was a strike. On the days when they weren't on the picket line, most of the men came down to the Knights' Hall to hear the latest strike news and just gather for moral support. The Knights organized sports contests inside and outside the skating rink almost every day so the men could either watch or participate in foot races, baseball and football games, and the popular roller-polo matches that were normally held in the rink. As an officer in the Knights, Richard went to the Hall every morning to plan strategy and take care of necessary business.

The leaders in the Knights made a point of making the rounds of the tanneries each day to talk to the picketers and see how things were going. On the twenty-third, as he approached Beggs and Cobb, Richard was alarmed to see a crowd of more than a hundred men outside the gates. They didn't seem agitated or violent, but they were shouting things at someone in the yard. When he got closer, his alarm changed to amusement when he saw several of the foremen and managers, including William Beggs himself, with their coats off and their sleeves rolled up on this raw day, unloading hides from the railroad cars. The men were getting the most out of the spectacle, shouting encouragement to the bosses and offering them work if they would come down to the other tanning yards. Beggs had come up through the ranks in the tanneries, and he knew what he was doing. The work was proceeding at a fast pace, but the bosses, unused to hard work, tired themselves out pretty fast in the men's opinion. Someone yelled, "try doing that for eleven hours a day!" every time a winded and red-faced man paused to rest.

The approach of Christmas made things more difficult for the families, especially ones with small children like the Terretts. The owners had of course timed their action so that a strike would come in December, and there was little money for celebrating and not much good cheer in Woburn that year. Richard told Maggie he thought they should forego their usual Christmas dinner and just give token gifts to the children unless the strike was settled.

"But Dick," she said, "the children have been looking forward to this day for weeks, for months. They've been eating nothing but eggs and milk and bread and our potatoes and canning from the garden. Surely we can afford to give them a decent Christmas dinner. The neighbors haven't been as prompt as usual in paying, but I've still some egg and milk money that I can spend on treats."

In the end, they decided that Maggie would kill a chicken for their dinner and buy the raisins and currants and candied fruit for a Christmas cake. She would make the children's favorite vegetable dishes, mashed potatoes and gravy, glazed carrots and candied sweet potatoes. They would let the children hang up their stockings, but would fill them with oranges and gingerbread men rather than toys or more expensive gifts. Maggie had been knitting new mufflers and mittens for the children in odd moments, and she was ready with those gifts. With the bit of spare change she had left, she planned to buy some penny candy and little gimcracks to add to their stockings. Richard felt bad not to be giving each of the children a nice gift, as was his custom. Eleven-year-old Tom had been talking for weeks about a new sled to replace his broken one. The little girls pulled at Richard's hands and dragged him over to Meyer's window to see the particular dolls they admired every time they passed the store. He knew just which ones they were. He tried to explain the strike and the reasons for it to the children, but they were too young to understand. And Maggie wasn't any help. He knew that she didn't really believe in the strike. Try as he might to explain the Knights' position, she just didn't see the necessity for it.

Tuesday, Christmas Eve, was a clear day with a bite in the air. As he walked to the Knights Hall, Richard felt that the delayed winter was definitely on the way. The strike news was promising, though. The Manufacturers Association had finally agreed to a meeting to begin arbitration. The men immediately became more cheerful, and "Merry Christmas!" was heard often as they left the hall that day. As Richard passed Meyer's, he noticed that everything had been marked down for pre-Christmas sale. The stores were having as hard a time as the workers this Christmas. He looked at the window display. Both of the dolls were marked down to twenty-five cents, and there was a sled for forty-five cents. After hesitating for a few minutes, he went in and bought them, as well as a pair of warm felt slippers to replace the ones that Maggie had long since worn out. Today he felt that Maggie was right. Regardless of how long the strike went on, they should all have one happy day at least.

When he got home, he rather shamefacedly told Maggie he'd spent a dollar on gifts for the children. She was only a little surprised. "I knew you'd relent in the end," she said, "but I didn't know how much. The children will be so happy."

Maggie was more surprised when she opened the box with the slippers after they'd come home from midnight Mass. Dick actually thought he saw tears in her eyes. And he was touched when he saw the fine warm scarf she had knitted him. A lot of work had gone into it, as well as the egg money. "Well, we've done it," Maggie said to him on Christmas night, after the dinner and the singing and the reading of the Christmas stories. "We made a holiday. It makes me think of the old days back in Athenry when a candle in the window and some singing and dancing with the neighbors made us forget about the hard times and just enjoy Christmas."

"You were right, Maggie," he said. "I should listen to you more often."

"Yes, you should," she said, smiling up at him.

He laughed. "I know I haven't been the easiest person to live with during all this, and it's a hardship to be without the money. It's all a terrible worry, but I hope the outcome will be worth it for all of us."

"And I hope so too," she said. Given her feelings about the strike, it was a big concession.

The strike negotiations proceeded slowly. The conference took place on the afternoon of Christmas Day. The Knights submitted their wage list, which was about 15% higher than the one the owners had published two weeks earlier, but about the same as the list they had agreed to back in 1886. The Manufacturers countered that it was not the wages but the issue of who controlled the amount of labor in a day's work, how many hides a man would work on, that they cared about. After some fruitless negotiating, the Knights offered to concede the question of what constituted a day's work and submit the wages to arbitration.

On December twenty-sixth, a second conference between the negotiating committees was held, and the Manufacturers Association rejected their offer and refused to alter their list of wages. The men could come back to work at the lower wages. The Knights said they would take the matter to the whole assembly, which met that night in Carter's skating rink. More than a thousand men stood shoulder to shoulder in the rink with their eyes trained on their union leaders on the raised dais. After reviewing the history of the strike, David Moreland reported the result of the conference and asked for a vote on the question of whether the Manufacturers Association proposal should be accepted. The vote was seventeen yes to 1,115 no. Moreland gave a rousing speech to the enthusiastic men, saying "you must not go into this fight with drums and cymbals, but in cold blood, and keep up the flag of free labor, and see to it that we are not obliged to put out the black flag of surrender."

Finally, at a conference on January seventh, the Manufacturers Association offered to come up on wages and the Knights offered to come down. The full meeting of the owners endorsed the Knights' offer to submit to binding arbitration by the state board. On January tenth, a freezing cold day, the Knights met in the skating rink, and were warmed by cheers and shouting when Moreland ordered them back to work, pending arbitration.

When the Arbitration Board released its decision on January thirty-first, it noted that, other than the fifty-nine-hour week, the amount of work required in a day was expressly excluded from consideration, and released its new compromise list of wages. This list fulfilled one of the primary goals of the

Knights in that it raised the lowest-paid workers to a living wage. No worker was to be paid less than nine dollars a week, which meant a twelve percent raise for the lowest-paid workers over the Manufacturers Association's proposed eight dollars. On the other hand, while the pay of most workers was raised by from fifty cents to a dollar a week, the wages of the highest-paid, most skilled workers remained at what the manufacturers had set, thirteen or fourteen dollars. As a leather setter, Richard's wage was set at eleven dollars a week, a dollar more than the manufacturers had posted, but the same as he had been making before the strike. The blackers, whose wage went from ten-fifty to ten dollars, were particularly incensed.

Richard wasn't pleased when David Moreland, who was the chief negotiator, implied that he was to blame. Those who weren't at the meeting read in the Boston *Globe* that Moreland had reminded the men that the resolution for binding arbitration, which everyone knew Richard had authored, had gone through at the first meeting "with a rush and without a dissenting vote." At that time, he said, "the executive board had not uttered a word or recommended anything, but they took the mass meeting at its word." In his skillful way, he suggested that every action the negotiators had taken on behalf of the men was all with the intention of carrying out this resolution. As to the new wage list, he said, "an agreement had been made to abide by the decision and we are in honor bound to it." After this meeting, some of the men who had lost wages by the settlement grumbled that Terrett had gotten them into a bad deal by binding them to arbitration.

In mid-February, Richard was finally back at work, after being locked out or on strike since December twelfth. The strike had been hard on his family. Financially, they were all right, better off than most, because Richard was always careful with money and had savings to fall back on, as well as the milk, eggs, and canning from Maggie's garden. With Richard out of work, however, the routine that he and Maggie had established in the household was disrupted.

Although he went out every day to the Knights' hall or to take his turn on the picket line, Richard was at home more, something that Maggie said she almost regretted that she had ever wished for, because he was always advising her about saving money, shushing the children so he could read, or quizzing them on their school work, which made them nervous and sometimes ended in tears. And he was on edge himself. His disposition, never sunny, was not helped by constant worry over the strike news and anger at the latest action by the bosses. Although he kept his vow of secrecy about the Knights' meetings, he complained to Maggie about the owners, the latest problem with the strike, the mistakes Moreland and the executive board were making. And as time went on, Maggie became more and more anxious about the strike herself, questioning whether the bosses would ever take the men back. She suffered from "sick headaches," and these increased as the strike went on. It was a great relief to them all when Richard went back to work.

David Moreland was elected to the State Legislature on February 11, 1890, on his third try, by two votes. Moreland was largely given credit for avoiding a prolonged strike or violence at the tanneries. Richard still resented him for having gone out of his way to block his candidacy for mayor the year before. And, despite his high rank, Moreland was not devoted to the Knights of Labor or the cause of the workingman in the way that Richard was. He knew that now. But whatever his personal feelings about Moreland, Richard thought that having the chief negotiator for the Knights of Labor assembly elected to state office was a good sign for the future.

In the fall, Richard talked the political situation over with Tim Malloy and some of the other men who had developed an interest in local politics. They wondered whether the time was right for a real run at the mayor's office by one of the city's well-known union men. Between them, Richard and Tim decided to try it. Rather than risk being disqualified again, Richard put together his petition and Tim collected the signatures before the nominating convention. He filed his papers with Moreland on November eleventh.

The *Journal*, Woburn's Republican newspaper, wrote favorably of his candidacy, "Richard Terrett, for many years a prominent and influential member of the Democratic party in this city, is a candidate for the office of Mayor and will make a bold, hard push for victory. Mr. Terrett has led the Woburn Democracy in many a tough battle in years past (sometimes to success and again to defeat) and it is only fair that the party should now turn to and place their old leader and honored champion at the head of our city government. In justice to Mr. Terrett the *Journal* would say that he is 'in it' to stay."

William Kenney, owner of the Kenney and Murphy tannery and one of the prominent figures working on the manufacturers' side in the strike, was the favorite to become the Democratic candidate. Word went around immediately that Terrett was aiming to undercut William Kenney by declaring as an Independent. On the eighteenth, Richard clarified his intentions by telling a newspaper reporter that he was not in the field for the nomination with any intention of assisting the Republican candidate.

At the Democratic nominating convention on the twentieth, Richard received two of the twenty-three votes, with six going to George F. Bean, a liberal lawyer, and thirteen going to Kenney. Kenney had served as alderman from the Third Ward for several years, running on both the Republican and Democratic lines, and was the current chairman of the city council. On the same day, he was nominated for mayor by the Republican convention as well, and Bean received one vote. The Boston *Journal* reported that the uncertainty of his election on a nomination by the Democrats alone had led Kenney to announce that he would not stand as a candidate unless nominated by both parties, and "sharp work has finally brought this about."

Meeting Mr. Moreland's deadline, immediately after the meeting, George F. Bean filed the papers to run as an Independent candidate. The list of candidates printed in the Boston *Globe* on November twenty-fourth included George F. Bean, Citizen, William C. Kenney, Republican and Democrat, and Richard Terrett, Independent Democrat.

A story in the Boston *Journal* suggested that "Mr. Terrett will receive the votes of many workingmen unless he withdraws in favor of Mr. Bean, as it is rumored that he will, both he and Mr. Bean being opposed to Mr. Kenney's candidacy." It added that "Mr. Terrett has been a leader among the workingmen for a number of years, and his honesty of purpose has gained him many friends." But many of Richard's friends and supporters voiced their doubts about continuing with the campaign. The prospect of a workingman running against a popular tannery owner who had a great deal of political experience in the city as well as the endorsement of both parties was bleak in the best of times. And things had changed in Woburn since last year. With the memory of the lockout and strike still fresh, the election would inevitably be seen as a repetition of the battle between laborers and manufacturers, pitting Richard against the most popular figure among the owners. With a number of the men disillusioned by the arbitration's outcome, the enthusiastic support of labor that he would need to make a showing was in doubt. And Bean would get the liberal Democratic vote that might otherwise have gone to him. He was certain to lose, they felt, and the broader issues that he hoped to address would never be heard. Most of them advised against running.

Accepting the inevitable, Richard wrote to Moreland, sending a copy of his letter to the Boston *Globe*.

"David F. Moreland, city clerk of Woburn:

Having carefully inquired from those who were my steadfast friends heretofore as to the possibility of my being elected as mayor in the coming contest, about six-tenths of them have advised me to withdraw my name.

This I regret to do, because I believe the workingmen of Woburn by their demands on me to do so, are carelessly throwing away a grand opportunity which would otherwise be to their benefit had they remained faithful to me.

However, it may be to the best interest of the citizens at large to have Mr. Bean instead; therefore I do hereby withdraw as an Independent Democratic candidate for mayor of Woburn, on account of the above stated reason. Yours, Richard Terrett."

On December third, most people were surprised to find that George F. Bean was elected Mayor of Woburn. It was a defeat not only of the manufacturers but of the entrenched interests of political insiders in the city. Richard, who had supported Bean, was pleased at the outcome, but he never got over what he felt was the desertion by his brother Knights at the most crucial time in his fight for political recognition. With Bean and Kenney splitting the Republican and middle-class vote, he felt that labor could have carried the day.

The experience made Richard bitter, not only about politics, but about the Knights of Labor. The Knights was not what it had been six or seven years earlier. What use was a fraternal order if the members didn't stand by each other? Many of the men who had joined or become active members before and during the strike had drifted away from the organization in its aftermath. Their commitment had never really extended beyond the strike anyway.

The Woburn assembly of the Knights followed the organization's national pattern in the 1890s, as it had during the extraordinary growth in membership from 1885 to 1889. The effect of several high-profile failed strikes, the association of the Knights with the Haymarket anarchists in Chicago, and the failure of the national assembly to provide the financial support they had promised some strikers was driving the people whose commitment had never been very deep away from the organization. What's more, in 1890, the fraternal brotherhood of workers, with its code of character and its secret rituals, was beginning to feel like a quaint anachronism. The American Federation of Labor, founded by former Knight Samuel Gompers in 1886, seemed the more modern approach to labor organizing, with its locals based on trade or craft, its limited focus on hours and wages, and its independent political agenda. By 1900, the Knights still existed, but it was a non-factor on the labor scene, which the AFL had come to dominate.

By 1891, Woburn assembly 2956 of Tanners and Curriers had met its end. The Knights' hall on Main Street, where hundreds of men had gathered daily during the lockout and strike, was empty. Carter's skating rink, the scene of thousands of men joining in tumultuous meetings and the triumphant celebration of their win in 1890, was again a quiet place where young people skated together and boys played roller polo after school. When he stopped in to watch Tom sometimes, Richard thought of those days almost with disbelief. He continued to renew his membership, but as far as he was concerned, the Knights as a fraternal and labor organization was finished.

Chapter 7

1891–1901

As the Woburn Assembly of Tanners and Curriers came to an end, Richard began to look for a group that could supply the fellowship he missed from the old days at the Knights, when everyone seemed to believe sincerely in the great things that could be achieved by men who shared an ideal of brotherhood and mutual assistance. He began to think about the possibilities for the Ancient Order of Hibernians, an organization that professed similar high ideals. When Richard came to Woburn in 1869, the Hibernians were still a somewhat secret organization, reflecting their origins in 1836 as a force to protect church property and church members against the assaults of anti-Catholic and anti-Irish thugs like the Know-Nothing party. He didn't think there had ever been violence in Woburn as there had been in places like New York and Boston, but there had been plenty of anti-Irish feeling.

As they moved toward the new century, the Irish had moved into positions of leadership in the city. Now many of the town officials and the leaders in both parties were Irish. There were a few Irish tannery owners as well as workers. The Irish Roman Catholic St. Charles's was the largest and most active church in the city. The Hibernians now operated like the other fraternal organizations in the city, focusing mainly on fellowship and charity, and holding picnics, parades, and sports competitions. They still helped the new immigrants to find jobs and housing, but there were many fewer now than there had been at mid-century. The focus now was more on the insurance fund that paid benefits to widows and orphans.

In 1885, the several Irish societies in the city had combined to provide support for the efforts of Charles Stewart Parnell and William Gladstone to secure Home Rule for Ireland. Like most of the other Irish-Americans he knew, Richard followed the Home Rule campaign avidly, and always made donations to the movement when he was asked. He began to talk with some of the other Hibernians about making the local A. O. H. more relevant to the struggle for Home Rule. Together, they founded Woburn's Division 1 of the A. O. H., Board of Erin, in April of 1890, leased a membership hall on Main Street, and began a membership drive. Richard was elected Vice-President.

In January of 1891, he wrote a letter to the newspapers announcing plans for a St. Patrick's Day celebration and noting that the new division was "the only one in the city connected with the mother country," and the members intended to make it "a credit to the sons and daughters of the Emerald Isle beyond the seas." He became as devoted to the Hibernians as he had been to the Knights, working for the cause of unity among all members. In 1898, when the two national factions of the A. O. H. reunited with ties to Ireland, the group dissolved, and he joined Woburn's old Division 3, quickly becoming an officer.

As he worked on developing the A. O. H.'s ties to Ireland and the Catholic Church in the early 1890s, Richard did some soul searching as well. He contemplated his own identity, particularly his Catholicism. Since his childhood, when his mother had insisted on raising her children Catholic and the Protestant Terretts had thrown them out of their house, Richard's Catholicism had always been a fiercely defended part of his identity. He had gone to Mass every Sunday, even when Bernard Kernan had made it difficult for him, and he had fulfilled his other obligations as a good practicing Catholic. But he began to feel that his religion should go deeper than that. Now that the Knights and the Democrats weren't claiming most of his time, he was able to read something beyond the newspaper again, and he discovered Cardinal Newman, who had founded the Catholic university in Dublin, and some of the other Catholic thinkers.

Richard had always considered his children's education his major responsibility beyond feeding and clothing them. Having felt his own lack of education, he was determined that they would all go to high school and perhaps beyond. Tom went to the Cummings Elementary School in the neighborhood, but Josie and Mary he sent to St. Charles's parochial school, which opened in 1884. When he was at home, and this was more often now, Richard sat with the family around the kerosene lamp on the dining room table in the evening, he reading and supervising the children as they did their lessons, and Maggie knitting or sewing. At nine o'clock, he called a halt to the work, and they all knelt at their chairs as he led them in the rosary. He began to add prayers for the repose of the souls of relatives and friends, some of whom had died years before in Ireland, three Hail Marys for each of them. The children complained that this took longer than the rosary, and they didn't know most of the people, but he wanted them to understand the deep connection they had to the members of their family and to Ireland.

As soon as they were old enough, Richard insisted that Josie and Mary join the Young Ladies' Sodality, which met at St. Charles's church on Sunday afternoons. It was the sort of fraternal society his active public life was built on, but for girls.

With its emphasis on religion, purity and virtue, charity, and a social life with Catholic values, it was just the kind of training he wanted for his daughters.

When Mary was fourteen, she told her parents that she was sure she had a religious vocation. She wanted to join the Sisters of Notre Dame de Namur, the nuns who taught at St. Charles's. This would mean entering the order's novitiate in Cincinnati as a postulant. Richard was pleased that Mary wanted to become a nun. It was an honor to give a child to the Church. But at fourteen, he thought she was too young to know what she wanted for the rest of her life, and he didn't want her leaving home. And in an uncharacteristic show of determination, Maggie made her opposition clear. She told both of them she would not sign any papers giving up her only child at fourteen. To Richard she was more blunt. She said Mary had no fitness for religious life.

"Mary is spoiled,"' she told him. "She could never bow to the rule of obedience that the nuns have. She's had her way about everything since she was a child. She even had her way about the furniture. And I surely don't see her taking a vow of poverty."

The furniture was something of a sore point between them. A year earlier, the girls, especially Mary, had talked incessantly about redecorating the parlor until they had convinced Richard to buy new furniture. Since Maggie wanted no part of making the decisions, Richard brought Mary with him to the furniture store, trusting in her taste and knowledge of what was up to date. They bought three chairs—a platform rocker and two side chairs upholstered in green plush—and a beautifully carved second-hand upright piano. Because they were buying so much, the salesman threw in a corner "what-not" for one dollar.

Maggie was stunned. Even a second-hand piano was an enormous extravagance for the Terretts, and Richard was not given to extravagance. But a piano in the parlor was also the symbol of middle class life, a proof that his children had a better lot in life than he had had. Richard justified the purchase by saying that Mary was making real progress in her lessons and needed an instrument at home to practice on. But Maggie saw it as another instance of Richard's blind indulgence of his younger daughter.

Although Richard grew more skeptical about local politics after 1890, his interest never wavered. He believed that labor could gain enough power on the local level to make a difference in the lives of workingmen and their families. In February of 1893, a series of bank failures precipitated a two-year depression that was the worst the country had experienced up to that time. It affected the manufacturing centers of New England, including the Woburn tanneries, most severely in the winter of 1893–94, when a number of mills, factories, and tanneries were shut down for periods, and some smaller operations closed for good.

The cities took different approaches to the problem of suddenly having large numbers of unemployed people facing a New England winter. Several adopted the "Lynn plan," in which the city employed heads of families at public works, like road building and chopping wood, at a rate of three dollars for three-and-a-half days of work per week. This enabled them to feed their families, but nothing more. In Woburn, under the newly elected mayor, a leather manufacturer named Hugh Murray, some unemployed men were put to work in a wood lot, cutting and cording the wood, which was stored by the city to be sold or distributed to the needy. But nothing systematic was done to address the issue of unemployment and relief for the destitute, who were dependent on the charity of churches and other private organizations. Business began to pick up in the spring and summer, and the hands began to be hired again, but there were still hundreds of unemployed workers in Woburn in the fall of 1894.

For Richard, the experience of the depression had emphasized the precarious position of Woburn's working people and the gulf between the owners and the workers that was elided when times were good and they met on cordial terms at churches and political meetings. With the Knights out of the picture, there was no strong union presence in the tanning industry, and the men in each tannery were pretty much left on their own to try to negotiate wages and conditions with the owner. Beaten down by the severe unemployment of the previous winter, the men were demoralized.

As he had for the last ten years, Richard believed that the future was in the ballot box. There would never be any security for the workingmen until they elected officials and legislative bodies that would make laws to protect them and take positive action when they needed it. He decided that the time had come for him to run for mayor on his own terms, with a straight-out labor platform.

While most of the men called him foolhardy, Tim Malloy and some of his other old friends and supporters shared his belief that workers needed and deserved a voice, however unlikely it was that their advocate would be elected. They easily collected the signatures for the nomination. David Moreland had resigned from the City Clerk's job, but Richard didn't take any chances in filling out the papers. On November tenth, he sent a letter to the newspapers that laid out his agenda. He addressed it to "the citizens of Woburn and my Fellow Workingmen in particular, irrespective of past party affiliations" and thanked his "warm-hearted fellow citizens who had the manly and undaunted courage to sign my nomination papers." Then he laid out his platform, starting with the general principles that had been shared by the city's workingmen since the heady days of the Knights of Labor:

"My political principles are well known, vis. equality of rights, equality of justice and equality of privileges to all men, irrespective of party, color or creed.

I believe in economy, but not in parsimony. I believe in an honest day's wages for an honest day's labor. I believe in reducing the hours of labor whenever and wherever it is necessary to do so. I believe in the elevation of all mankind from poverty to prosperity. I believe there is enough of food and clothing in this country for all its inhabitants, if properly and honestly divided."

Then he got down to particulars, proposing a version of the Lynn plan for Woburn in times of economic depression:

"I believe the main support of the citizens of Woburn is the tanning and currying industries, and I believe that when those industries are dull it should be the duty of our city government to provide employment for our citizens who seek it on our highways and sidewalks, which are in a very poor condition, notwithstanding increase of taxation, and hundreds of men seeking employment.

I believe that money paid out of the city treasury for the maintenance of our highways and sidewalks is only loaned and properly expended because it remains in the city and is divided between the grocer, the butcher, the baker, the clothier, the milkman, the landlord and others and finally returns to the city treasury again by way of taxation."

Then came the heart of his message. He had believed for years that the rights and interests of working people would never be secure until they had real political power. No one was going to give it to them. It was up to them to take it. Knowing that it was probably the death knell of his candidacy, he still made this absolutely clear in his statement:

"I believe in the Constitution of the Commonwealth of Massachusetts, wherein it says the end of the institution, maintenance and administration of government is to secure the existence of the body politic, to protect it and to furnish the individuals who compose it with the power of enjoying in safety and tranquility their natural rights and the blessings of life, and whenever these great objects are not obtained the people have a right to alter the government and to take measures necessary for their safety, prosperity and happiness.

Now, it is a well known fact that people of Woburn are not enjoying the prosperity and happiness the Preamble to the Constitution speaks of, therefore it behooves us to alter the government when we believe in so doing it would be a benefit for the people.

I do not believe in strikes or lockouts between employers and employes, where peace and harmony should prevail; but I do believe and coincide with General Master Workman Sovereign that ballots are more effective than bullets. Therefore there is no need of bullets to strike with, if we only strike properly and unitedly.

The fault is our own if we allow ourselves to be led astray by wily politicians and flowery speeches, as we have in the past, and we will have to stand another year of misgovernment or non-government."

Richard knew that such a straightforward statement of a labor agenda gave him no chance of being elected, but that wasn't really his object. What he wanted was for working people to recognize that their votes were a force to be reckoned with. The race was between two lawyers, George F. Bean, the Democrat who had won with Richard's support in 1890, and Montressor T. Allen, a Republican. But if Richard received a substantial number of votes with his avowed pro-labor platform, the parties would have to consider the factory workers as they formulated their policies in the future. This time, he was able to campaign full out, and he enjoyed himself. He gave speeches all over town, and he campaigned with good humor. The Woburn *Journal* reported that when he was advised to withdraw his candidacy, Richard said, "he pulled for Mr. Bean once and it would be no more than fair for Mr. Bean to return the compliment."

In the election, Allen won, with Richard receiving only a smattering of votes. This was the moment of truth for him. Although he knew better than to let politics become personal, at some level he felt personally betrayed by the men for whom he had given the last ten years of his life, men who had eagerly drafted him to run for Mayor in 1889. More devastating, though, was his recognition that this was end of the fight. He had known there was no chance of winning the election, but he had expected his fellow workingmen to support his platform. When they didn't, he realized the fight was futile. Tim Malloy, faithful to the end, tried to cheer him up on the day after the election. "Don't get downhearted, Dick," he said. "We'll live to fight another day."

Richard put his hand on Tim's shoulder. "No, Tim, we won't," he said. "At least not this fight. But we've given it our all."

In the Spring of 1897, Richard was nominated for Constable by the administration of Democratic Mayor John P. Feeny, and elected. After all his involvement in politics, it was the first time he actually held an office in the city. He appreciated the gesture as well as the extra income, and the job was a welcome excuse for not being more active politically. He had also moved from the leather-setting room where he had worked for many years to join Tim in the stuffing room at Beggs and Cobb. It was a job that paid two dollars more a week than leather setting, but was more demanding physically, especially in the summer. It required heating the hides with hot air, and then adding a tallow mixture that was heated to 130 degrees. In summer, the stuffing room got very hot, and Richard was more tired out by his work now.

At the end of June, 1901, there was a heat wave in Woburn. On Thursday the twenty-seventh, the temperature reached ninety-six degrees, and on the twenty-eighth, ninety-seven. The temperature in the stuffing room at Beggs and Cobb was much higher. On Friday, Richard, who was now in his fifties, became exhausted from the strenuous work in the heat. He felt dizzy and nauseous, and then he passed out. Jimmy Kearns, his young apprentice in the stuffing room, got scared as Richard's skin turned pale and his breathing became labored. He called the foreman over.

"Looks like he fainted," said the foreman. "Douse him with some cold water."

Jimmy poured some water from the drinking bucket over Richard's head and chest. He didn't come to, so the foreman went to tell his supervisor. Tim Malloy came over, and together he and Jimmy tried to rouse Richard, without success. A few minutes later the foreman came back with a teamster.

"Jimmy, you can help Dennis here to take him home. Do you know where he lives?"

Jimmy shook his head. "It's in Woburn. I live in Winchester."

"I know the house," said Tim. "I'll go with them. I'm ahead on my hide count."

"All right," said the foreman.

So Tim lifted Richard by the arms and the others lifted his legs, and they carried him down the stairs from the fourth floor stuffing room. When they reached each landing, Tim called in through the open door, "It's Terrett!"

The three men laid Richard in the wagon bed. Tim climbed in next to him, holding a tarp over his face to shield him from the sun. As the wagon started off, he looked up to see hundreds of men at the windows, silently watching.

When they stopped in front of the house on Arlington Street, Maggie opened the front door, her face ashen.

"What happened, Tim?"

"He just passed out from the heat, Maggie. It's like blazes in there today." The men carried him up the stairs and laid him on the bed.

"Thanks for bringing him, Tim."

"We're happy to get out of there today, Maggie. He should be all right soon, but maybe you should have the doctor look at him. I'll stop in on my way home." The three men clumped heavily down the stairs and out to the wagon, then drove slowly off toward Winchester.

Maggie did her best to cool Richard down with sponging and cold cloths, but he did not rouse, and his breathing became more labored. She went next door and got Ann, who glanced at him and quickly took his pulse. She said, "Go over and tell my Richard to run for the doctor right away. He's very sick."

The two women worked for half an hour to try to rouse him, but they got no response. When the doctor came, he diagnosed heat stroke, and administered spirits of ammonia, but Richard still did not regain consciousness. In another half hour, he was dead.

Richard was buried in Calvary Cemetery. His funeral Mass was held on July first at St. Charles's Church. The Boston *Globe* reported that "the service was attended by a large number including division 3, A. O. H., of which the deceased was treasurer, the bearers being from that organization. There were many floral pieces." The Woburn *News* said that "Mr. Terrett was a very worthy man and a model citizen, a man of more than ordinary intelligence, open to conviction, tolerant of others who disagreed with him, a loving husband and father."

Richard Terrett portrait, about 1895

Tom Terrett, about 1908

Part Three

Tom Terrett

Chapter 8

1898–1901

At 8:00 on a March morning in 1898, as Tom made his way toward the *Wabash* in the Charlestown Navy Yard, he was relieved to find that there were not hundreds of men who had gotten there before him. In the last week, while he worked at convincing his father to let him enlist, he had fretted as each day went by and the papers reported hundreds showing up at the recruiting headquarters. He had read in the *Globe* that they were taking only four or five out of every hundred men, though, so he figured they weren't going to fill up the Navy in five days.

In the end, Tom was glad he had taken the time to talk his father around to it and tell the foreman at work he was planning to enlist. That the Navy would take him he hadn't had a doubt, until now. Looking at the other men around him, he knew most of them thought the same. It was a motley bunch that was there waiting for the barge to take them to the ship. Some of them were old enough to be Tom's father, looking pretty shabby and in need of a job. But there were plenty of young men and boys too. The first test came with the marine sentry at the end of the gangplank on the barge. As each man came up, he asked, "How do you intend to ship?"

Tom had decided not to claim to be an expert machinist. He had read that machinists had to be able to take full charge of the engines, take them apart, and make any new part that was needed. He was still in his apprenticeship, and his skill did not extend nearly that far.

"Fireman," he said.

When they reached the landing and climbed up to the ship, another marine asked the same question. The men who wanted to be seamen he kept on deck, but he sent Tom along with the other machinists, firemen, and coal passers below to the gun deck. Another marine lined them up, and they were sent in one by one to the recruiting officer to be examined. When his turn came, Tom concentrated on trying to look older and more experienced than he was.

"Want to enlist?" The officer asked.

Tom stood straight and tried to appear military. "Yes, sir."

"What as?"

"Fireman."

"Ever been to sea?"

"No, sir."

"How old are you?"

"Twenty. I'll be twenty-one in August."

"Schooling?"

"High school graduate."

All this time, the officer had been examining Tom's sturdy frame. He tried to look as tough as he could.

"You play baseball?"

"Yes, sir."

"What position?"

"Catcher."

"Football?"

"Lineman."

"Are you strong?"

"Pretty strong, sir."

"Do you have experience with fires and boilers?"

"Yes, sir."

"All right, take this card and report to the Chief Engineer."

When he got to the Chief Engineer, he had to answer more detailed questions about building and banking fires, replacing grate bars and such like, which he passed thanks to years of maintaining the coal furnace and the steam radiators at home. "I guess I owe you for that one, Pa," he thought. The physical exam was not nearly the ordeal he was expecting. They checked his vision, hearing, teeth, heart and chest. He passed the exam easily, as he had been sure he would. At the end of it, he and eight other men were sworn in and issued their Government outfits. And that was all there was to it. In a couple of hours time, he had become a sailor in the U. S. Navy.

March 20, 1898
U.S.S. Wabash
Charlestown

Dear Papa, Marm, Josie, and Mary,

Sorry it's taken this long for me to write. I know you've been anxious to hear what's become of your son and brother. You've probably guessed that I passed the exams, and I'm in the Navy now. It's been quite a week, and I just now on Sunday have time and paper so I can use the grand fountain pen you gave me. The ship is a little rocky right now, so I'm sorry my penmanship won't live up to the pen.

I enlisted as a "Fireman 2nd Class," or "bilge rat," as we're referred to on the ship. Everything is slang here, Pa, so I don't know if I can follow your rule to speak good English all the time. The pay is thirty dollars a month, not bad, considering there's no cost for food, clothes, or rent. We were given our Navy bags and uniforms when we signed in and issued hammocks, which are the best contrivances for sleeping you'd ever see. We string them up at night and stow them in the morning. There are no berths, and we just have assigned places for stowing our gear. Otherwise, the engine room is my home. So far, everything has been learning. I feel like I'm back at school. It's mostly learning to handle the furnaces and boilers and drilling the Navy manual, but there are all kinds of other drills we have to learn, battle stations and so on, and they're pretty strict about getting things right. Some of the fellows among the recruits have been in the Navy before, and they make it pretty warm for the rest of us when we mess up because we have to keep repeating the drills.

I miss your cooking already, Marm. The food is mostly hard tack, which Marm and Pa are well familiar with from their voyages from Ireland, pretty bad coffee, and some kind of meat the sailors call "salt horse," salt pork or beef. They make it into "cracker hash" or this kind of stew made from salt pork and hard tack that they call "dandy funk." Along with that, we usually have peas or beans and some kind of stewed fruit. I'd give a lot for Marm's roast chicken with mashed potatoes and gravy and a big piece of mince pie.

We're going to be on board the Wabash until we finish our training and receive orders for a ship. The word is that the Oregon has left San Francisco on the way to Cuba, so things are heating up. We're all expecting to be sent to Cuba before long.

I miss you all and hope you are all well and Mary is enjoying my room.

Your loving son and brother,
Tom

March 27, 1898
U. S. S. Wabash
Charlestown

Dear Mary Elizabeth,

I hope you don't mind if I write to you. Manny gave me your address. I'm very glad he brought me to St. John the Baptist to see a Portuguese Mass.

If you don't want me writing to you, you can just ignore this, but I hope you will write back. You can consider it doing your patriotic bit for the war. Writing to Manny doesn't count because he's your cousin. I promise to give you the real story on him as opposed to what he tells you.

Yours truly,
Tom Terrett

April 3, 1898
U. S. S. Wabash
Charlestown

Dear Family,

Thanks all for your letters. It was good to get a little touch of home, and to hear the news. Woburn seems far away. To answer your question, Marm. You needn't send me anything now, thank you. We have no place to keep anything but just a black bag, a foot in diameter and three feet high, for clothing, and what they call a "ditty box," a wooden box about 18" square where we keep things like toothbrushes, brush and comb, writing materials. I brought what I needed from home, and some of that I've had to get rid of. All our clothing is Navy issue—canvas and denim—and we take care of it ourselves. You should see the boys on their knees on the deck working the scrub brushes when the order comes to "wash and scrub clothes." I'm afraid it would not do your heart proud to see my Navy whites on the line, Marm, but we have to scrub away with cold salt water. I wish I'd taken a few lessons in scrubbing and sewing before I left.

I'm getting into the routine now, and getting used to living in stretches of four hours on and four hours off. At the beginning, it was pretty hard to turn out at 4:00 a.m. when we only got into the hammocks at midnight, but we're all learning to sleep in snatches. I've pretty much mastered the fires and the boilers, at least my part of the work, which is managing the fire under the boiler, monitoring the gauges, and managing the water levels to generate exactly the level of steam that's wanted. The machinists and the boilermakers have a lot to learn in a hurry. It makes me glad to be a humble fireman. The Chief says not to think we know what we're doing, though, because the conditions on board a battleship that's underway are nothing like this old tub in the harbor (his words). I guess he's right. We have no idea what it will be like when the order for "full steam ahead" comes.

A lot of our time now is taken up with drills—general quarters, fire drill, abandon ship, everything to get us ready to face a fight at sea. In the engine room we pretty much have to build up the fires and the boilers so we're ready for full speed. The worst battle station below is in the coal bunker, where it's black—as coal, I guess—and you can't see your hand in front of you. I don't want to be there when a real battle starts. We've even had what they call physical drill, which is exercises you would do in a gymnasium or to warm up before a football game. I guess they don't want us getting soft while we're sitting in port. There are quite a few fellows on the Wabash now, and we're all getting pretty eager to be assigned to a ship and get underway.

I have to stop now, as my watch is coming up. I miss you all, and Marm's good cooking.

Your loving son and brother,
Tom

April 3, 1898
U. S. S. Wabash
Charlestown

Dear Mary E.,

Thank you very much for your letter. Yes, I'm keeping an eye on Manny, and so far he is behaving himself, although he does eat a lot.

In answer to your questions, my family lives in Woburn, and I have a father, a stepmother, and two younger sisters, Josie and Mary, who are in high school. My mother died when I was little. Before I enlisted, I graduated from high school and then went to work as a machinist in Winchester. I don't know that I would call myself a patriot. I did want to do my bit after the Maine, but I've wanted to join the Navy since I was a kid. I love ships and boats, and I've always wanted to see the world beyond Massachusetts. The Navy seems like the one chance for someone like me to do it. I think Manny feels pretty much the same. My father is not too much happier about my enlisting than Manny's, from what I hear. I guess fathers generally want their sons to do what they do, only do better at it and get further. My father works in a tannery, but he is a leader in the Knights of Labor and the church, and everything else he does. He's also in politics. He's a constable, and he ran for mayor of Woburn a couple of times. He would love for me to follow in his footsteps, but I'm just not like him. He did finally see that it's time for me to get out and see the world, though, and I'm grateful. I can't imagine settling down in Woburn right now.

Well, this is certainly more than you wanted to hear, but you did ask! How about you telling me about your family. Manny says that Portuguese families are pretty strict and old-fashioned, but you don't seem that way. How do you spend your time when you aren't at the factory or church? I want to know all about you.

Yours truly,
Tom

April 10, 1898
U. S. S. Wabash
Charlestown

Dear Mary E.,
Thanks for your letter, which I am very glad to have. No, you haven't told me too much at all. I want to know all about your family and your life. It does sound like your father is very

strict, even more than mine, and he keeps a pretty close watch on my sisters. If you can't keep company with boys, does that mean you can't go to dances or anything? That would be hard. My sisters can go, as long as they're escorted. I take them sometimes, or I used to. How would it be if a fellow visited you? Would it be OK to escort you home from church or visit on Sunday afternoon? I'm just curious.

We're all getting anxious to get off the Wabash and onto a regular ship. The ship is pretty much full to bursting, and the rumor is that some of us are about to be ordered to one of the new ships they've bought and are refitting in New York. I hope so! This life of drilling and make-work is getting hard to take, and they won't give us shore leave, even to go to church. One of the old salts who is instructing us says that they don't like to give shore leave to the firemen and coal passers in Boston and New York because they get in too much trouble, or they pawn their uniforms so they can buy more whiskey. Well, we aren't all like that!

It's time to go on watch.
I hope you will write again.
Yours truly,
Tom

April 15, 1898
U. S. S. Wabash
Charlestown

Dear Family,

This is just a quick note to let you know that I'm being deployed at last. About 50 of us are taking the train for New

York tomorrow. I figure we'll be boarding a ship at the Brooklyn Navy Yard. The rumor is that it's a hospital ship. I don't care, as long as it's going somewhere soon!

I'll try to mail this on the way. Wish me luck.

Tom

April 19, 1898
U. S. A. S. Solace
Brooklyn

Dear Family,

This is going to be short, as I only have a few minutes to rest before the watch. They did send us to the Solace, which is a hospital ship, not an ambulance, but a full floating hospital. It's the first ship to fly the Red Cross flag, which means it is an unarmed vessel tending to the wounded and sick on both sides. It's forbidden by the Geneva Convention for the ship to be armed or for anyone to fire at the ship. Let's hope the Spaniards got the message!

This is a beautiful ship, almost brand new. Now I know what the Chief meant by calling the Wabash an old tub. The machinery in the engine room is like nothing you've ever seen. I haven't seen all of the ship yet, but they say it has regular operating rooms as well as berths for the patients, and even a sun lounge for the ones who aren't too bad. According to the rumor mill, there's a death room with coffins and embalming fluid, but I don't know if that's true. There is a laundry. I don't know if that's for us, or just the patients. There are four surgeons and a bunch of nurses (male) on board, so we should do pretty well by the wounded. I'm going to try to live up to the engine room.

Have to go now.

Your loving son and brother,

Tom

April 25, 1898
U. S. A. S. Solace
Hampton Roads, Va.

Dear Mary E.,

Thank you for your letter, which just caught up to me in Virginia. Manny and I have both been ordered to a new hospital ship, the Solace, and we are hard at work getting her ready to sail for Cuba, where we will pick up the sick and the wounded and bring them back here. It's a real hospital, with doctors and nurses, and operating rooms, and everything.

I was glad to hear that your father doesn't mind visitors, even if he doesn't let you out of his sight while they're there. Maybe if we come to Boston, we'll get shore leave and I can come. Should I bring Manny with me, or would it be OK to come on my own? I wouldn't want them to think I wasn't proper.

I don't know what's going to happen to the mail after we sail, so I wanted to make sure I wrote to you from here. I hear that the mail just piles up while the ships are at sea, and then gets taken off the ships when they're in port, and whatever is coming their way is loaded on. Sometimes people get six-months' worth of letters at once. I would love to have a letter or two from you the next time we get mail call, wherever it is.

Yours truly,

Tom

May 3, 1898
U. S. A. S. Solace
Hampton Roads, Va.

Dear Family,

We have a little break in the work, so I'm going to try to send a few lines. Now that war has been declared, the "scuttle-butt navigators" all seem to agree that we will be departing for Cuba sometime in the next few days. I can hardly believe we have gotten the Solace ready to go in the last two weeks. She has been painted white with a green stripe to distinguish her from the other ships, and all the operating rooms and quarters for the sick and wounded are squared away. I've seen all of the ship now, and it's true that there are coffins and an embalming station aboard. There are also big steam launches that will be lowered to collect the wounded from the other ships, and there's a complicated system of cables and tackles to load the wounded. We sailed down here from New York like a breeze. Everything in the engine room has been checked and re-checked, and we are ready to go.

I don't know if I'll be able to send any mail now for a while, but you can probably follow the movements of the Solace in the newspapers. Wish us luck.

Your loving son and brother,

Tom

*****

"From Sampson's Fleet," Woburn *News*, May 28, 1898, page 4.

The following letter from Thos. A. Terrett, a Woburn boy, who is fireman on the Solace, a U. S. Hospital ship, will be read with interest. Young Mr. Terrett is a son of Mr. Richard Terrett. Thomas was born here, and attended the Cummings School. He is in the very forefront of the conflict and this word from him will be enjoyed by his friends here.

On Board the U. S. A. S. Solace
Key West, May 18, '98

To the Editor of THE NEWS:—I will write you a few lines for your paper as I suppose you would like news regarding the movements of this fleet of which Admiral Sampson is Commander and I can thus let my friends know of my whereabouts.

I am now on the U. S. A. S. Solace. We left Norfolk, Va., May 7 and arrived at Key West at 8 a.m. on the 11th. At 6:30 p.m. we received orders to go to Porto Rico with all speed. On the 13th at 3 a.m. as we were steaming on, we were suddenly stopped by a shot passing close to our bow. We ran to the ports to see what was the matter, and found guns levelled at us and a flash-light on us which proved to be from the Detroit. When the sun rose we were in the midst of a part of Sampson's fleet. . . .

It seems now that I will not have a hand in the fighting, but we cannot pick our choice here. We must do as we are told. We on the Solace, which is a Hospital ship, will be fighting indirectly, so we must be content. I wish you would be kind enough to forward me THE NEWS each week, and if you publish any of this letter please state that I would like very much to have some of my old schoolmates write me as it seems good to get letters here. I must now close as we have reached Key West, so here's hoping this will find Woburn and its people getting along well. Success to THE NEWS.

Yours respectfully,
THOS. A. TERRETT

*****

May 22, 1898
U. S. A. S. Solace
Brooklyn

Dear Family,

We are back from our first trip to Cuba, and it was a baptism of fire, or rather a baptism of fire, wind and water. Less than two days out of New York we hit a hurricane, which lasted a day and a half. The ship was pitching and rolling like a bronco, and for green sailors like us it was pretty hard to make your way ten feet at times without pitching forward on your head or getting thrown against a stanchion. Lucky for me, I must have inherited Pa's sea stomach, because I weathered it pretty well, compared to some of the boys, who were not ready for this on their maiden voyage. The engine room was pretty wild, too, with everything flying around and the waves so high that the engine's screws were sometimes up in the air instead of in the water. The noise they made sounded like the ship would split apart. With that on top of the wind and the waves, I have to admit we were pretty scared. Nobody got much sleep during those two days except a few old salts who have probably been in the Navy since the Civil War and have seen everything. They laughed at us, which, in an odd way, made us feel better.

Now I know what the engine room is like when we're going full steam ahead at sea, and it's hot as blazes. Down in Cuba, where it's already hot, the engine room was up to 130 degrees. Add in the coal dust and ashes being blown around by the engine's ventilators and it gets pretty rough down there. They rotate us out fast when it's like that, but some of the boys haven't been able to take it. We made our trip back from Cuba with some sick sailors and soldiers in five days, and we have two firemen now that are in the hospital part of the ship with heat prostration, but I don't think they were too strong to begin with. I feel fine, so you needn't worry about me. I drink about a gallon of fresh water when I get out of there and either dump a bucket of sea water over me, or, when I can, get a shower bath of cold sea water from the hose on deck. I admit it is nice being in Brooklyn for a while, though. The scuttle-butt is that we will be going back in a couple of days because things are heating up in Cuba.

I hope you are all well, and I think often of what everyone must be up to at home. I hope you will keep sending letters because we do get mail when we are in port here.

Your loving son and brother,
Tom

May 25, 1898
U. S. A. S. Solace
Brooklyn

Dear Mary E.,

We're back from Cuba, and we had mail call. Thank you for your long letter, which is a peach! I can picture you in that new taffeta shirtwaist you're making. By the way, if you have a picture to spare, I would like very much to have it. We are short of pretty things to look at on the ship.

The trip to Cuba was exciting, with a hurricane on the way down. The noise from the wind and the engine's screws, which are lifted out of the water at times, is really something at first—but we got used to it. It lasted a day and a half, and I have to say that I it's hard to believe I slept in a hammock on a ship in the middle of a hurricane.

Manny is fine, although a little tired out from the trip. The engine room was very hot in Cuba, and they had us speeding back pretty fast with the wounded, so we were keeping the steam and the fires up the whole way. A couple of the fellows got sick from the heat and the strain, but Manny and I are both in pretty good shape, so we managed. The secret is lots of water.

It's almost time for the watch, so I will put this in the mail. Manny sends his love to you and all the family (as I'm sure you know, Manny is not much on writing).

Yours truly,
Tom

June 24, 1898
U. S. A. S. Solace
Brooklyn

Dear Family,

We have come back from Cuba, where we went to Santiago and were anchored with the fleet at Guantanamo Bay for a while. You probably read about the engagements there. The fort is in pretty rough shape after all the shelling it got from the Navy, but old glory is flying from it now, and the marines are there in camp. We picked up some men who were wounded in the battle and got them up here in less than five days. The steam launches are sent around the harbor to the various ships, and they lower the wounded and sick men into the launches. The launch comes aside the Solace, and they have a system of cables and tackles forward that lifts the wounded man onto the ship in a chair or stretcher, then they are carried to the hospital area. I don't think I'd like the raising and lowering too much if I was wounded, but once they're on board, the ship is set up so they aren't jostled around too much.

Thank you all for the letters. I was the envy of mail call. It's good to know what you are all doing and to be reminded of home. I don't mind if you paper the room, Mary, just so it's not too flowery. To answer everybody's questions, we do get some food besides hardtack and salt horse or cracker hash. We have rice, and oatmeal for breakfast, canned meat, and sometimes fresh meat in port, and peas or beans with salt pork, and once in a while, stewed fruit. And the mess—that's the group of sailors assigned to eat together—chip in some money for other things. We also have the bumboats in port. These are private boats that sell all kinds of supplies like writing materials and needles and thread and shoe blacking as well as food. At Hampton Roads, they had cakes and pies to sell, nothing like home, but plenty good to a sailor. In the tropics, they had all kinds of fruit, not only bananas and oranges and limes, but things I've never seen before, like mangoes and pineapples. The prices are outrageous, but nobody cares when the bumboat shows up.

Now I'm hungry for some of Marm's home cooking, but it will probably be cracker hash again. I miss you all.

Your loving son and brother,

Tom

June 25, 1898
U. S. A. S. Solace
Brooklyn

Dear Mary E.,

Thank you for your letter. It was a real lift for me. This trip was kind of hard for us—not the physical work—Manny and I are both doing fine as far as that goes. But this time we took on a lot of men who were wounded, and it was tough to see them. Both of us volunteered for stretcher duty, carrying the men to the hospital part of the ship after they've been hauled on board. They have a good system for raising and lowering them, but you could see it was very tough for them. And some of the wounds are awful. They say the Mauser bullets were supposed to be better for the ones who are hit, but they are actually worse. It made you wish you could do something for them, but of course that's not our line. We have good doctors and nurses on board to take care of them.

Well, I didn't mean to write all that. Here, I was thanking you for giving me a lift, and I'm telling you about the wounded. But it is better now. The boys are all in hospitals on land, and they say that the treatment they get here on the ship will save a lot of lives and limbs.

I wish I could have been with you on the factory picnic. I would love to do the three-legged race with you! Seriously, it sounds like you have a pretty good employer. Anything like that in Woburn and Winchester is always organized by the union or the Hibernians, not by the factory owners. Of course my Pa would say that they just do it to keep the workers from forming unions.

We are having a little holiday in Brooklyn, although they're not letting us go ashore. It's nice to be at anchor in a cooler place and resting for a while.

Write when you can. I would love to see a picture of you in that taffeta shirtwaist.

Yours truly,
Tom

*****

"From Fireman Terrett," Woburn *News*, July 23, 1898, page 5.

Dagaree, July 10, '98

. . . Since I wrote you last there have been many changes here. On June 23, the batteries at Guantanamo were silenced. On July 3rd, while at Guantanamo, we received a cable that the Spanish fleet were annihilated at Santiago. We hurried there with all possible speed but on account of darkness had to keep off till the morning of the 4th. We took from the Iowa thirty-five wounded Spaniards, and from other ships of the fleet till we had ninety-six. The loss was terrible to the Dons. . . . When we arrived at Guantanamo the Vulcan's launch was in waiting for us with three blue-jackets from the yacht Hornet. One died, and on the sixth, I and seven more firemen took him ashore and buried him in the cemetery with others who have been killed here. There is one by the name of McColgan of Stoneham, and another Dumphrey of Gloucester, Mass. . . . The 7th, 8th, and 9th of July passed quietly, except for the moaning of the wounded. Three of the Dons have died and were given a watery grave; sewed in canvas with two grate bars tied to their feet, they were slid over the side. . . .

Yours Respectfully,
THOS. A. TERRETT

*****

Boston *Daily Globe*, Jul 23, 1898, page 6.

NURSES GO WITHOUT SLEEP
Joshua Clarke Writes to His Brother About His Experiences on Board the Solace—Had to Punch One Spaniard

SHELBURNE FALLS, July 22—George L. Clarke has just received the following letter from his brother Joshua, who is a trained nurse in the employ of the government and is now stationed on board the steamer Solace:

"You will doubtless wonder how we are getting on during genuine warfare. Of course the news of the American success has reached you long ago. On the 4th and 5th we received more than 100 wounded Spaniards from Cervera's fleet. My recent experiences have been novel and hard to endure. I have been on the night watch and have stood on guard over 50 of these men. The first night or two it seemed tough. One fellow made it lively for me. He did not obey orders. As he could not speak English the orders were conveyed to him by gestures. It seemed to be absolutely necessary to use force with him. His language, spoken in broken English, was not choice.

"I was forced to tap him under the chin. He did not seem to enjoy this. He proposed to fight. Then I gave him a fairly hard tap and as he closed his teeth upon his tongue he was furious. A fight was on at once, but it ended soon. When he struck at me I dodged and made a light reach with my right which he stopped with his left and in doing so left his throat exposed. I deemed it my duty to plant my left squarely upon his larynx. He gave a yell and the fight was over. I had no more trouble with him.

"Some of the prisoners are terribly wounded. We have done everything we could do to relieve them. We have gone without sleep in order to serve them."

*****

July 25, 1898
U. S. A. S. Solace
Brooklyn

Dear Family,

We are back from the latest trip to Cuba, and getting a little bit of a rest because they're making some repairs to the engines and also putting in an ice machine for the hospital. We were hoping for shore leave, but so far, it's N. G. (No Go). We're not on the best of terms with the officers right now, because of a letter that was written by Josh Clark, one of the nurses. You probably saw the story in the Globe. He wrote about how he beat up a Spanish prisoner while he was on guard in the ward, which isn't what a nurse is supposed to do on a hospital ship according to the Geneva Convention. And then his brother had the bad judgment to send the letter to the Globe. So the Solace is not looking too good right now. At general muster, Commander Dunlap addressed us in no uncertain terms about the necessity for treating all patients humanely and being circumspect in what we write in letters.

We took on about 150 wounded and sick sailors and soldiers from both our forces and the Spanish, more than 80 wounded in the battle of Santiago. The wards were crammed full, and the doctors and nurses were working very hard. All of us firemen who were not on watch at the time served as stretcher-bearers, and I can tell you a lot of our fellows were in a bad way, with bullet holes from those Mauser rifles. They do a lot of damage. I heard the doctors did quite a bit of surgery onboard. Now we have one of those X-Ray machines that lets them see through the skin and bone to the bullet so they can find it without using a probe. A lot of the boys were really suffering when we brought them aboard, but they give them morphine on the ship. Six or seven of the Spanish died between July 5th and the 17th, when we brought the prisoners ashore at Norfolk, after we had brought our boys to the hospital at Fort Monroe. It was pretty grim all told, the worst of the trips we've made so far, but I'm sure we saved some lives, and kept some legs from being amputated.

The time in Brooklyn has been good, especially with the beautiful weather for the last few days. Even if we can't get off the ship, it's nice to be in port and not steaming full speed ahead in the tropics. When we aren't cleaning up the ship from stem to stern, we get a little time to go up on deck and rest in the fresh air. We've even had some sports in place of physical drill—races and so on. I held up the honor of the firemen in a couple of them. We are the best at tests of strength, but the seamen always want to do things like climb the masts, and of course they win at that. When they call us "bilge rats," the men on our watch have taken to responding with "rig monkeys," but of course it's all in fun, most of the time.

It's almost time for mess, so I have to get my knife and fork and get into the fray before there's nothing left. The scuttle-butt is that we will be leaving in a day or two, as the ship is all repaired, but you can still write letters for me to get when we come back. Send me a piece of the wallpaper, Mary. I want to know what to expect.

Your loving son and brother,
Tom

July 24, 1898
U. S. A. S. Solace
Brooklyn

Dear Mary E.,

Thank you for your letter and the picture. It's a good likeness, just not quite as pretty as you are in real life. Anyway, it's the best looking thing on the ship, so I won't complain.

We had another bad shipment of wounded on the way here, and some of them died. You probably read that letter from Josh Clark that was printed in the Globe. Apparently no one told him that nurses aren't supposed to punch out the patients. He's in big trouble now, I hear. What a dope!

I wish I had been along on that outing on the 4th. Just the food alone would have made it heaven for me, not to mention the company. Maybe one day we will go boating on the Charles. What do you say? Of course we celebrated on the ship, but it was very formal. Just a ceremony and general muster in the morning, which was impressive, and a couple of speeches. No fireworks. Being a hospital ship, we don't have any guns, so we didn't even have a salute. But we all knew it was the 4th, and it made you thoughtful about what you're doing here.

We are glad to be at anchor in Brooklyn for a few days, and I hear there may be shore leave for the firemen and coal passers, since we've been such exemplary sailors. I promise to keep an eye on Manny if we go.

I have to go on watch, so I'll put this in the mail now. Don't forget to write!

Yours truly,
Tom

*****

Woburn *News*, September 3, 1898, page 4.

The 10:15 p.m. train Thursday, Sept. 1, brought Fireman Thomas Terrett of the Hospital ship Solace to Woburn. . . Mr. Terrett, who was on a 12-hour furlough, is looking finely, and reports his health as first-class. There has been little if any sickness among the ship's crew. . . . He says the soldiers tell pitiful stories of the lack of food and care.

*****

September 3, 1898
U. S. A. S. Solace
Charlestown

Dear Mary E.,

This is just a quick note to tell you that we are here in Charlestown, and if we can get leave on Sunday, Manny and I will be at Sacred Heart. I don't know if it will happen, but there's a chance.

Our mess caterer is going ashore and promised to mail this for me, so I have to get it to him right away.

Hope to see you soon!
Tom

October 16, 1898
U. S. A. S. Solace
Brooklyn

Dear Family,

We are at anchor in Brooklyn now, having delivered some sick soldiers and sailors from Porto Rico to the hospitals here. It's mostly typhoid, more soldiers than sailors. The fighting is over now, and a lot of the troops are coming home. I guess the island belongs to us. It's a beautiful place, what I've been able to see from the ship. Very green, and the water is very blue. Mostly it's steep cliffs, but there are some beaches where I'd love to dive in and take a swim.

The war in Cuba seems to be just about over, so we're all wondering what the Solace will be doing next. Some of the battleships, like the Oregon and the Iowa, have left for the Philippines. It looks like we will be fighting Aguinaldo and the native insurgents there when the U. S. takes the islands over from Spain. The experienced scuttle-butt navigators think the Solace will go along as a hospital ship, but nobody knows for sure. I will write as soon as they tell us anything, but of course we're usually the last to know. Watch the Globe.

It's nice to be up north for a while. I've been up on deck whenever I had a chance, enjoying the cool breezes, and even the rain. Send mail when you can. Who knows when I may be off for the Philippines!

Your loving son and brother,
Tom

October 16, 1898
U. S. A. S. Solace
Brooklyn

Dear Mary E.,

Thanks for your letter. I'm disappointed about the shore leave too. It would have been nice to look at the real you, and not just your picture. And if I escorted you home, we could have had the chance to have a real conversation, within the limits of your family, of course.

I don't know how much longer we will be making the run to Cuba. The patients all seem to be fever patients now, and not the wounded, which is a relief, although some of them are pretty sick. We just came back from Porto Rico, and brought quite a few of them. That is a beautiful place, by the way, an island paradise. Something like the Azores, from what you and Manny say, but warmer. Manny wants to stay there, now that it belongs to us and the war is all but over. I have to remind him of the little fact that we signed up for three years. Everybody seems to think that we will be going to the Philippines now to support the fight against the native insurgents. That means sailing halfway around the world. We'll see. We should learn a lot in the next month or so.

Right now, we have at least one more trip to Cuba to make. We're enjoying the rest in Brooklyn and the cool weather.

I'm hoping to find a letter from Cambridge next mail call. That will cheer me up quite a bit!

Yours truly,
Tom

January 6, 1899
U. S. S. Solace
Brooklyn

Dear Family,

By now you have probably seen the news that the Solace is being converted to a transport ship, and we are off to Manila in a month or so. Even better news is that I have furlough! There are all kinds of work going on to convert the ship, so they want most of us who aren't employed in the work out of the way. Firemen and coal passers are pretty much all getting leave if we ask for it. I am going to come home on Monday and stay until Wed. morning. I hope this letter reaches you before I do, or you're in for a big surprise!

Your loving son and brother,
Tom

January 6, 1899
U. S. S. Solace
Brooklyn

Dear Mary E.,

Did you see the news that the Solace is up here being converted to a transport ship, and we will be sailing to the Philippines in a month? Well, they've given both Manny and me leave next week, starting Sunday. We're going to get off first thing and take the train to Boston, so we may be able to meet you at Sacred Heart, or if not, Manny says we can visit in the afternoon and your family won't mind if he brings his Navy buddy. So either way, I will see you soon.

I hope you get this letter. If not, I hope it's a pleasant surprise!

Yours truly,
Tom

January 12, 1899
U. S. S. Solace
Brooklyn

Dear Mary E.,
I'm back on the ship after my visit to Woburn. I was sorely tempted to go absent without leave so I could visit you again yesterday. It was grand to spend the day with you, and I'm indebted to Manny forever that he maneuvered it so we could sit together and talk. I like your family, and I don't find your father so fearsome as everyone in the family seems to. I'm

glad he looks out for you, though he is awfully strict about keeping his daughters at home.

You look splendid in your new silk shirtwaist. Roman stripes, is it? Why are they Roman? You see I have so much to learn about you. You have to write and tell me.

The visit home was nice, although a little strange. It was good to see the family and my friends, but I had the feeling that they expected me to be the same person I was when I left, and I'm not. It's as if the last year never happened as far as they're concerned. They're interested in hearing the stories from the ship and funny things about my mates, but I couldn't begin to tell them about anything that really matters. I think my father still considers the Navy some sort of boyish adventure, when it's anything but that. I did appreciate that you were interested to hear more than funny stories, and to find out what the war is really like for the sailors, even if I have a hard time expressing it. It's not something you want to dwell on when you're in the middle of it.

I will probably not be able to send many letters now that we're sailing, but I hope you will write when you get the chance, and your letters will catch up to me eventually. In the meantime, I now have many happy memories to go along with your picture.

Fondly,

Tom

*****

"Fireman Terrett going to Manila," Woburn *News*, January 14, 1899, page 4.

Fireman Thos. A. Terrett sends us the information that the U. S. S. Solace is ordered to Manila. Good luck to Tommy on his long trip!

*****

January 29, 1899
U. S. S. Solace
Brooklyn

Dear Mary E.,

Thanks very much for your letter, which means a lot to me. I thought we said some important things too. It will be good to know I have such a good (and beautiful) friend back in Cambridge on this long voyage. I know you will remember your promise to write.

It looks as though we will be sailing in the next couple of days. We have been loading supplies and coal like mad. I'm hot to get started. We are going to so many places I've dreamed of seeing—not only Europe, but Egypt, the Red Sea, and places in the Orient. They probably will not let us off the ship on this trip, but you can see a lot just steaming in and laying at anchor in the harbor.

I look forward to having a chance to tell you all about it when I see you next!

Your affectionate friend,
Tom

January 29, 1899
U. S. S. Solace
Brooklyn

Dear Family,

The word is that we sail on Tuesday or Wednesday, and this will probably be the last chance I get to send a letter for a long time. We are ship shape here now, and the ship is loaded down with coal and all kinds of food—canned fruit and vegetables and meat as well as the usual salt horse and hard tack and oatmeal and rice. I hope it's not all for the Philippines, and we get a share of the good stuff. I don't know what they've said in the papers about our route. We are bound for Manila by way of the Suez Canal, Ceylon and Singapore. If you trace it on that big map you put up in the parlor, you can see that it is more than half way around the world! The plan is for the Solace and the Buffalo to alternate trips every three months, the Solace coming from New York and the Buffalo from San Francisco. They're going to want us to get there fast, so we probably won't be going ashore anywhere, but it will be something to see all these places, even from the ship.

I know I will be thinking of the visit home many a time during the months ahead. It was so good to see everybody. And I want to thank you for the keepsakes. It will be good to be reminded of all of you and home. The boys devoured all the food that I hadn't eaten on the train the day I got back, and now they want to see pictures of my sisters. They say they don't believe I have sisters, let alone ones who can cook and are pretty to boot.

I will send this off, and write when I can, but I have a feeling that we will be the first ship carrying mail from Manila home. Wish me luck. It looks like it's going to be a hard pull for the firemen to get her halfway around the world!

Your loving son and brother,
Tom

*****

"Sailing of the Solace," Boston *Daily Globe* , February 7, 1899, page 5.

Sailing of the Solace
Took Double the Quantity of Ammunition Intended at First and Many Stores—People Anxious to Get There

NORFOLK, VA, Feb 6—The U S transport Solace, which was held 30 hours beyond the time originally fixed for her departure from Hampton Roads, sailed at 4:30 o'clock this afternoon for Manila, bearing not only stores for Dewey's fleet as at first intended, but in accordance with his request made since hostilities began in the Philippines, about double the quantity of ammunitions she expected to carry, as well as numerous extra supplies for the army at Manila.

The officers and men aboard the Solace are anxious to reach the Philippines, not one of them but expresses the hope that our forces will speedily smash the savages, but every one wants to be in at the death.

*****

"On Board the U. S. S. Solace," Woburn *News*, April 15, 1899, page 5.
Colombo, Id. of Ceylon
Mar. 10, 1899

To the Editor of THE NEWS:—Since I wrote you last I have seen some fine sights. The Solace left Valletta, Malta, Feb. 22, and arrived at Port Said, Egypt, on the 25th. We stopped there about five hours, just long enough to await our turn to go through the canal. We started through the Suez Canal at 3 p.m. and arrived in Suez at 10 a.m., Feb. 27, the trip of 96 miles taking 43 hours, rather slow traveling.

The Canal, which connects the Mediterranean and Red Seas, is 96 miles long, and about 100 yards wide . . . Ships coming from Suez have the right of way, so that when a ship was sighted we had to tie up to the bank and let it pass.

We saw many camel trains along the Sahara, and were wishing to see a sandstorm but none came. There were many herds of sheep and goats along the banks of the canal. It was a mystery to us what they lived on as all we could see was sand. It was very hot in the daytime. How would you like some of it in Woburn? The nights were cool.

As we passed, the Egyptian camel-drivers would dismount, then tie the animal's forefeet together so that it could not wander, and then with others, who seemed to spring up out of the sandhills, would be seen running with the ship. Sometimes there would be twenty of them. We would throw hardtack to them and they would pile up like a football team to get it. . . . We steamed on for 80 miles through the Gulf of Suez, and came to the Red Sea. The old salts showed us where the sea parted for Moses and his army. . . . We arrived at Colombo today, March 10. This is a pretty place, with a high breakwater at the entrance, and cocoanut groves all along the beach. . . .

Respectfully yours,
THOMAS A. TERRETT

*****

"With Dewey at Manila," Woburn *News*, May 13, 1899, page 5.

Manila Bay, Philippine Islands
Mar. 23, 1899
To the Editor of THE NEWS:—We arrived here today safe and sound, and most of the crew are in good health.

The Solace now holds the record for a quick trip from the States to this port. . . . Admiral Dewey came aboard and complimented our Captain on our quick trip, and we are all glad it is over, for thirty-nine steaming days at a time is almost enough. . . .

Respectfully yours,
THOS. A. TERRETT

*****

April 21, 1899
U. S. S. Solace
Manila

Dear Family,

We are just about ready to sail now. The word is that we will be underway tomorrow. We are going to San Francisco instead of New York. That means we will have sailed almost around the world. The ship is full to the brim with coal, as well as about 160 sailors and a soldier or two that we are transporting home. Most are going back because they've finished their tours. Lucky dogs. Although there are some that have been invalided home. When I see some of them, it almost makes me wish the Solace were a hospital ship again. They probably would have been able to save some arms and legs if they'd had better operating conditions here. It looks like we will be going to Yokohama first, and then the Sandwich Islands and San Francisco. We're ready to go, you bet! It's a dull life here. The rest was good at first, but now it's time to get moving.

Your loving son and brother,
Tom

*****

"In Mid-Pacific," Woburn *News*, June 3, 1899, page 2.

On board the U. S. S. Solace
Honolulu, Sandwich Islands
May 15, 1899

To the Editor of THE NEWS: —

After laying at Cavite, a short run from Manila, and unloading stores, we received orders to go to Mare Island Navy Yard, California, and on April 22, just one month from the time we steamed into Manila Bay, we started out on another long run. . . .

On April 28 we dropped anchor outside the breakwater at Yokohama, Japan, the run from Manila being 1800 knots. The scenery, for about 345 knots before entering the harbor, was grand. The Bay is about 15 miles wide. Numerous cities can be seen on either side, and the shores are so well-fortified it seems impossible for an enemy to enter.

On April 29, my turn came to go ashore for twenty four hours' liberty and of this I was very glad as it had been 73 days since I had had such an opportunity. On landing at the dock the first sight I saw was at least 400 "Jin-rickshas," a two-wheeled carriage drawn by a Jap to be hired for, in our money, three cents an hour. There are but few horses in Yokohama. In twenty four hours I saw only four.

These "rickshaw" men are very fleet, and can run for hours. The streets are very narrow, so narrow that it is an easy matter to jump across some of them. The people seem to be always content, going along in their slow way over the pavements, with their wooden shoes making a noise like that of a horse with loose shoes. The houses are for the most part one story high, and always open except in bad weather. There are no doors; the whole front acts for that purpose, and when the weather will permit, all articles for sale are left on the floor which does duty for a counter.

The police very seldom move. At a distance they look like a hydrant, but on getting close to them you see a neat little man in blue uniform, topped by a peaked cap with a yellow band. They carry a sword, pistol, and club. I saw one running about 15 knots an hour, after throwing away his gear. Not very much like some of our Woburn police. The married women have their front teeth blackened and carry their children tied to their backs. There is hardly any machinery used here, nearly all work being done by hand. . . .

I took a train for Tokio, the capital, about twenty miles from Yokohama. The two places were much alike, only at the Capital a line of street cars passes the depot. I saw the Emperor's palace, but could not get very near it as mounted soldiers are stationed all around it. . .

Respectfully yours,
THOS. A. TERRETT

*****

June 4, 1899
U. S. S. Solace
Mare Island/ Vallejo
California

Dear Mary E.,

We are here in the Navy Yard north of San Francisco, and the mail finally came! Thank you for the letters. The boys were very jealous of my haul. It sounds like you had a pretty good winter and spring, all told. I hope you get some more entertainment in the summer. At least when there are church feasts and family picnics and things, you can get out of the house, even if it's always with your family. I would love to be in Cambridge for the boat races one day.

We had another tough run from San Francisco to Manila and back, but we got shore leave in Yokohama. You should have seen us trying to buy things in the market! The British built the port up, so most of the merchants speak some kind of English, but their English is limited, and if you aren't too used to shopping anyway, the results can be hilarious. I did manage to buy presents for my family, and a little something for you too. I think you will like it.

Now we've been resting for a few weeks while they overhaul the ship at Mare Island. It took a little while to get acclimated, but it's like heaven here compared to the muggy heat in the Philippines. It's sunny for the most part, and cool, but not cold. Not like November in Massachusetts. They've given us leave a couple of times, and Manny and I have crossed over to Vallejo, the small town on the other side of the river. Manny is thrilled because there are a lot of Portuguese people there, and we've found some good restaurants. I've become quite a convert to Portuguese food and wine. Pork and clams is my favorite dish. We've also hiked in the hills a couple of times with some of the other fellows, and there is nothing like the feeling you get at the top of the hill looking out over the landscape. The other day, we were there at sunset, and the view of the Napa river flowing out to the Carquinez Strait with the mountains in the distance surrounded by a red sky was just spectacular. This is a place where I wouldn't mind living when I get out of the Navy. There is plenty of work for civilians at the Navy Yard.

I often think of what it's like in Cambridge and what you are doing. It's kind of strange to get your letters, because they are telling me what happened months ago, like Christmas in June, but I'm still happy to catch up! I hope you and the family are all well. Manny sends his love.

Your affectionate,

Tom

Dear Josie,

I'm putting this note in with your birthday present, which I hope you like. I think it will look good on you when you make it up into a shirtwaist. Anyway, it's pure silk from the Orient. I bought it in Yokohama. You should have seen me trying to explain to the man what it was for and figure out how much was needed. Luckily an English lady came by and helped me. People are very friendly in Yokohama. She did get a good laugh out of it, though.

If I was at home now, I would make Jimmy Boyle sorry, I can tell you that. But now it's best to forget him. I always thought he was an all right fellow, but he behaved like a louse, and so he probably is one. You can do much better, and you will. And don't let Winn's get you down. I know factory life is tough—the hours, and the noise, and the boredom. I don't know how Pa has stood the tannery all these years. But you don't have to work there forever. Why don't you try getting some tailoring piece work to do, and see if you like it better? You could work at home if you did that.

I'll be looking out for something special for you when I go ashore.

Love,
Tom

June 21, 1899
U. S. S. Solace
Mare Island/Vallejo

Dear Family,

Thanks to all for your letters. It's grand to hear the news and what everybody is doing. I can picture all of you at home, coming home from St. Charles's and getting ready for Sunday dinner. I can picture that too! Quite a bit different than what we'll be getting today.

I can't complain too much, though These three weeks in Vallejo have been the best time I've had in the Navy. We've had a lot of time to rest and visit the other ships and we have had shore leave quite a bit. I think they mostly want to get us out of the way while they do some things to the ship. Vallejo is a small town, nothing like San Francisco, so there is not much to do here, and some of the boys complain. Of course, they're the ones who never get out of the waterfront district anyway. Beyond the Navy Yard and that part of Vallejo, this is a beautiful place. Manny Almeida and I have hiked up into the hills a couple of times, and the view of the Carquinez Strait and the mountains on the other side is just beautiful. We've found a couple of places to get some good food, almost as good as yours, Marm. And the weather is not too warm and not too cold, and sunny most of the time. They say it's pretty much like that all year round. It would be a grand place to live.

Time to go on watch.

Your loving son and brother,

Tom

June 27, 1899
U. S. S. Solace
Mare Island

Dear Mary E.,

Thanks for your last two letters, which arrived pretty quickly. No, I don't think the news from Cambridge is boring, and I hope you will write and tell me everything that happens. I'm glad I got to meet your family and see your house, so I can picture everything. I sympathize with George, having been in trouble most of the time when I was a kid too. When you're a boy that age, it just seems very hard to sit still and do everything every adult tells you to do when all you want is to be outside playing ball. I still feel that way a bit, although they tire us out so much that we're happy to hit the hammocks when a watch is over.

I'm sorry you've had such a hard time with your father. I always thought my Pa was kind of strict with the girls, but he is nothing like yours. My sisters have always belonged to

Sodality and gone to dances and parties. It doesn't sound like you get out at all, except to go to work or church or the market. I wish I was there so I could maybe talk to your father and get him to see things from more of an American point of view. You shouldn't think we're so free in the Navy, though. We're only free to do what we like on shore, which is why some of the boys go so wild once they set foot on land. On the ship, we are the slaves of the boatswain's pipe. It's not just when we're on watch or when there's a drill, of which there are many. They tell us when to go to sleep, when to get up, when to eat, when to wash our clothes, everything. That's one of the reasons why sailors live for shore leave. It's not always that they want to see the place, or even be on land, they just want to get away from that confounded whistle. Then they get on shore and the only thing they can think of to do is drink themselves into oblivion until they get hauled back on the ship.

That's not Manny and me, by the way. We both like to see the places. And waking up after a binge and facing the engine room is not something we want to do. We found some Portuguese restaurants and Manny has introduced me to some nice wine, which I approve of very much. But we're always perfectly capable of getting ourselves aboard afterward.

Speaking of which, it's almost time for me to go on watch. Not that there's anything particular to do, but they will come up with enough make-work to tire us out.

Don't forget to write!

Your affectionate friend,

Tom

June 28, 1899
U. S. S. Solace
Mare Island

Dear Family,

I got all your letters, and it was a treat to read through them, almost like a visit home. Thanks for your photos, Josie and Mary. You are both looking so pretty and grown up. And congratulations on your graduation, Mary. I know Pa is proud as punch to have two high school graduates in the family. The boys have been asking to see pictures of my sisters for a while. They don't seem to believe you exist. These should shut them up pretty well.

We have been in port here almost a month now, and it looks like we will be sailing for Manila in a day or two. The ship is weighted down with supplies and coal and fresh troops for the Philippines. We will probably be stopping in the Sandwich Islands and Yokohama again. I sure hope we get shore leave. I got to spend a 24-hour liberty in San Francisco, and I saw quite a bit of the city. It's an exciting place, kind of rough and ready, especially near the docks. A few of us got around the city. We took a look at Chinatown, which is very crowded and dark, and seems to be a town with only men, all dressed in black. I don't know if there aren't any women, or if they just don't come out in public. All the walking gave us an appetite for the giant steaks we consumed. We won't be seeing any food like that for a while, but we brought back some canned food for the mess that will be very welcome in a couple of weeks.

I miss all of you, and often think about what's happening at home. I guess it will be another 4 or 5 months before I get any letters, so I'll have to make do with these for a while.

Your loving son and brother,
Tom

*****

Woburn *News*, September 16, 1899, page 4.

On Board the U. S. S. Solace
Off Cavite, Manila Bay, P. I.
August 18th, 1899

To the Editor of THE NEWS:—The Solace left Mare Island Navy Yard, Cal., July 1st, and arrived at Honolulu on the 8th, coaled and started the 12th for Guam. . . . The island of Guam is a most desolate place, and ships cannot get nearer than two miles, as coral reefs extend very far from shore. . . . On March 17th a whaler was wrecked on this reef, and one of its crew was a Frank Morrisey, born in Billerica, who knows many of the people around Woburn. He was very glad to meet me, and has had some hard times trying to get away as very few vessels ever stop there. . . .

The sunrises and sunsets are grand in the torrid zone, and I don't think it is quite as warm in Woburn. The temperature often reaches 110 deg. when steaming 11 knots. We came very slowly, and sighted nothing in thirteen days. The firerooms often reach 150 and 160 deg. . . . I must close with best regards and wishes to all, and success to the NEWS.

THOS. A. TERRETT

*****

September 15, 1899
U. S. S. Petrel
Manila

Dear Family,

As you see from the above address, I've been ordered to the Petrel. You probably know about the Petrel since you've been following the war news. She is a little gunboat about 1/6 the size of the Solace, but she's been in almost all the important battles here in the Philippines, including Manila Bay, Panay Island, Cebu, and Neveleta. It looks like I will at long last see some military action, and I won't have any more full-speed-ahead 39-day cruises for a while.

I need to get this into the mailbag, since I'm no longer traveling with the mail. Wish me luck!

Your loving son and brother,
Tom

September 15, 1899
U. S. S. Petrel
Manila

Dear Mary E.,

As you've guessed from the address, I have been assigned to a new ship, the Petrel. It's a small gunboat that has seen a lot of action. In fact, it's kind of famous for the important role it's played in several important battles here in the Philippines. Manny is still on the Solace, and I will miss him a lot. I'm sorry I won't be able to send regular reports on him for a while, but we do a lot of visiting back and forth when the ships are at anchor, so I'm sure I'll be seeing him before too long.

I have great hopes that I will at last see some action myself, so I am happy to be here, but I have mixed feelings I never expected. It's strange to be on a ship other than the Solace. I will miss all my mates, and I won't be seeing anything but the Philippines for a while. But so far the crew seem like good mates. The engine is much smaller than the Solace's, and the watches aren't quite so hard, which is a relief. I think I will like it here, once I get used to it.

I'm putting this in the mail so you'll know about my new address, and the mail doesn't have to chase me around even more than usual. I think of you often, and hope all is well.

Your affectionate,
Tom

*****

Woburn *News*, November 18, 1899, page 5.

News from Luzon
U. S. S. Petrel
Cavite, P. I.
Oct. 9, 1899

To the Editor of THE NEWS,

Dear Sir:—Hoping you have received my last letter OK, I will tell you and my friends through your columns of some of our recent work . . .

On the 7th the soldiers had a brisk engagement with the insurgents at Imus. On Sunday, the 8th, we up anchor at daylight and went to the opposite side of the Causeway. The soldiers advanced from Imus and Bacour, the Marines from Cavite, and about 11 a.m. they had a brisk engagement with the Filipinos, but it was soon over as the Petrel dropped a few 6-inch shots into the trenches, and the soldiers say the insurgents were flying in every direction, but not until two marines were dead and 19 wounded.

In the evening we returned to our anchorage, and are still here. The rainy season is over and it is very hot now.

Yours,
THOS. A. TERRETT

*****

December 26, 1899
U. S. S. Petrel
Manila

Dear Family,

Today I've been thinking of you all at home, and what Christmas was like. I have a few Christmas presents for you, but I'm afraid you won't be getting them for a while.

Yesterday was busy, and a big distraction from missing home. This is the first time that I've been in port for a holiday, and I have to say this is the best day I've spent in the Navy, hands down. A party of us went to the Solace for the holiday, and I got to spend it with many of my old mates. We had the run of the ship with no assigned duties from colors in the morning until sundown. All of the ships had fancy dinners, the best they could put out. The men in all the messes pooled their money in order to turn it over to the caterers to buy food in the market, and the market was ready for the holiday. We had roast pig, which is the best thing you can get in the Philippines, as well as mutton, beef from Australia, birds of various kinds, fruits and vegetables, and even fresh bread and puddings. I have never seen such a feast. They invited crews from the foreign ships to come and join the festivities, and in the morning, we had boat races and all kinds of sports to work up our appetites.

The big event of the day was the international boat race, where each country puts up their best crew, and they race for three miles across the harbor. It was us against the British, the Russians, and the Japanese. There is no end of excitement aboard all the ships over this one, added to by the betting that takes place. This can get pretty high, but I stayed clear of the high stakes. I did bet on our boys to win, and they did, but there wasn't much of a return because most everybody was betting on our boys. The most fun was the open race, where all boats can compete, with men from every part of the ship doing the rowing. It's one place where us firemen and coal passers are in demand by the seamen, because we are the ones with the muscles. I was on a big twelve-oared cutter that was manned three to an oar with one seaman, one fireman, and one marine. We did pretty well considering how heavy we were, and got cheers from all sides.

After the boat races, the meal pennant went up, and we headed for the gun deck, where the feast was spread out buffet style. You should have seen it. Some of the boys had decorated it to look something like Christmas back home, though it was bunting and flags instead of holly or evergreens. Everybody lined up and filled up their plates, and came back as often as they wanted. We all tried to show our hospitality to the foreigners, and they seemed to appreciate it. We had a constant stream of visitors, and the cooks kept refilling the table all afternoon. I don't know where all that food came from. In the afternoon, there were all kinds of contests, from foot races and boxing and climbing the mast to things that aren't too naval in character, like climbing a greased pole. I'm told that in other ports there are swimming and tub races, but that wouldn't be safe here with so many sharks around.

So good a time was had by all that we didn't have time to be homesick. It's a little different today, now that it's just a Tuesday and I'm back on the Petrel, but it gives me something to remember and laugh about.

Here's to a grand New Year for us all.

Your loving son and brother,

Tom

*****

Woburn *News*, June 9, 1900, page 5.

From the Petrel
U. S. S. Petrel
Cavite P. I.
April 22, 1900

To the Editor of THE NEWS:—Since last writing there has not been much of importance, everything seems to drag slowly especially on the Petrel, "Bird." There are about twenty Chinamen repairing our boilers and we are good for about five or six months more here unless transferred. . . .

On the "Bird" we are all somewhat sorry she is laid up as all the fleet are going in turn to the north—that is China and Japan—to cooler climate to give the crews a chance to recuperate, as this climate will in time tell on the hardest.

As for food we have plenty of fresh beef and ice as three refrigerator boats the Celtic, Gologoa, and Glacier run between here and Australia on that mission, and by chipping in extra, from the commissary we can get food and live well, but as the old song goes, "There is no place like the old home after all," and it proves very true in the cases of those who have spent any length of time in these islands. . . .

Respectfully yours,
THOS. A. TERRETT

*****

April 30, 1900
U. S. S. Celtic
Manila

Dear Family,

I've been transferred! I'm now on the Celtic, formerly the Celtic King out of Belfast. How does that sound? She is a supply ship that goes back and forth to Australia once a month or so, mainly with food. The boys tell me it takes about 15 days, and we stop in Brisbane on the way. This is a clean, modern, fairly new ship. The engines and boilers are in great shape. So far I like the firemen on our watch, so I think it will be good. And I'll get to see Australia.

I think we're off tomorrow, so I will put this in the mailbag and hope you get it fairly soon.

I miss you all. I hope we get a mail call soon!

Your loving son and brother,
Tom

May 1, 1900
U. S. S. Celtic
Manila

Dear Mary E.,

I've been ordered to the Celtic, which is a supply ship that goes back and forth to Australia. It's going to be a lot like the Solace, but with much shorter cruises. We will mostly bring food and other supplies to the fleet in Manila and Cavite. This sounds boring, but at least I will get to see Australia. The fellows who have been there say there's nothing like it, with the kangaroos and so on.

I think we're off tomorrow, and am putting this in the mail so you know where I am.

Your affectionate,
Tom

May 15, 1900
U. S. S. Celtic
Cavite

Dear Mary E.,

Mail call! Thank you for the letters. They were just what I needed right now. I'm feeling a little low. It's just being on the new ship with strangers instead of my old mates. There's nothing wrong with these fellows. They do their work, and they're fine to get along with. It's just that they're not my mates. But I'm sure they will be before too long. Sorry I didn't get to see Manny before they left for San Francisco. The last time I saw him he was fine.

The trip to Australia was interesting, but I didn't get to see any kangaroos. They have an epidemic of fever in Brisbane and Sydney, and they wouldn't let anyone off the ship. No need to worry. They took all kinds of precautions so it wouldn't get on board, and so far, everyone is healthy, and we're back in Cavite. I'm anxious to get underway, though. It's much hotter and muggier here than in Australia, and I'd rather be at sea anyway.

I've been thinking this week that I now have two years in with the Navy, and less than one year to go. I suppose I could spend it in worse ways than sailing back and forth to Australia, but I miss the excitement of the early days on the Petrel. Except for all the discipline, sometimes I think it's not like we're in the Navy at all, but just sailing around in the merchant marine. Sorry to let my low spirits out on you. I didn't really know I was low until I started to write.

I loved the story of your Christmas dinner. Your uncle must be a real character. On Christmas, we were at anchor in Cavite, and I spent it on the Solace. It was the best day I've had in the Navy. We had the bulliest banquet, with roast pig and beef and different kinds of birds, and all kinds of vegetables and fruit, and even pudding. You could just keep filling your plate all afternoon. You should have seen what Manny put away! Then there were boat races and other contests with the men from the foreign ships. We were like boys again.

Well, I want to say that I am looking forward to seeing

you next April. Is it a date? Don't worry, I will abide by all the rules to make your Papai happy.

Your affectionate,
Tom

May 15, 1900
U. S. S. Celtic
Cavite

Dear Family,

Well, we finally had mail call and the Quartermaster was generous to me. Thank you for all the letters. It's good to hear you are all well and to hear about everything at home, especially now that I'm on a strange ship where I don't have any old mates around. So far, the new ship has been good. I like all the men, and there are no shirkers among the firemen, which is important.

The cruise was a breeze as far as I was concerned, ten days to Brisbane with a stop for coal, and then two days to Sydney, where we took on supplies and water. The weather was good, hot, but not muggy like the Philippines. The boys say it can get over 100 degrees, but it wasn't anything like that on this trip, and the skipper, Cmdr. Patch, isn't as set on breaking a record every time we weigh anchor as Cmdr. Dunlap was. On the whole, this is a less exciting, but more relaxed ship than the Solace or the Petrel, and the food is better. We get fresh meat and vegetables from Australia, even beef!

It was an interesting voyage among all the islands around there, but I don't think we'll be getting ashore in

Australia for a while. They have an epidemic there, and they aren't letting us off to pick up any disease. We are all fine. I hope it's over soon, though. I would like to see Sydney, which looks like an impressive city from the docks.

Meanwhile, we're back here in Cavite for a couple of days to unload and then go back again. I haven't had a chance to see my old mates on the Solace, but we have visited around.

Your loving son and brother,

Tom

August 18, 1900
U. S. S. Celtic
Cavite

Dear Mary E.,

Sorry to upset you with my last letter. I'm in much better spirits now. The ship is beginning to feel like home, and I've made a couple of good friends. Most of the boys are from New York or Brooklyn. My best mate is Frank Kelly, another fireman on my watch who's from New York. I wish I'd known some of the things he's told me about the city when I had shore leave in Brooklyn. There's a lot to see there. Now that we're allowed to go ashore in Australia, I'm enjoying the trip down there much more. What a strange place it is! I'll have lots of stories to tell you when I see you. And I have some souvenirs. Have you ever heard of a boomerang? You throw it and it comes back to you. Kind of like me. I'm not bringing you a boomerang, though. I think I have something you will like better than that.

I'm starting to think about getting home now. It will take about two months to New York by way of the Suez Canal, or about five weeks to San Francisco, and then ten days or so on the train. Maybe they'll send me back to the Solace, but meanwhile, I have a few more trips to Australia to make.

I was glad to hear about your promotion at the factory. They must really value you if they're willing to pay you nine dollars a week and give you that kind of responsibility. It will give you a chance to put away some more money too. That's one good thing about the Navy. If you aren't a wild man who drops all his pay the minute he hits the waterfront, it's easy to save. There is not all that much to spend your money on. I have a pretty good stake saved up.

I think we sail tomorrow or the next day, so I'll get this into the mail bag before we go.

Your affectionate,
Tom

August 18, 1900
U. S. S. Celtic
Cavite

Dear Family,

Thank you for your letters, which I got at mail call today. It was good to be reminded of home, and I appreciate the birthday greetings. Yes, Josie, I am quite an adult at 22, though I'm not sure about the mature part. We got back from Australia yesterday, and for the first time, I was able to go ashore in Sydney, since the bubonic plague epidemic is over now. They are still demolishing buildings around the wharf area, as they think the poor living conditions there contributed to the disease. I read that they have killed 44,000 rats! The mates I was with also told me they have cleaned up the city quite a bit. It did seem to be a very clean place, especially around the docks, which is not usually the case, to say the least. It's a very big city, and it seemed quite a lot like San Francisco, with some pretty rough neighborhoods, but a busy, prosperous downtown with impressive public buildings. I rode the trolleys around the city and saw a lot of it. The Australians are a very friendly and open people. Also very talkative, which can be a problem, because it's hard to understand their accent at first, and it's so broad that it can give you the sense that everybody is doing a comic vaudeville routine until you realize that they're quite seriously telling you something. I like the Australians very much, and they seem to like Americans, too.

We're back in Cavite now, and will start again for Brisbane once the cargo is unloaded. We go back and forth regularly. It takes about 15 days to make the trip, so every month or so, we go there and back. I'm anxious to get going, as it's very hot and muggy here now, and it's much nicer down there.

I have to get this in the mail bag before we leave. I miss you all, and think of home often. I should be there before too long. It's hard to believe I have just a few months left of my tour of duty.

Your loving son and brother,
Tom

*****

Woburn *News*, October 20, 1900, page 5.

In the Typhoon Belt
U. S. S Celtic
Manila, P. I.
Sept. 10, 1900

Dear Mr. Weatherell:—

The rainy season is now on for fair and when it rains it pours. We have seen several waterspouts in the bay, but don't care for any closer acquaintance than five miles at which distance these generally were. . . .

Mail is coming slowly on account of the China trouble. We expect to stay here for about two months and I for one hope to start for home before it is time to leave for Australia as this country is N. G.

All ships and other craft are stormbound as typhoon signals are flying, and since the eighth it has been blowing a gale. . . .

Most respectfully,
THOS. A. TERRETT

*****

November 12, 1900
U. S. S. Caesar
Cavite

Dear Family,

As I'm sure you noticed, I've changed ships again. The Caesar is a collier that saw service in Cuba. I remember her coaling the Solace. She's been refitted as a supply ship, and arrived in port about a month ago. She is getting ready to put out for home via the Suez Canal with extra crew, which includes me!

I have less than four months left of my tour, so I figure this ship will be taking me home. I don't know which will arrive in Boston sooner, this letter, or me, but I thought I would send it anyway. So by the time you get this, you will be seeing me very soon, or you will already have seen me.

Your loving son and brother,

Tom

November 12, 1900
U. S. S. Caesar
Cavite

Dear Mary E.,

As you can see, I've changed ships. The Caesar is a supply ship. She came here by way of the Suez canal, and she will be returning the same way, with me on board. I'm glad to be taking that trip again, and not in the mad rush we were always in aboard the Solace. I'm an extra crew member, so although I will probably be put to work in the engine room, I don't expect it to be nearly as tough as the Solace was. I don't know if this will reach you before I see you. I think we're the ship that will be taking the mail. But I thought I would let you know, anyway.

Your affectionate,

Tom

*****

"On His Way Home," Woburn News, January 12, 1901, page 5.

U. S. S. Caesar
Colombo, Island of Ceylon
Dec. 7th, 1900

Mr. Editor:—As I am homeward bound I write to you these few lines to let you and my friends know of our trip since leaving Manila for "God's Country."

We left Manila on Nov. 12 at midnight for Hong Kong, 640 miles, and arrived there Nov. 18, at 12 noon, 5 ½ days in the China Sea, in very heavy weather, the northeast monsoons blowing hard, and a rough sea running.

There was much grumbling, and many of the fellows who are anxious to get home said we would not reach Norfolk before 1902, and were much disappointed at our craft, which is built like a scow. . . .

The Old Caesar has given us a happy and welcome surprise; we are making a quick trip, but she can't go any too quick. The weather is red hot, but if it don't get a white heat we can stand it O. K. . . .

Most respectfully yours,
THOS. A. TERRETT

*****

December 31, 1900
U. S. S. Caesar
Malta

Dear Family,

First, Happy New Year to you all! I think 1901 is going to be a good year. I hope you had a Merry Christmas. We were in the Mediterranean Sea on Christmas, and didn't have anything like what we had in Cavite last year, but the cooks and the mess caterers really put themselves out to make sure the meal was special. They had picked up a lot of things in Port Said that made the dinner almost a banquet, though not a traditional one. So far, I'm having a good time on this cruise. Since the firemen always need an extra hand, I've been assigned to a watch, but it's not really hard work. This ship is in no particular hurry, and the weather is cool, so it's nothing like what I'm used to.

In the Indian Ocean near the Island of Socotra, I saw a whale that looked like a small island, and we were escorted almost all the way through the Red Sea by porpoises. We've had shore leave in a couple of places. I got to see Hong Kong on this trip, and I just had shore leave in Valletta, Malta, which is a beautiful place. I have a surprise for you too. I picked up a little abandoned puppy in Valletta, the funniest little ball of fur you've ever seen, and the officers let me keep him because the ship's mascot they'd had died a couple of months ago. Everybody who's seen him loves Malty. I think he might make even Mary a dog lover. We'll see.

It looks like I'm going to be on this ship a little longer than I'd thought. The scuttle-butt is that we're not going home from here, but to several ports in Europe, and possibly the Azores and Bermuda. I don't mind that. I'm in the Navy until the end of March, and I'd rather be at sea and looking at new countries than sitting in Virginia or Brooklyn. Maybe we'll get shore leave in England.

I am sending this letter, thinking some other ship will be taking the mail bag home before we get there. Whether you get this or not, Malty and I will be seeing you soon!

Your loving son and brother,

Tom

February 11, 1901
U. S. S. Caesar
Hamilton, Bermuda

Dear Mary E.,

I'm writing to you although I'm pretty sure this letter will not be making it to you much before you see me. This ship has taken her sweet time getting from the Philippines home. We stopped in several ports in Europe, to bring the mail, I guess, but we only had shore leave in Liverpool. We did put in at Ponta Delgada, in the Azores. That is a truly beautiful place. It must have been very hard for your family to leave. But I could also see that it must be a very hard place to make a living as a farmer, with all the mountains. It seems quite a bit like Ireland as my parents describe it. It's a beautiful place that they loved, but a place where it would have been impossible for them to live.

Anyway, I just wanted you to know that we're on our way now. We have been stormbound here in Bermuda for twelve days, but we should be weighing anchor tomorrow, and we'll be in Virginia in a week or so. It's hard to believe that I'm this close to home and the end of my tour. I should be seeing you in a couple of months!

Your affectionate,

Tom

*****

"Home At Last," Woburn *News*, March 2, 1901, page 5.

On Board U. S. S. Caesar
Norfolk Navy Yard Va.
Feb. 24, 1901

To the Editor of THE NEWS:—I have at last arrived in "God's Country" after a most trying experience of thirty-two steaming days from Gibraltar and one month and 14 days all told, that is counting the twelve days we were stormbound in Bermuda. We left that place Feb. 12 at 10:30 a.m. and after seven days of heavy seas and head winds we dropped anchor off Fortress Munroe, much to the relief and happiness of all hands, at 6:15 p.m. on the 19th.

The temperature was 27 degrees and us Filipinos were very near frozen after two years of that Asiatic climate, and it will take some time to get used to our own.

It is two years this month since I left this same Hampton Roads for Manila and in that time I have steamed something like 55,000 miles and this is the best part of it all, from the Rip Raps to the Navy Yard.

It is stated we are to put this "old tub" out of commission and turn her over to a merchant crew and we will then finish our time on the Receiving Ship Franklin; that is, those who have time to do . . . All hands hope the weather will get up to 90 degrees in a short time as this is a fearful experience.

With kind regards and best wishes to all my friends and success to the NEWS,

I am most respectfully,
THOS. A. TERRETT

*****

"The Navy Yard at Norfolk," Woburn *News*, March 9, 1901, page 4.

U. S. S. Caesar
March 2, 1901
To the Editor of THE NEWS:—The Ajax formerly the Scindia arrived yesterday from Manila with about 250 short and overtimers aboard. This will make about 350 here now to be paid off this month. There will be a big shortage in the Navy by May 1 and the officials will have to offer great inducements for many of those whose time is short to re-enlist as the general opinion of the men forward is in other directions. I could write a whole lot on the way men are often treated in this line but will refrain. In time of peace our Navy is going to be far behind what it should be. . .

We have got a fine lot of ships in our Navy but where are the men to man them? The officials are recruiting young men and boys inland to see the world and send them on a European cruise but they mostly fetch up in that far away Asiatic station where they will finish their four years away from civilization, that is if they live. Many will go there who will be wiped out by fever and improper care and treatment.

Yours most respectfully,
THOS. A. TERRETT

*****

March 12, 1901
U. S. S. Vermont
Brooklyn

Dear Mary E.,

Here I am! The Vermont is a receiving ship which takes in new recruits and musters out old salts like me. It's easy to tell the ones coming in from the ones going out. I still have another couple of weeks to serve, so they're putting me to work here with the new recruits. I look at them and think, I was that green once. They have no idea what's ahead of them. I try to be brusque and tough with them like an old salt, but it's hard when they're so eager and scared they will mess up.

It looks like I will be free to go by Sunday the 31st, and I will either meet you at Sacred Heart or come in the afternoon to visit before I go out to Woburn. I hope you don't mind if I bring the little dog I picked up in Malta. I think you'll like him.

This is going in the land mail, so hopefully you will get it before you see me, and I won't be surprising your family too much. See you soon!

Your affectionate,
Tom

March 13, 1901
U. S. S. Vermont
Brooklyn

Dear Family,

I've been ordered to the Vermont, which is a receiving ship processing sailors in and out. The cruise home from Gibraltar was not enjoyable, to say the least. I've written about it for the News. I had shore leave in Liverpool though. I remembered hearing Pa and Marm both talk about people going there to work during the bad times in Ireland, and you could see that there are a lot of Irish people there still, judging by the names on the businesses. It's a very lively city, a big favorite with sailors, although most of the boys just stay around the waterfront. The fish and chips I had there are something I'll remember for a while.

I'm hoping to get your last bunch of mail while I'm here, but it might not catch up with me. It's a long time since I've heard anything from you, and you will probably say the same. This letter will go out by land mail, so at least you will know that I'm here, and will be seeing you in a very short time, probably the first or second of April. I'm going to take the train up to Boston, and then out to Woburn. So don't be surprised when you see me walking through the door with my Navy bag and my dog!

Your loving son and brother,
Tom

Chapter 9

1901–1908

April 18, 1901
19 Arlington Street
Woburn, Mass.

Dear Mary E.,

This is just a note to say that I won't be able to come up to Cambridge this Sunday. One of Pa's Knights of Labor friends has found me a machinist's job in Salem, and I'll be moving up there on Sunday. It's probably the best that could be hoped for right now. I can't see myself settling down to a machinist's bench, but I told him I would try it. I need some kind of job, and this is a good one. My father is pretty set on the idea that I can do better than the kind of manual labor that a fireman does. I understand how it looks from his point of view. He's spent his life doing hard manual labor when what he wanted was to use his brain, and he wants a better life for his children. But he doesn't see that sitting at a machine or a machinist's bench seems like a kind of death to me. I don't know how else to say it. Anyway, I'm going to try it. Maybe now that I'm older it will be easier. And, in Salem, I can be looking out for something maritime. I found a nice room in a boarding house a couple of blocks from the harbor.

I left Malty in Woburn for now. The girls love him, as everybody does. Even Mary, who's been afraid of dogs all her life, is fond of Malty. They've promised to take good care of him.

When I see you a week from Sunday, I'll let you know how the job is going.

Your affectionate,

Tom

July 3, 1901
110 Harbor Street
Salem, Mass.

Dear Mary E.,

I wanted to write and say how much it meant to me to have you and Manny at the funeral. It's been a week now, and I still can't seem to realize that my father is dead. He was always the most important person in my life. We didn't always agree, but I loved and respected him very much, and I always knew he had my interest at heart, even when he thought I didn't measure up. It was so moving at the wake and funeral to hear from all the men who looked up to him and told me about the things he had done in the old days with the Knights of Labor or in politics. To me the saddest thing about his life was that he had to put so much of himself into a hard job that meant nothing to him. I think he sacrificed a lot to support his family, and I know we meant more to him than all the success in the world, but I do wish he'd been able to get out of the tannery.

I'm going to spend this Sunday in Woburn with Marm and the girls, but I will see you a week from then. It's going to be a hard week. Pa loved the 4th of July. He was in his element then, with all the celebrations and speeches.

Anyway, thanks again, and I will see you soon.

Your affectionate,

Tom

September 3, 1901
110 Harbor Street
Salem, Mass.

Dear Mary E.,

This is just to tell you that I got the job on the tugboat. There will just be two of us working the engine, boiler, and fire, but it's a small "lunch bucket boat," and it shouldn't be bad at all. I'm mainly responsible for the fire and the boiler, and the mate is going to teach me what I don't know about the engine, which will be good experience. It will be good to get out on the water again, even if it's just around Salem and Boston. And the good news is I get Sundays off, so I will see you in a couple of days!

Love, Tom

September 8, 1901
110 Harbor Street
Salem, Mass.

Dearest,

Marm has told me to invite your whole family and Manny to dinner in Woburn next Sunday. She wants to have an engagement party for us, and there will certainly be plenty of food, and maybe some music and dancing after, if I know Marm. I'll come up to Boston for church. We could go to St. John the Baptist, and then take the streetcar to Woburn. What do you think?

Let me know right away who can come, so I can tell Marm.

Love,
Tom

October 14, 1901
110 Harbor Street
Salem, Mass.

Dearest,

I broke the news to Marm about our plans to move to California, and she is taking it pretty well. I think having me away for three years has made it easier for her to imagine than it is for your family. Now that the estate is all sorted out, I feel that I'm leaving them in good shape financially. The house is paid for, and they have a thousand dollars in insurance as well as the savings account Pa left. Josie is working, and when Mary finishes her business course, she will get a job that pays more than I'm likely to make.

I feel a little guilty leaving them, but I also feel that this is our chance to really begin a new life. I hope you can bring your father around to it. I'll be there on Sunday to do my best.

All my love,
Tom

November 27, 1901

Dear Josie,

This note goes with the ring we wanted you to have as a reminder of this day when Mary Elizabeth joins our family. We have always had a special bond between us, little sister, and Mary hopes that you feel the same way about her now. The ring is engraved with the date so it will always remind you of us, and how much we love you.

Your brother,
Tom

~~~

Thomas Augustine Terrett and Mary Elizabeth Grace were married at Sacred Heart Church in Cambridge, Massachusetts on November 27, 1901, the day before Thanksgiving. Two days later, accompanied by Mary's reluctant mother and father, they took the Atlantic Avenue Elevated to Boston's new South Station, where they boarded the train for the first leg of their journey to Los Angeles. They boarded with Malty and with all their belongings packed in a small trunk, Tom's old Navy bag, and two traveling bags. Tom was excited to be leaving Woburn behind at last and seeing the world again, and Mary
~~~

was thrilled to be with him on this adventure and not just reading about it.

Mostly they ate from a big basket of food that Mary had packed for the journey, replenished along the way with things that Tom hopped off the train and bought in the stations. But they did splurge on the dining car in Colorado and Nevada, when it was the only source of food for a hundred miles around. For most of the journey, they sat up all night in the day coach resting on each other, the price of a Pullman sleeper being far beyond their means. A healthy twenty-four and twenty-two, they could pretty much sleep anywhere, and they were too interested in each other and what was going on to notice any discomfort.

They stopped overnight in Chicago, in Omaha, and in Ogden, Utah, luxuriating in the chance to eat a meal sitting at a table, take a hot bath, and sleep in a real bed together. In Chicago, they walked from their hotel near the Union Depot on Canal Street to the downtown Loop, where they marveled at the traffic, the masses of people, and the Christmas display at Marshall Field's department store, all on a grander scale than anything in Boston.

Both Mary and Tom were entranced as the country sped by them, especially when they got out West. They had never imagined anything like the western mountains and the giant red stone formations of Utah. At night in Nebraska and Wyoming, they got out at nearly all the coal and water stops, partly for Malty, but mostly to stand together in the frosty air and look at the sky. In the darkness, complete except for the occasional oil lamp in a farmhouse window, they felt enveloped by the stars. It took Tom back to his nights at sea and his sense of the immensity of the world, but for Mary, it was the first time. She and Tom were beginning a new life together, free from her father's house and the factory, and the world felt boundless before them.

When they reached San Francisco, they stayed over for two days. They really felt they were on their honeymoon. Tom showed Mary some of the things he'd found on his earlier visits, and they explored the city together. But their ultimate destination was Los Angeles, a city new to both of them, where they had been told the weather was perfect year-round, and there was plenty of work. On the third day, December twelfth, they took the train south, expecting to emerge from it in a summery climate. They were disappointed to find it was fifty degrees, not much warmer than San Francisco. Tom also had a hard time finding work that he wanted to do. He finally signed on as an apprentice steamfitter with a heating and ventilating company, thinking the skills would give him a wide choice of employment, but the job paid only half of a journeyman's wages. Mary found work in a small factory. Her wages helped while Tom was in his apprenticeship, but she had to quit a month before their first child, Richard Joseph Terrett, named for his grandfathers, was born on November 5, 1902.

The lack of money hadn't bothered them before the baby came. They were happy to live in a single room together and spend what little leisure they had from work in exploring the city. But the baby changed it all. Tom arranged to speed up his apprenticeship, and with his Navy experience, he took only a few more months to qualify as a journeyman steamfitter. They found a three-room apartment at 218 South Daly Street, close to his work, and finally felt like a family. When another son was born in 1904, they named him Tom Jr. But they never grew comfortable in Los Angeles. As aggressively American as Mary was, she missed seeing Portuguese people and joining in community life. Stuck on the Northeastern side of the city, Tom missed the ocean and being around ships and boats.

When a daughter was born in the spring of 1905, they named her Veronica Grace, after Josie and Mary's family. But little Veronica, small and delicate, didn't grow and develop as the boys had. As the hot summer dragged on, she grew more and more frail. Her appetite fell off, and she started losing weight. They took her to the doctor, who couldn't find anything wrong with her. "You have to get her to take nourishment," he said, and they tried everything they could think of, but she couldn't hold her milk down. She grew more and more listless until she didn't even cry anymore. On the last night in July, she fell into a deep sleep. Mary put her in the cradle while she put the boys to bed. When she looked at her an hour later, she was no longer breathing.

Tom and Mary were devastated by the death of their baby daughter. It got so they couldn't stand to be in their apartment because everything around them recalled some sweet moment with Veronica or some desperate attempt and failure to save her. After two weeks in which Mary seemed unable to stop crying, Tom said, "We need to get out of here, Mary. We have to try to make a life for the children we still have. And I don't mean just this house. I think we should leave Los Angeles. We've never liked it here anyway. We can go to San Francisco. There is a lot of work for steam fitters in the shipyards there, and we can make a fresh start."

Mary was not ready to think about a fresh start, but she felt it would be a godsend to be released from Los Angeles. Tom quit his job, and they took their little savings and set out for San Francisco. They went first to Berkeley, where they found a small apartment on Eighth Street, not far from the waterfront, and Tom went to work making repairs. But the work was not steady, and Mary couldn't seem to get over her sadness. Tom asked Mary to move one more time, to Vallejo, where he knew there would be steady work at the Navy Yard on Mare Island, and where he remembered from his Navy days that there was a thriving Portuguese community. They found an apartment at 661 Ninth Street, far enough from the waterfront and the saloons of South Georgia Street that it was quiet, but close enough for Tom to walk to the ferry that would take him to the Navy Yard. Tom was hired immediately as a steamfitter. At St. Vincent's church, they were welcomed by both the Irish and the Portuguese communities.

Tom liked working at the Navy Yard. He would often say that it was like being in the Navy without the boatswain's whistle. He got his daily dose of the water riding back and forth across the Napa River on the ferry from Vallejo, and he liked the active, big muscle work of the steam fitter much better than the precise work of the machinist's bench. And then, of course, he came home to his family each night.

With his father on his mind, Tom joined the local Steamfitter's Union as soon as he could. Although his interest in the union never took fire as his father's had, Tom diligently attended all the union meetings. There wasn't much action there. The men knew the pay at the Navy Yard was lower than at the private yards in San Francisco, but they were mostly satisfied with their steady work and the lower cost of living around Mare Island.

Tom himself was more interested in taking Mary and the boys on outings, like watching boat races on the channel or having a picnic and a swim at Blue Rock Springs, than in union activity. When roller polo came to Vallejo's skating rink, he found that the skills he had developed in Woburn were not too rusty, and he quickly became known as one of the best players in town. Soon he was selected for a Vallejo team, and Mary and the boys loved coming to the rink to cheer him on.

As for politics, when Tom registered to vote, it was with no party affiliation. He felt that he was letting his father down, but there was no point in being a Democrat in overwhelmingly Republican Vallejo. The Terretts became an integral part of the Portuguese community in town, and Tom got as involved in helping with the Saint's Day feasts as Mary did. A third son, born in August of 1908, was named Harold. Tom said they already had Tom and Dick, so they might as well have Harry. With their growing family, they moved to a larger apartment at 230 Sacramento Street.

On Saturday, the fourteenth of November, Tom worked a shift at the Navy Yard and picked up his pay envelope, which contained a notice that he was laid off. It was quickly evident from the noise around him that a number of other steamfitters had received the same notice. Tom talked the situation over with his friend Clyde Nevins on the ferry home, and they decided the best thing to do was to inquire for work at the C & H sugar refinery in Crockett, on the other side of the Carquinez Strait from Mare Island and Vallejo, before too many of the other workers had the same idea. They decided to take the ferry, which had more frequent service than the train, and planned to meet at the boat right after early Mass the next day.

Mary supported Tom's determination to find work as soon as possible, but worried that they would be late for the church supper at St. Vincent's where she was supposed to help serve. Tom told her there would be no problem getting back in time, and promised to be on the two o'clock boat. While Tom and Clyde were walking to the sugar plant in Crockett from the steamboat landing, they came to a sharp curve in the road. As the two men rounded the curve, a fast-moving freight train came alongside.

"I'm going to jump this," Tom yelled to Clyde. "I don't want to miss that two o'clock boat." Clyde shook his head and waved. He was not the athlete Tom was. There was no way he could jump that train. Tom ran alongside, and, as he had done many times since he was a boy, jumped to grab the ladder on the back of a freight car and pull his legs up after him.

*****

Vallejo Daily Times, 17 November 1908.

The body of Thomas A. Terrett, well known Spanish-American war veteran, crackerjack polo player and until Friday last employed as a pipe-fitter on Mare Island, lies cold in death in J. J. McDonald's undertaking parlor, while at 230 Sacramento Street, a little woman and three fatherless children are stunned by the horrible accident that on Sunday robbed them of a husband and father . . .

Train service between Vallejo Junction and the sugar town is poor and so the men started to walk from the steamer landing. A half mile away is what is known as Horseshoe Head, but which Crockett people call 'Death Curve,' owing to the number of lives that have been lost there. When that point was reached Terrett attempted to jump a rapidly passing freight train. He missed his step and fell under the cars. The rain passed over both legs near the knee and mangled him terribly. The train was stopped and he was hurried to the railway physician at Port Costa. A hopeless effort was here made to save Terrett's life, but of no avail. He passed away about 5 o'clock, Sunday afternoon.

*****

Tom was buried in the Spanish-American War veterans section of Sunrise Cemetery in Vallejo. A few months later, with the help of two hundred dollars in insurance from the Steamfitters Union, Mary Elizabeth opened a rooming house at 320 York Street, near the waterfront, where she kept house for five lodgers as well as her three sons. Maggie Terrett and her daughter Mary regularly sent her Tom's share of the rent on the Woburn house, and then his share of the proceeds when it was sold in 1919. When he was seventeen, young Richard went to work in the Navy Yard, and Mary bought a smaller house at 1016 Eldorado Street, where the family lived along with one lodger, Joseph Garofalo, whom Mary later married. Tom Jr. died in 1922 at eighteen, and Harry died in 1928 at nineteen, both of tuberculosis. After Joseph Garofalo died in 1938, Mary continued to live in the house with Richard and his wife Angel until her death in 1967. Like his father, Richard was a dog lover. He and Angel became well known among dog breeders in the San Francisco Bay area for the French bulldogs they raised. Richard died in 1981. Since he and Angel had no children, he was the last of the family to bear the Terrett name.

Tom and Mary Elizabeth Terrett with Richard J. and Tom Jr., about 1908

Harold Terrett in 1911

Richard J. Terrett and Angel Viault on their wedding day

(from left) Mary, Maggie, and Josie Terrett at 19 Arlington Street, about 1890

Part Four

Josie Terrett

Chapter 10

1883–1900

As Maggie Terrett finished up the lunch dishes on a hot July day in 1883, she looked out her kitchen window at the flourishing vegetable garden with satisfaction. It hadn't been easy to tend it this year. At five and three, Tom and Josie were a handful, always into something. And at two months, Mary was still claiming a lot of her mother's attention. For this moment, though, everything was quiet, with Mary asleep in her cradle in the parlor and the other two playing together upstairs. Then, as she gazed absently out the window, some motion at the corner of the garden caught her eye, and she saw Josie slowly making her way across the yard toward the Connollys' house. She must have slipped out the front door again and gone around through the side yard.

Suddenly, Ann came running out her back door, stopped, and began moving slowly toward the little girl, bending her head and stretching her arms toward her, speaking with an uncharacteristic calm. Then Maggie noticed that Josie was carrying a big rag doll under her arm. One she hadn't seen. For a moment, she wondered where it had come from. Could Dick have given it to her? But he wasn't one to spend money on extravagant toys, and her birthday was last week. Then the recognition struck. It wasn't a doll, it was the baby. Josie lugged Mary under her arm as she toddled unsteadily across the yard.

As Maggie flew out of the house, she could hear Ann saying with a strained cheerfulness, "Come to Auntie, Josie. Let me see your new dolly. Be careful not to drop her."

Josie looked up at her Aunt and Ann quickly took hold of the baby.

"The baby's all right," she said to Maggie. "You need to keep a closer watch."

As they grew, Josie continued to think of Mary as her own special doll. She enjoyed spoiling her almost as much as their father did. In fact, she put him to the test on Mary's tenth birthday, when she got up a big party for her. The neighborhood children joined in together to buy her a ring to commemorate the occasion, but twelve-year-old Josie went to the grocery store to order the food on her Papa's account. When Josie finished ordering cake and ice cream and party food for the neighborhood, she'd spent nearly half a week's pay on the party. Her Papa fumed and sputtered at Josie for her extravagance and forbade her to charge anything else at Haney's. But after all, it was for Mary that she'd done it, and he forgave her.

Josie doted on her little sister, and she didn't mind being in the same grade at St. Charles's, even though she was nearly three years older. Since Josie always struggled with her school work and Mary was so quick, Mary got into the habit of explaining things to her big sister and helping with her lessons at home. Josie did much better in school when Mary was there. And Josie was there to help Mary when she got into trouble in the school yard. Mary was often teased for being the teacher's pet, but it never got too far because everyone knew they would have to reckon with Josie if they made her cry.

When they entered high school, their father insisted that the girls join the Young Ladies' Sodality together, and attend the Sunday afternoon meetings at St. Charles's. Mary needed no persuading to join. For a girl who loved religious ritual and dreamed of being a nun, but also loved clothes and parties, the Sodality was a perfect way to socialize. She enjoyed marching with the group in church processions, all dressed in white with blue ribbons, and she was usually chosen to carry the banner or place flowers on the altar of the Blessed Virgin on the feasts of the Assumption and the Immaculate Conception. Josie liked the parties and church dances, and she didn't mind the various fundraisers to buy altar cloths and vestments, but in her view, she got more than enough of St. Charles's between Catholic high school and Sunday Mass. She did not enjoy spending Sunday afternoons praying the rosary and learning how to conduct herself according to the Sodality's "Rules of Comportment."

About once a month, when the two girls would head off to the Sodality meeting together, Josie would go visiting instead. Occasionally, she was able to tempt Mary into going with her. On one beautiful Sunday in June, she talked her into visiting their Aunt Mag in Arlington, arguing it would be an act of charity because she had been sick, and wasn't it one of the Corporal Works of Mercy to visit the sick? They decided to walk along the Mystic River instead of taking the streetcar home, and they planned to take their shoes and stockings off and wade in the water when they got to a little grove of trees they knew. But as they made their way down the steep bank, Mary tripped on a tree root, and fell head first into the river. She couldn't seem to get her footing and splashed around wildly for a minute, so Josie ran in after her and dragged her to the shore. They dried off as best they could, but their Sunday dresses were all muddy, and Mary's hair was a sight.

On the way home, they decided that their best hope was to slip in through the back door of the house without their father seeing them. Marm would surely help them. It was not a pleasant walk, with their squishy wet shoes and their clammy stockings, but they made it home, and luckily, Maggie saw them through the kitchen window and, though she had a good laugh over it, helped them to get their dresses into the wash tub, clean up, and put on their regular dresses while Richard read his Sunday paper in the parlor, none the wiser. Fortunately, the Connallys were off visiting and didn't see them go by the house, or he'd have gotten an earful.

Smart and pretty and pious, the golden-haired, blue-eyed Mary was the darling of the nuns at St. Charles's. Though the youngest in the class, she was always at the top, while the plainer Josie, with her pug nose and dishwater blonde hair, hovered near the bottom, even with Mary's help and her father's constant admonitions to study harder. It went without saying that Mary would continue on to the girls' high school at St. Charles's when they graduated from the eighth grade, but Josie had not been so sure that she wanted to. As she had watched Tom struggle through his first two years at Woburn High, she had thought she would avoid this if she could. Tom at least had sports and high school dances to make up for all the book work. The girls would have only the same academic and religious activities they had always had. She told her father that at fifteen, she could easily go to work in one of the factories and start earning good money, and they both knew that she had no head for books. But Richard was determined that she at least try the high school for a year or two. Any education was better than none in his eyes, and he said she could take the courses in sewing and cooking at the school rather than the more academic subjects. Both of those things would be useful to her as skills for earning a living, and certainly later, when she married. So Josie went to high school for two years, and although she didn't enjoy it very much, she did become adept at sewing and tailoring and making hats, and Sister Tabitha thought she had a good eye for trimming.

When Josie left St. Charles's, her father got her a job at the Winn watch hand factory in Winchester, about a mile's walk from the house on Arlington Street. As factories went in the Woburn and Winchester area, it was a good one. Built on the site of an old grist mill, it was isolated in the country between the two town centers and away from the tanneries, and Josie had a pleasant walk there each day if the weather wasn't bad. But she found her work as a cutter of watch hands both tedious and exacting. Josie hadn't thought it was possible to be bored and nervous at the same time, but that was how she felt at Winn's. She had to work fast, with the same careful movements over and over again. At the end of the day, her fingers were sore and her back and head ached from hunching over her table to see the work. For each day of the first week, she thought she couldn't do this work another day. But it was a good, clean job that paid well for a girl hand, and she had to stick it out, if only to prove to her father that she could do it. Eventually, she learned to do the work with her hands, very quickly and neatly, while her mind wandered wherever she wanted. She found that hours could pass in this way, and she managed to get through her days and collect her seven dollars a week.

Winn's became a lot more tolerable when Jimmy Boyle started to talk to her. She knew him slightly because he was on her brother Tom's roller polo team. He lived not far from the house on Arlington Street, and on a few mornings, he fell into step with her when she walked to work. With her pug nose and long chin, Josie was far from the beauty her sister was, and had never been singled out by a good looking and popular boy like Jimmy before. She felt at ease with his jokes and teasing, so much like Tom's, and they had a good time together. Jimmy took to waiting for her at the corner of Belmont and Garfield Streets, a couple of blocks from her house, and they walked together to the factory. He hung back a little when they got to the factory gate, but this didn't fool the Winn gossips a bit. Plenty of people saw them walking together to and from work, and they were quickly considered a couple. Not that Josie minded. She was happy to have her name linked with Jimmy's, and she enjoyed the attention of the teasing she got from the other girls.

Before long, Jimmy's attentions became more physical. He knew where the little hidden spaces on the walk to Winchester were, and he would often steal a kiss or put his arm around her waist, things Josie liked. But as the days grew shorter and it got dark on their way home, he got bolder, and she started to feel uncomfortable. She knew she wasn't acting according to the Sodality Rules of Comportment or the way her father would expect her to act. But she liked Jimmy a lot, and she didn't really see that what they did was so bad, if you cared for the person. And she did care for Jimmy. On the night of the Sodality's big fundraiser, the annual Autumn Dance, she was proud to have Jimmy escort her and Mary, and he acted like a perfect gentleman in the hall.

After an hour or so, he took her by the hand and said, "Come on, Josie. Let's go out for some air."

He led her around the back of the building, where there were no windows. When they were in the dark, he kissed her as he had never kissed her before, with his tongue in her mouth and his hand on her breast, and pressed her against the side of the building. She pulled away.

"Stop it, Jimmy," she said quietly. When he only grabbed her and pressed harder, she tried to break away, but he was stronger than she was.

Pinning her against the wall, he kept saying, "You owe me this, Josie. This is what it means to be my girl." Finally, when another couple came around the corner of the building, he moved away, and they went back in. He was a perfect gentleman for the rest of the night.

More than at any other time since Tom had left for the Navy, she missed him. He could tell her how to think about this and what to do. She knew what her parents and the Sodality would say. There was no sense talking to Mary. It would only shock her. She decided to tell Jimmy they had to draw the line at kissing.

On Monday, as they walked home in the dark, he put his arm around her as he often did once they got beyond the crowd from the factory, and she felt comfortable. But when they got to the grove of trees where he would kiss her, he pushed her up against a tree and started doing the same things he had done at the dance, only more roughly, and started pulling her skirt up. She told him to stop, but he wouldn't, and then she started to feel afraid of him. When she heard some people coming, she broke away from him and hurried back to the road, keeping close behind them. He didn't follow her, and he was not waiting for her the next morning. After work, she made sure to walk out with some of the girls, just saying hello to him and walking by when she saw him in the yard.

Josie was very downhearted and confused after that. She knew she had done what she had to do, but she still felt sad to lose Jimmy's company. When he wasn't pawing at her, he was fun to be with, and she had felt proud to walk into the dance on his arm. The girls teased her about her lost beau, and she wondered if she had made a mistake in giving him up. Maybe all men were like this. Maybe in the world outside the Young Ladies Sodality, that *was* what it meant to be somebody's girl. But it was also the reason so many girls got pregnant and had to get married. She didn't know if she wanted to marry Jimmy. She wrote to Tom about it, and when she at last received his reply, she felt good that she had done the right thing when she saw how angry he was at Jimmy. Meanwhile, she kept her distance from the boys at the factory.

Chapter 11

1901–1909

Shortly after her father died in June of 1901, Josie started working at the sewing she was trained for. She got a chance to do some piece work at home and found she enjoyed it much more than she had at school, particularly after two years at Winn's. She quit the factory and began to build a business in ladies' tailoring, which paid better than plain seamstress work. Her flair for trimming and her pleasant way with customers resulted in a number of referrals, and before long she was making almost as much as she had at Winn's, without the uncomfortable conditions.

In November, Tom, recently discharged from the Navy, married Mary Elizabeth Grace, a girl from the Azores he had met while stationed in Boston. Josie loved the girl Tom called "Mary E.," whom she thought a perfect match for him, with her spirit and her love of life, and she was delighted when she asked her to be a bridesmaid. Mary E. and Tom made Josie an extravagant bridesmaid's gift, a ring with three turquoise stones surrounded by seed-pearls, with her initials, "JVT" for Josie Veronica Terrett, and the date of the wedding, "Nov. 27 1901," engraved inside. Josie cherished the gift and wore it on her right hand for the rest of her life.

When Tom and Mary E. moved to California after their wedding, Josie was left with her sister Mary and Marm on Arlington Street. Mary, who had been taking the entrance examination for Salem Normal School on the day her father died, decided to do a short business course instead of training for teaching, and found work as secretary in a firm of Boston architects. The three of them had a pleasant life together, with Mary commuting to Boston, Josie working at home, and Maggie selling her milk and eggs and keeping house for them all.

At St. Charles's annual church social in 1906, Josie introduced Mary to a young man she had known since Winn's, Felix O'Connor. Felix was a jovial, red-faced man a few years older than Josie who had pursued her at Winn's without success, and whose interest revived immediately when he heard that she was still unmarried. He had brought along his friend George McGlynn, an outgoing, handsome man of thirty-five, and he made use of him to pry Mary from Josie's side so he could have some time alone with her.

To everyone's surprise, George, whom Felix thought of as a confirmed bachelor at thirty-five, was smitten with the twenty-three-year-old Mary. Josie and Felix's romance didn't last, but George courted Mary avidly. Maggie thought it was a good match for her daughter. George was an easy-going, steady man with a good job, a skilled machinist at the United Shoe Machinery Company, and he made extra money at night playing the cornet in a band.

After George and Mary were engaged, he was transferred to the United Shoe's new factory in Beverly. He moved into a rooming house while they made plans for their Beverly home after the wedding. It was decided that Maggie would rent out the Woburn house and move with Mary to Beverly. Josie had been tired of life in Woburn and Winchester for a long time and was determined to move to Boston, a step that Maggie tried to discourage.

"Where would you live, Josie, when you know no one? And what kind of work would you find? You couldn't just start up a tailoring business on your own in the city."

Josie had an answer when a friend of her cousin's told her that there would soon be an opening for a second maid at the house on Beacon Street where she worked. The pay wasn't much, but there was room and board and every other Sunday off, and with two maids they could spell each other in the evenings so that half of them would be free. Anyway it would be different from endless, boring factory work or sewing from morning to night.

Maggie was unconvinced. "But Josie, you've never done that kind of housework. It's drudgery, and the days are so long. And you don't know how to act in a big house. You have to kowtow to everyone in the family."

Josie laughed. "Well, Marm, I've done plenty of kowtowing to bosses and ladies I'm sewing for. I'm strong enough to do the work, and what better teacher could I have for how to be a housemaid than you with your ten years' experience? Anyway, the work isn't as hard now as it was thirty years ago. The big houses have electricity and oil stoves and central heating, and indoor bathrooms, which is more than we have here."

In the end, Maggie gave in and helped her. She decided that if Josie was determined to go to Boston, it would be better for her to live in the servants' quarters of a big house than on her own in the city. Mary and George were married at St. Charles's in November of 1906, and Maggie moved with them to Beverly. Josie went to work in the Back Bay.

Once she got used to the work, Josie didn't mind being a housemaid. She liked being busy and moving around much better than hunching over a factory bench or sitting still and sewing all day long. She was at the bottom of the ladder in the house, but she and Jane, the first girl, got to be good friends, and the cook was easy to get along with. Josie did plenty of kowtowing to the family, but that sort of thing wasn't much of a bother to her. She was usually able to show a cheerful face, even when the mistress was piling on the work or the master was ill-tempered. Miss Sarah, the fourteen-year-old daughter, was inconsiderate sometimes, dropping her clothing all over her room and raiding the kitchen and leaving a mess behind, but she was young, and for the most part Jane and Josie, who went by her birth name Bridget in the house because Maggie had told her it would be considered more suitable for a servant, got a kick out of her. On the whole, it was better than putting up with ill-tempered factory foremen and fending off the advances of the men.

One warm Sunday evening in June of 1908 when the family was out, Josie went with Jane to walk through the Public Garden and the Common. They were attracted by the sound of singing on the Southeast side of the Common and went to see if there was a free concert. It turned out to be a choir, all young men and women, who were singing on the steps of the Methodist Episcopal church at the corner of Tremont and Concord Streets. The churchyard and the sidewalk in front of it were crowded with people who had stopped to listen. Josie and Jane joined them.

The music was much different than the Gregorian chant Josie was used to in church. It was rousing, loud, full of life. The people in the crowd were urged to join in. They stayed to listen to the pastor, who read the twenty-third Psalm and proceeded to talk about it, not admonishing the crowd, but explaining the passages of the psalm and how it meant that they could find the comfort of God in their lives. Josie had never heard a sermon like it. At the end, he explained that this was a meeting of the Epworth League, an organization for young people sponsored by the church, and invited all the people in the crowd who were between eighteen and thirty-five to come to a meeting the next week.

Jane, a Protestant, knew all about the Epworth League, but it was new to Josie, so different from the prim Young Ladies Sodality of her youth. Jane was too old for the League now, but she told Josie about some of the pleasant excursions she'd been on as a girl back home in Providence. On the next Sunday, Josie's day off, she decided to go to the meeting. She had nothing to lose, and it was a chance a housemaid didn't often get to meet some nice young men. She found the people warm and welcoming and fun, and kept going to the meetings.

When she went to a morning church service with some of the girls, she found that the congregational singing and the Reverend Henry Wriston's sermons made her feel much closer to God than the distant ritual of the Latin Mass ever had. In July, she decided to join the church, and was received by the Rev. Wriston on probation. It was a decision she kept from her family, knowing that Marm and Mary would be horrified at her abandoning her faith to become a Protestant, but she felt that she belonged in her new church more than she ever had at St. Charles's or a Boston Catholic church. It seemed to be the right thing for her to do.

Chapter 12

1909–1910

In the Spring of 1909, the household where Josie worked was upset a bit when the master bought an automobile and hired a chauffeur, Terry Burns. Terry was a brash young man in his early thirties, a sandy-haired, blue-eyed Scotch-Irish Protestant who came from County Armagh. In some ways it was good for the other servants because Terry helped with some of the heavy work, but he could be fresh sometimes and free with his hands around the women servants. Jane thought he was funny, but Josie, who had seen his type at Winn's, was careful how she acted around him and mostly stayed out of his way.

One Thursday afternoon in April, Josie was coming down the walk from the back entrance to the house on her way to the moving pictures when she ran smack into Terry on the sidewalk. He laughed off her apologies and asked where she was going.

"How would you like to go to a real show, Bridget? You look so nice in that pretty new suit, you don't want to go to the movies tonight."

"With you, Mr. Burns?"

"Sure. And you can drop the Mr. Burns. We'll just be good friends tonight. Keith's has a new vaudeville show."

Josie hesitated. It had been a long time since she'd had a real night out. There were not many chances for a twenty-eight-year-old housemaid to meet suitable men to socialize with in the Back Bay. This young man was a member of the household, offering to take her on an outing. Why not?

"That's very nice of you, Mr. Burns," she said.

He laughed, and they headed down Beacon Street toward Keith's, on Tremont and Washington. Josie thought the vaudeville show was wonderful. There was a hilarious play about an acting school, and a comedian and an impersonator and blackface singers and Russian dancers and Japanese acrobats and trained animals. There was also a lovely piece in which someone read verses that were illustrated with actors posing in living pictures. She remembered some of the poems fondly from her father's reading to them at night, and nearly cried at "Maude Muller." After it was over, Terry took her to a little restaurant and insisted on ordering beer with their supper. He made her feel at ease and entertained her with stories about his adventures on the road with the automobile. She had a marvelous evening.

As a final luxury, they took a cab back to the house. Terry told the cabbie to drive around the Common and then down Charles and around the Public Garden before he turned on Beacon. It was during the slow cab ride that his fresh side came out. He kept crowding close to her and putting his hands where they shouldn't be while he kissed her. She kept him away as well as she could, but she didn't want to seem rude. A kiss was not something to upset a modern girl of her age. Then before she knew it, he had pulled her skirt up and was on top of her, forcing her legs open. She struggled, but he was too strong for her, and he knew what he was doing. In a minute he had her corset and her drawers open. It hurt, but it didn't take long.

After it was over and they had straightened themselves up, he looked at her. "Gee, I'm sorry Bridget. I thought you would have been around the block a few times."

She looked down and didn't answer. When the cab stopped at the house, she got out and went around to the back door without a look back. The next morning, she said good morning to Terry as always, but she did not lift her eyes to his. She kept out of his way as much as she could and gave her two-week notice, telling Jane she would miss her, but she had had enough of service.

Josie found a room at 45 Worcester Street, in the South End. After persistently making the rounds of dressmakers and milliners for weeks, she started to pick up piece work and finally began to make enough to cover the rent and food. She had savings that would last a couple of months until she found a job, not as a housemaid. In May, she began to suspect there was something wrong. She denied it as long as she could, but by July, she was sure. In August, when the bulge was unmistakable, she went to see Dr. Hayes on Columbus Avenue.

He gave her a quick look when he was examining her, and said, "You haven't had relations many times, have you, Miss Terrett?"

"Just once," she said.

"I see. Was it voluntary?"

"No."

"Do you have a family, or anywhere to go?"

"No. My stepmother lives with my half sister, and she has her own family. I couldn't tell her about this. I don't really know what to do."

"Well, maybe I can help."

When she came out of Dr. Hayes's office, instead of walking the few blocks down Worcester Street to her room, Josie turned right toward Mass Avenue and walked up to catch the Huntington Avenue trolley that took her out to Jamaica

Plain. At the 800 block, she got out and stood across the street from the massive brick facade of the House of the Good Shepherd, surrounded by its seven-foot red brick wall and iron gates. This was where Dr. Hayes had offered to place her.

Like any single woman who had worked in Boston for a few years, Josie knew plenty of stories about the House of the Good Shepherd. It was supposedly a "home for the correction of wayward girls," and it did take in poor girls and women who got pregnant as well as people who would otherwise be on the streets because they couldn't support themselves, but it was also one of the places where girls and women were sent on probation by the courts when they were caught stealing or selling themselves. Stories of escapes and near-escapes appeared in the papers from time to time. Given the choice between this place and jail by a judge, many a girl chose jail. The place certainly looked grim, but what choice did she have? She would be showing soon. She was too old for the smaller, more homey North End Mission on the block next to her lodging house. She had to go somewhere. Dr. Hayes was really very kind to help her.

In early September, Josie gave notice at the lodging house and wrote a letter to Marm and Mary, saying that she wouldn't be able to visit with the family in Beverly for a few months because she was going south to Florida for the fall and winter with the family she was working for. Two weeks later, she packed all her belongings in a bag and a box and took the trolley to the House of the Good Shepherd.

A girl of fifteen or so answered her ring and took her to Sister Mary of St. Genevieve, who would see to admitting her. Sister Mary was brusque but seemed kind enough, offering her a chair while she filled out the paper work. Josie's role in the interview was familiar territory to someone who had spent her girlhood in parochial school.

"You are Veronica Josephine Terrett?"

"Yes, Sister." No need to tell her that her name was really Bridget Veronica.

"Your age?"

"Twenty-eight."

"Dr. Hayes writes that you are expecting a child in January and you have no husband."

Josie dropped her eyes. "Yes, Sister."

"Is the baby's father going to give any support for it or you?"

"No, Sister."

"I see. We have many women and girls like you here, Veronica."

She went on as if reciting her catechism. "We are proud of our record of reclaiming the fallen and uplifting and encouraging the weak. Many have left our charge after a period of months or years strengthened and uplifted, and are leading good moral lives. Others have chosen to remain here and dedicate their lives to atonement for their past sins. They are called the Magdalenes, and they follow the third order of St. Theresa under the direction of Sister Amanda. Some have even gone on to join our order, the Sisters of the Good Shepherd, to help carry on our work. These may be examples for you to follow as you begin your life here, Veronica."

Josie hoped she didn't look as alarmed as she felt.

"The more than four hundred women and children who find shelter here are separated into three classes. The Penitents are women who have already fallen to temptation. The Preservation class includes young girls who have begun to show a lack of self-control and are in danger of falling. The class of Homeless Children includes those poor innocents who may be exposed to perverse influences on account of neglect or abandonment. The classes are kept separate, and each is subjected to a discipline that combines moral, intellectual and industrial elements. You will be assigned to the Penitent class."

"Yes, Sister."

"Everyone who is able works here, and we will expect you to work up to the time of your confinement, and then six months afterwards to help repay your expenses. We maintain a commercial laundry and a sewing room where we make a variety of garments for women and children. Do you have any skills at sewing?"

Anything but the laundry. Josie dreaded spending the remaining months of her pregnancy on her feet, bending over a washtub scrubbing clothes. She tried to switch from her docile, penitent demeanor to an air of confidence. "Yes, Sister. I've been sewing for a long time. At twenty-one, I was working independently as a tailoress out of my family home in Woburn, and I've worked for several shops since I came to the city."

"That's good, Veronica. We need skilled hands in the sewing room. You have Catholic training? "

"Yes, Sister. I went to Catholic school and my parents always saw to it that we went to Mass on Sunday. My father led us in the rosary every day."

"It's unfortunate that you didn't profit better from your training. Does your father know of your condition?"

"My mother and father and only brother are all dead." She would not mention her step-family.

"Well, since you are Catholic, you will understand that our home is cloistered. Only a few Sisters like myself communicate with the outside world. The women and children under our care share the same retirement from the world as the Sisters. We believe that they profit greatly from the isolation from evil influences."

"Yes, Sister."

"Now Mabel here will take you to the Penitents' dormitory and answer any questions you have about day-to-day life. We are all on a strict schedule that emphasizes a balance among prayer, work, education, and recreation."

Josie followed Mabel to the stairs. "The Penitent sleeping room is on the fourth floor," she said. "So is the Preservation. The laundry and the kitchen and dining room are in the basement. Here is the chapel. The second floor has the children and the school rooms and the packing and shipping room, and the third floor has the sewing room."

"What's the schedule like?"

"We pretty much live like nuns here. Up at 5:00, wash, dress, pray. Then breakfast, work, lunch, more work, an hour for recreation, supper, prayer, bed. And then it starts all over again. We aren't allowed to talk, except during recreation. During meals, somebody reads a religious book. There's always a Sister wherever you are. Sunday we don't have to work, but we spend a lot of time in the chapel."

"Do we get outside at all?"

"Sometimes they take us out in a line two-by-two for a walk around the grounds during recreation. The children get to go out just about every day."

"How is the food?"

"I've had worse. It pretty much depends on how the laundry and the sewing factory are doing. We all live off them. Slow times, it's pretty much bread and potatoes and mush, along with whatever's going from the garden. We get eggs a lot, and they make sure the pregnant girls have milk. On Sundays we usually get a real dinner with meat."

"How long have you been here?

"Two years. I'm a Preservate. My father died, and my mother couldn't really take care of my sister and me. We were Orphans at first, but now we're Preservates, and we work. My sister runs a sewing machine and I'm learning office work. I'm hoping to be able to get out and get a good job when I'm sixteen, but usually they keep you until you're eighteen."

Mabel took Josie to the laundry, where she was given a shapeless blue dress, some underwear, and a nightgown.

"Plenty of room to grow," said Mabel, holding out the dress. Josie had to turn her clothes and most of her possessions in to Sister Mary Brennan, who was in charge of the dormitory. They would be kept for her until she was released in June.

841 Huntington Ave.
Boston, Mass.
September 19, 1909

Dear Mary Elizabeth,

I hope you and the boys are all well and happy. You've probably noticed that I've changed addresses, so I should explain right away that I'm in a bad spot. The chauffeur at the house where I was working took shameless advantage of me, and so I left. It only happened once, but all the same I find myself in trouble. My kind doctor helped me to get placed in The House of the Good Shepherd. I don't know if you have one in California, but they're in many cities in the country. The Sisters here take in women and girls who are in trouble or are placed here for other reasons. My baby is coming in

January, so I will be here until then and deliver at the Boston Lying-In. After the baby comes, I will be staying another six months so that I can work long enough to repay the Sisters for my expenses.

I hope you don't mind me writing to you about this. I miss Tom so much. I trusted him with everything, and I know he would have given me good advice. But I trust you in the same way, and being all on your own at the rooming house with the boys to bring up, I know you'll understand better than anyone what I'm going through.

The life here is very regulated. I'm lucky to be employed at my profession, as a trimmer and finisher of ladies suits. There are eight of us, and we sit at the back of an enormous sewing room, with about 140 machines. It's a big place, and there are women of all ages. We have girls as young as thirteen in the sewing room and I met a woman in her sixties who works in the laundry.

I'm able to write to you because the Sisters give us an hour on Sundays to write home, and I thought I could confide in you rather than Marm or Mary. They would just be upset to hear about this. I know I can trust you not to mention it to them.

They've just given the signal for five minutes, so I will close. Please write and tell me how you and the boys are getting along.

Affectionately,
Josie

841 Huntington Ave.
Boston, Mass.
October 3, 1909

Dear Mary E.,

It was so good to get your letter, and to hear that everyone is well. I admire you so much for taking hold the way you have with the rooming house and taking care of the boys so well. I sometimes think I can't even take care of myself. I knew you would understand how a thing like this can happen. I searched my conscience, and I can honestly say that there is nothing I did to lead him on or suggest it was all right. But that's water under the bridge now.

I'm settling in here, and getting used to the routine. It's quite a bit like working at the factory in Winchester, though there is more praying than even Pa made us do at home! We get up at 5:00 and are in bed by 9:00. Probably good hours for the baby. I sleep in a huge open room with the other women. Many of us are expecting babies, and the women who have had children are a help. I've made friends with the other trimmers and finishers, especially two married women, Helena Sculling and Emma Smith, who are about my age. We sit together in the sewing room. We aren't allowed to talk while we're working, but it wouldn't be possible anyway with the noise from more than a hundred sewing machines around us. We get an hour a day for recreation, though, and we sit and talk, and they give me advice about the baby. Emma has five children who are downstairs in the orphanage. She only gets to see them for a few minutes once a day, and misses them all the time. Helena and Emma are helping me to make a layette out of remnants from the sewing room.

I think I'm getting better at my work all the time. We have to work fast, as the sewing room is on a quota and this is the busiest season. Everything here has to turn a profit in order to support everyone. The other women have shown me some tricks to make the finishing go faster, and it still looks good. To answer your questions, the food is fine. It's very plain, but filling. I wouldn't want anything fancier in my state. I've been very lucky not to have any morning sickness with the baby. I do feel tired a lot of the time, but at least I get to sit down while I'm working. I hope I'll be able to keep the baby. Most of them are put up for adoption, but if you have a skill and are able to make enough money when you come out, you can come back and claim the baby. I'm hoping it's a girl because the boys get adopted much faster than the girls. I'm working hard to improve my skills and speed. Sister Anastasia, who's in charge of the sewing room, can put in a good word that will help get a job if she thinks you're a good worker.

Well, time to stop. Thanks again for writing, Mary. It means so much to hear from you. A kiss for the boys.

Affectionately,
Josie

*****

New York Times, February 23, 1909, page 14.

GREENWICH ADOPTS WAIFS
Five Families There Take Children from Boston House of Good Shepherd

GREENWICH, Conn., Feb. 22—Greenwich residents have now no further objections to rural lack of facilities, for added to electric lights, a first class post-office, and daily deliveries from the big New York department stores, there has appeared as a crowning convenience the system by which children can be supplied on a few hours' notice at any age or nationality wished. To interested persons they will be brought out on inspection.

Five Greenwich families were thus supplied Sunday, and it is said that several wealthy families are waiting for more. The agency which supplies the little ones is St. Mary's Roman Catholic Church, the wealthiest church in the diocese of Connecticut. The Rev. J. J. Fitzgerald, a week ago last Sunday, announced from the altar that a number of children would be brought here from the House of the Good Shepherd in Boston, and asked all those of his parishioners who wished to adopt children to select some of those. A number of the members of the church, who were either childless or whose children are grown up and have gone from home, signified their willingness to take children.

On Sunday Daniel Pine, agent for the House of the Good Shepherd, came with seven bright looking boys, and those who wanted the children appeared at the parochial residence and made their selection. Some who desire children older or younger were told they could have them to suit.

In each case, Father Fitzgerald supplied the House of the Good Shepherd with a guarantee that the children would be well cared for and educated. If, after two years, all is well and the families who have taken the children wish to, they may, according to the laws of Massachusetts and Connecticut, adopt them, provided that the pastor of the church still thinks that they are proper persons to have the children. Among the families here who took children brought by Mr. Pine are those of John Diffley, Fletcher Lewis, Mr. Florentine, and Henry Hines.

*****

841 Huntington Ave.
Boston, Mass.
October 31, 1909

Dear Mary E.,

Thank you so much for sending Harry's baby clothes! Now I can stop worrying about putting together enough nice, comfy clothes so the baby doesn't have to wear the ones they have downstairs, which are very plain and kind of rough for a baby. You made such beautiful things. My baby will be the best dressed one here. It's especially good to get the clothes for when it's a little older. Emma keeps reminding me that there isn't much point in having a lot of clothes for when they're tiny because they grow so fast.

I'm hoping to get a good job when I get out of here in June and save enough so that I can bring the baby home a few months later and pay someone to look after it while I'm at work. One of the women who was here a year and then got out and got a job was just able to get her daughter out of the orphanage.

Things are picking up very fast in the sewing room, as all the stores are getting ready for the Christmas rush. I didn't know I could sew this fast! All of us are just dead at the end of the day, but it does make the time pass quicker. As the Sisters keep reminding us. I have to admit my tailoring skills are much improved. And now that there is more money coming in, the food has improved too. We have meat almost every day now. The women who have been here a while say the fall is always the best for food, because both the sewing room and the laundry are very busy. The worst is after the first of the year, when the work orders fall off and there's nothing coming in from the garden.

I hope you are having a good fall, and you were able to rent that empty room. It's good that you're so convenient to the Navy Yard. Do you have the fall colors out there, or do you miss Mass. at this time of year? I have to say it has cheered me up to look out the window on the fourth floor and see the maple trees all red and gold in the side yard here. The leaves are almost gone now, but I try to think of it as one season closer to the baby coming.

Thanks again for the lovely clothes.

Affectionately,

Josie

841 Huntington Ave.
Boston, Mass.
November 25, 1909

Dear Mary E.,

Happy Thanksgiving! I'm sure you were run off your feet getting the dinner for nine people, but it's so nice of you to invite your lodgers. I know how it feels to be on your own and away from home on Thanksgiving, and I know they will appreciate it. We had quite a time here. There was no work for the sewing room or laundry, although I'm sure the people who work in the kitchen and dining room had to work extra hard. They put out a beautiful turkey dinner with all the trimmings, and most everyone rose to the occasion to celebrate the holiday.

Now there's a group of bigwigs from the city being shown around. We had to be extra careful in cleaning up the sewing room yesterday and making up our cots this morning because they're going to look everywhere, apparently. They fed them dinner separately, and they just left the recreation room here, where we've been given silent recreation, which is reading and letter writing. They kind of walked around and looked at us like we were livestock at the county fair. It's the first time I've really felt embarrassed about my condition. The Sisters just take for granted that you're a sinner and they're helping you to repent. Everybody else is in the same boat, pretty much, so we don't think too much about it most of the time.

I'm looking forward to actually taking a nap after this. I'm getting pretty big, and I haven't been sleeping well, which I'm sure sounds familiar to you. This baby is a kicker, and it's hard to get comfortable on my cot.

I'm thinking of you all, and hoping you had a lovely day.

Affectionately,
Josie

841 Huntington Ave.
Boston, Mass.
December 26, 1909

Dear Mary E.,

Thank you so much for the beautiful Christmas presents! I don't know where you found the time to do all the embroidery on that Baptismal gown. It is just gorgeous, and I will treasure it forever. This dress will be my reminder of all your kindness to me and the baby, the way my ring is a reminder of my love for you and Tom. And the beautiful handkerchiefs will remind me that I will be getting out of this place in a few months, and I can live a normal life and have pretty things.

My time is very close now. I am huge, and tired all the time, but I'm excited to see the baby. All the attention to the baby Jesus at Christmas has made me sentimental, I think. I have dedicated my baby to the Blessed Virgin. I will try to be as good a mother as I can.

I hope you got my Christmas greetings and my love.

Affectionately,

Josie

When her labor started on January fifth, Josie, like the other inmates of the House of the Good Shepherd, was taken to the Boston Lying-In Hospital, a charity institution that had been established in the 1850s for the "care and relief of poor and deserving women." The birth was complicated, and the baby, a girl, died of asphyxiation. She was taken away by the undertaker J. Waterman and buried in an unmarked grave in the Paupers' Cemetery in Tewksbury, Massachusetts. After recovering in the hospital from the difficult birth, Josie was sent back to the House of the Good Shepherd and went back to work in the sewing room.

841 Huntington Ave.
Boston, Mass.
February 6, 1910

Dear Mary E.,

Thank you so much for your letters. I'm sorry I haven't written before this, but I've just been too downhearted. My baby, a little girl, died just a few minutes after she was born. It was a very long and hard labor, hours and hours, and the doctor said she just didn't get enough air at the end. I'm so very sad about her.

I'm sorry to say that the Sisters took the baby clothes for the orphanage without asking me. Sister Mary said that they didn't want them around to remind me. I asked one of the girls who works in the orphanage to see if she could get the Baptismal gown back, but she said it was already gone. They dressed Nora Cummings' baby in it when he was adopted. I pray that he's gone to a loving home, and the gown will bring him happiness.

I am back at work in the sewing room now, and just trying to get through the months until I am released and can get back to a normal life. Some of the women tell me that there was only a slim chance I would get to keep my baby anyway, so maybe it's better this way, but I'd much rather have her alive, even if she was adopted. I'm grateful to have Emma, who understands how heartbroken I feel. I know that you will too, having lost little Veronica Grace. I will never forget my baby or stop mourning for her. I'm so sorry to only be sharing my sorrow with you, Mary, when you've been so kind to me.

My love to you and the boys,
Josie

When the federal census was taken in April, 1910, the census taker was not allowed into the House of the Good Shepherd. Instead, Sister Mary of St. Genevieve went through the building and took the census information from everyone who lived there, beginning with the Sisters. Although there are birth and death certificates recorded for Josie's daughter, under the number of children born to Veronica J. Terrett, the census records nothing.

Chapter 13

1910-1917

Josie eventually paid her debt to the House of the Good Shepherd with her free skilled labor, and was released. With what was left of her savings, she found a hall bedroom in a lodging house for three dollars a week, and began the search for piece work. Even skilled tailors like her had trouble finding work in the summer months. Most women who did piece work could make eight to fourteen dollars a week while they worked overtime during the busy season in the fall, but had to plan and save for the dull time, about six months out of the year when work was scarce. In June, she was right in the middle of the dull time. But with her old contacts, she managed to pick up enough work to keep body and soul together.

Josie scanned the papers for work constantly, and was excited when she saw that Filene's was hiring for the fall, and there were openings in the alterations department. Filene's was one of the biggest stores in Boston, and was known as one of the best places for girls to work. It was also a place where Sister Anastasia's recommendation would mean something, as Filene's was open to hiring women from the House of the Good Shepherd.

Josie got up early on the designated day for interviews for the alterations department, and, dressed carefully in her navy blue ankle-length skirt and a plain white, business-like shirtwaist with a blue ribbon at the high neck, her freshly washed hair in a neat pompadour, she arrived at the employees' entrance of Filene's before 7:00 a.m. The employment office didn't open until 8:00, but there were already quite a few women in line. Some of them looked her up and down, but most ignored the new additions to the line, happy with their superior positions. Josie looked carefully at each woman and girl as she came out of the office, judging whether she'd been hired or not. She decided that only a couple had. When she got to the door, she put on her most confident air and smiled at the rather harassed-looking man who sat at a desk behind the name plate "Mr. Gilman," scribbling on some form.

"Good morning," she said.

He looked up. "Morning," he said shortly. "What's your name?"

"Veronica Terrett."

"Applying for?"

"Work in the alterations department."

"Experience?"

"I've been doing professional tailoring since I was twenty-one. I operated a business out of my home for several years, and I've done piece work for several different companies in Boston. I've worked on clothing that's being sold in Shepard Norwell and Conrad's."

Mr. Gilman perked up a little at the mention of these high-end rivals, and looked her over.

"What did you work on for them?"

"Mostly spring suits, lately." Josie smiled. "I've done a lot of silk collars and braid trim this year."

Gilman smiled a little himself. "Let's hope that's over. References?"

This was the moment. She placed her letter from Sister Anastasia on the desk. He looked up, a little surprised, but said, “This reference is OK by me. Sister Anastasia has never steered me wrong yet. But you’ll have to be very careful to follow the store’s code of conduct. No fraternizing.”

“Yes, sir.”

“No one in the department will know that you came from the House of the Good Shepherd. So this is your chance to make a fresh start. Get me?”

Josie’s cheeks burned, and she was dying to explain her story to him, but she knew it was pointless. “Yes. Thank you, sir. I appreciate it.”

“The salary is eight dollars a week while you’re on probation. After ninety days, it goes up to ten dollars.”

“That’s fine.” Josie had never made ten dollars a week in her life.

“OK.” He handed her a card with the salary filled in. “Fill out your information on this card and bring it to Miss Secker, next door. She’ll give you your locker key and so on.”

“Thank you very much, Mr. Gilman.”

“OK. We’re taking a chance on you. Make sure you live up to it.”

Josie did her best to live up to it. Working in alterations, she was not expected to look fashionable for customers. But she paid attention to her dress and her appearance, worked hard, and watched her opportunity, and when she saw a position in the millinery department advertized within the store, she applied immediately. She was able to demonstrate both her skill at trimming and her winning way with customers during her trial period, and the promotion was hers.

When she came to Filene's in 1910, Josie became Vera J. Terrett, and dropped six years from her age, youth being an advantage to a sales girl. At thirty, it wasn't hard for her to pass for twenty-four. She had a slim figure when she got out of the House of the Good Shepherd, and her face, with its big round eyes and pug nose, had always looked younger than her years.

Josie settled into a quiet life as one of Boston's thousands of single working girls. For fear they might learn her story, she was careful not to get too close to anyone at work, and she kept her distance from her landladies and the other people in her lodgings, moving every six months or so, always to another room in the Back Bay. It was lonely, working for ten hours a day and then returning to her room at night and barely speaking to anyone, but she was determined not to raise any suspicion about her morals, either at the store or in her landladies. She never entertained visitors in her room, and when she did go out to the movies or on a rare excursion with other women from the store, she always came back early. She made sure the landlady knew that she was visiting her family in Beverly when she left on Saturday and came back on Sunday.

On the whole, she loved her job in the millinery department. The hours were long, and it meant standing on her feet all day, but the work was easier than she was used to. With her naturally cheerful disposition and instinct for avoiding conflict, she got along well with customers and the other women in the department. There were no men around except for the floorwalkers who supervised the sales force, and she kept her distance from them. She liked working with the hats, helping a customer to find the perfect one to set off her good points, or suggesting ideas for new trimmings if a new hat was out of the question. For most women, buying a hat was a major decision. For a working girl, it represented a week's pay or more. Josie respected that. She had the same decisions to make herself.

The difference between working in the clothing store and working as a piece worker or maid was that she was expected to look good and dress stylishly, not easy when you made ten dollars a week, the price of a new dress, and had to pay about the same for a stylish hat. She followed the lead of the other sales girls and kept an eagle eye on the basement, with its famous markdowns, bought a few good pieces with her 15% employee's discount, and washed them often.

As "Vera," Josie was more reserved than she had ever been, wary that any hint of her past might get into the store's active gossip factory. But it was impossible to ignore little Esther Berger, who shared Josie's inclination to see the humor in everything, and constantly entertained her with a running commentary on unreasonable customers and pompous floorwalkers. Esther delivered her remarks deadpan and under her breath as she stood at the counter or arranged the merchandise, but it was hard for Josie not to burst out laughing some of the time. She often covered a giggle with a fake sneeze or cough. When they had a break at the same time, they usually went to the cafeteria together and laughed through their lunch, but they didn't quite become friends. Esther was fifteen or so years younger than Josie, and much as she enjoyed her company, she couldn't confide in her.

Though she didn't have any close friends at Filene's Josie enjoyed a level of sociability she had never before had on the job. Being downtown at the center of the shopping district was fun, and she sometimes went to the movies or to hear a band play on the Common with a group of women from the store. And Edward and Lincoln Filene, well-known progressive figures in Boston's business and political scene, provided unusual benefits for the employees, like health insurance at five cents a week and a health clinic right in the store. The employees ran their own restaurant, library, insurance fund, and credit union. They had their own baseball and bowling teams, and even an orchestra. The employees' association held dances, organized outings, and put on elaborate annual shows, full-scale revues or minstrel shows, sometimes presented at the Boston Opera House.

On many weekends, especially in the summer when the store was closed on Saturdays, Josie took the train from the North Station out to the Beverly Depot and walked to the house on Summer Street where Marm lived with Mary and her growing family. She loved her nieces and nephews. Edna, who had been born in 1908, was quickly followed by George, Andrew, Everett, and Doris. Josie was always on the lookout for little presents to bring them, some penny candy or little toys, or a bit of ribbon from the store for Edna and baby Doris.

In warm weather, Josie met Mary's family downtown when she got off the train, and they all watched George play the cornet in the United Shoe band. Whatever the weather, Sundays were for church and relaxation. In 1914, George bought a secondhand Ford touring car, which was his prized possession and demanded all his skills as a machinist to keep on the road. On Sunday afternoons, if the weather was passable, he took the whole family to the beach or for an outing he had thought up during the week, like picking blueberries in North Beverly. In the evening, Josie took the train back to Boston to be ready to get up at 6:00 the next morning and start another week.

It was during intermission at the Filene's "Jollies of 1916" that Esther introduced Josie to Leonard Brown, the assistant manager of the shoe department where she used to work. He was about Josie's real age, thirty-six. He was nice looking, not that you would pick him out of a crowd, but he had a warm smile and lively brown eyes. He was a couple of inches taller than she, and was of course dressed well, in a slim three-button suit with a nipped-in waist and the latest style of pointed low-cut shoes. As an assistant department manager, he had to pay attention to his clothes. Josie enjoyed talking to him, and he really seemed to be interested in what she had to say. It had been years since Josie had felt the full attention of a man. After the show, Mr. Brown insisted on walking her to the streetcar. They had a long conversation, stopping along the way several times, and found they had a lot in common. He was interested in her views about the store and the Filene brothers' way of doing business. He waited at the stop with her, and helped her up the streetcar step.

When she turned, he gave her a smile and a wave, saying, "Good night, Miss Terrett. I hope we'll meet again."

On Monday morning, Josie took extra time doing up her hair, coaxing fashionable spit curls at the sides, and she wore her nice silk shirtwaist with the v-neck. She took the elevator to the fifth floor and walked through the shoe department to the stairs rather than going directly to ladies' hats on the sixth floor. She didn't see Mr. Brown that morning or the next, but on Wednesday, he was fussing with a display near the elevator, with his eye on the people coming off.

"Good morning, Miss Terrett," he said.

"Good morning, Mr. Brown."

"Are you looking for shoes?"

She smiled up at him. "Just browsing today. I'm trying to find just the right pair."

"Well, I would be happy to assist you." They walked past the elegant display of Nettleton shoes, the most expensive in the store. "If they made pumps for women," he said, "these would suit you perfectly"

She laughed. "And they would cost a month's rent."

When they had made their way to the stairs at the back of the shoe department, Josie said, "I have to get upstairs now, but I'll be back again."

"You're always welcome here," he said.

Leonard Brown watched for her every morning after that. He always greeted her, and most days they had a little conversation before she went upstairs to work. One evening as she walked along the Common toward Columbus Avenue, he caught up with her, and they walked together until she turned left on Columbus and he went off to catch the trolley. They started walking these blocks together every night, chatting about the events at the store and the people they knew in common.

Then one rainy July night Leonard asked Josie to stop into a tea room and have some supper with him. They had a long talk, and she realized that she had a different feeling about him than she had had about any other man. Beneath his glossy exterior, she felt, Leonard Brown was a good person, a serious person, and he thought a lot of her. He really paid attention to what she said.

"I enjoy your company, Miss Terrett," he said. "You . . . you lift my spirits."

Josie laughed. "I enjoy your company too, Mr. Brown, but you can call me Vera when we're away from the store."

He looked uncomfortable. "I enjoy your company," he repeated, "but I should tell you that I can't . . . *keep* company with you. I'm engaged to a girl back in Boxboro—Rosemary.

She's a very sweet girl, just twenty-one years old. Our families have been friends for years. I should have mentioned it earlier, but I've tried to keep it a secret. You know what gossips there are at the store."

Josie knew. She did her best to smile. "That's wonderful, Mr. Brown. She's a lucky girl."

"I hope I haven't given you the wrong idea by spending so much time together, but I do like talking to you."

Josie managed to smile directly at him. "There's no reason we can't be friends. Have you set the date for the wedding?"

"We can't afford it yet. I'm trying to save, but with rent and clothes and everything else in the city, it's hard. I've put a little by, though, and I'm hoping to get the promotion to head of the shoe department when Matthews moves on. He's dead ambitious, and the word is that Mr. Kirstein has his eye on him for one of the buyers. On the department manager's salary, we could afford to live somewhere in the South End."

Josie went vague. She would make no allusion to her life at 45 Worcester Street. "I suppose so. I've always lived in the Back Bay, but I've heard that rents are cheaper in the South End."

"Anyway, I'm on my own for now, and it's nice to have a friend who's a good listener to talk to. I know you won't give anything away at the store the way the fellows would."

"Of course not. Now we'd better be going while there's this break in the rain."

Josie was crushed, but not really surprised that a nice looking, steady man of Leonard Brown's age was already taken. Still she didn't see any reason why she shouldn't spend time with him, and she continued to walk with him in the evenings. Occasionally, they would stop into the tea room for a longer conversation, and Josie would console him about his long wait for Rosemary and his problems in the shoe department.

One Tuesday evening in August, when Leonard was in particularly low spirits, he asked Josie to have supper with him and cheer him up. He took her to a rathskeller, something she had never seen before. They went down the steps from the street level into a dimly lit sort of tunnel leading to a cool cellar room that smelled strongly of beer, sauerkraut, and sausage. As Leonard had promised, the food was good and abundant. He had beer with his meal, and his mood lightened as they ate and talked. He even laughed when she repeated some of Esther's comments about floorwalkers that he knew.

"That Esther is a card," he said. As they made their way back through the tunnel, he took her arm, and then quickly kissed her on the lips. When she looked up at him, wide-eyed with surprise, he put his arms around her and kissed her again, a kiss that became long and passionate, a kiss unlike any she had ever experienced. And without any thought whatever, she responded, her feeling for Leonard at last finding its outlet. When they separated, he looked down at the ground, and said, "Forgive me, Vera, I got carried away."

"There is nothing to apologize for, Leonard," she said. "I feel the same way you do."

He became more uneasy. "But Vera, you know there is nowhere this can lead."

As she looked him in the eye, her calmness surprised her.

"Leonard, I'm over thirty years old, a sales girl living on my own. It's not very likely that I'm going to find a beau who wants to court me. But I'm very—fond of you, as I can tell you are of me. I don't see anything wrong with our taking a bit of happiness that has come our way. It won't affect your promise to Rosemary."

He gave her his arm, and they walked over to Columbus and parted as usual. They began to make a habit of stopping for tea or supper on Tuesdays and Wednesdays. Leonard found more out-of-the-way places where no one from the store ever came, and they discovered some isolated park benches that no one could see after dark. Soon the meals became just a preamble to be gotten through as quickly as possible so they could be together in the dark. And then the night came when both acknowledged that they had fallen in love.

"I want to be yours completely," said Josie. "Whatever else happens in my life, I want to have that."

"I want it too," said Leonard. "I can't tell you how much."

"Well, then," she said. "This one time in my life I'm going to have my heart's desire."

They planned it for the last Saturday in September, when they would have all afternoon and all night together. This was one weekend when Leonard didn't go to Boxboro, and Josie didn't go to Beverly. Leonard found a small hotel in the South End where they registered as Mr. and Mrs. Nettleton, Leonard's little joke, and they spent one day and night as if they were on their honeymoon.

Although they were in their thirties, both were inexperienced at love-making, but they made up for what they lacked in technique with desire and delight in each other. They explored together for hours through the afternoon, went down to the dining room for dinner, and then dove back into the bed for the night, laughing. When they left the hotel on Sunday,

Josie found that she knew what it meant to be head over heels, though she tried not to show Leonard how wildly in love she was. After that, they repeated their hotel stay twice a month, and those two days were Josie's life.

They were very careful, both about observing the proprieties at work and about taking precautions against a pregnancy. People in the store saw them walking or talking together, and she knew there was a certain amount of gossip, but there was no law against two store employees being friends. Josie kept the same early hours at her lodging house that she had always kept, and Leonard never visited her there. But they often managed a few stolen minutes and hours together that were all the sweeter for being their secret, shared with no one else.

In November, Josie began to suspect, but she put it out of her mind. And then in December, she was sure. Despite all their precautions, the pregnancy had come. She worried over what she could do. She had to keep it from her family. After her first experience, she didn't see how she could go through another pregnancy and birth. One thing was certain. She was not going back to The House of the Good Shepherd. No matter what.

Josie went to Beverly as usual for Christmas, and Leonard went to Boxboro. After the holidays, she told Leonard. She had a kernel of hope in the back of her mind, but the thought of marrying her did not enter his head.

"We have to get rid of it, Vera. You can't let this happen to you."

She felt that he was right. Together, they made a plan. There was a midwife that Josie had heard the girls whisper about, who would also help a girl out of trouble for a big fee. Leonard said he would help if she didn't have enough money.

So on Saturday afternoon, Josie walked down Boylston Street near the fens until she saw the house with the modest card reading "Midwife" in the window. She went up the three steps to the stoop and rang the bell. A middle-aged woman answered the door.

"Good afternoon," she said.

"Good afternoon," said Josie. "I would like to see the midwife."

"I'm the midwife," she said. "Come in." She led Josie to a stuffy little parlor to the right of the door, and gestured to a worn horsehair sofa. "Sit down and we'll talk," she said.

Josie sat on the edge of the sofa. The woman set a side-chair close to her and sat down. She looked at Josie's hands.

"That's a lovely ring," she said. "Is it an engagement ring?"

Josie looked at the ring. "No," she said. "It's a keepsake."

"How can I help you?" asked the woman.

"I'm afraid I'm in trouble," said Josie.

"How far along, do you think?"

"About six weeks."

"And you will be needing a midwife?"

"I can't keep the baby. I had a very bad birth six years ago, and the baby died."

"And you need help preventing that from happening again?"

"Yes."

The woman looked at her with some kindness. "I can help you," she said, "but the fee is very high."

"How much is the fee?"

"Fifty dollars."

This was what Josie had heard, but it still took her breath away. Five weeks' salary.

"I know it's a great deal of money," said the woman, "but there are risks, for you as well as me. You shouldn't do this lightly."

"I've thought about it," said Josie. "I can pay the fee."

"All right," she said. "Do you have a private room and bath? You will need privacy for a couple of days."

"That can be arranged," said Josie.

"You will need a hot water bottle and some towels."

Fifty dollars was more than Josie had to her name, but Leonard helped to make it up from his savings. She made the appointment for January eleventh, a Thursday. After the frenzy of the holiday shopping and the after-Christmas sales, it was a slower time at the store, and it wouldn't be so bad if she asked for sick leave for a couple of days. She found a room with a private bath on Haviland Street, not far from the midwife's house, where she could go right after the appointment. It was farther out on Boylston and farther from the store than her room on Huntington Avenue, but it was about the same price with a bath, so she thought she might as well move. As a precautionary measure, she engaged the room under the name Mrs. Nettleton, telling the landlady she was a widow, working in Boston to support her daughter, who was with her parents.

On Wednesday morning, she left her room as if for work, but took her few belongings with her in a hand bag and a Filene's hat box, and went to the new room. Then she kept her appointment.

The woman took the fifty dollars and led her to a small room at the back of the house, where there was an examining table and a glass cabinet with various medical implements. It made Josie feel better that the place was like a doctor's office.

She was told to take off her garments below the waist and lie on the table with her knees up. The woman gave her a sheet to put over her. Josie couldn't see what she was doing very well, but she took a stiff tube and inserted it between her legs.

"There will be some pain," she said, but it won't last long.

She felt a sharp pain, and then some liquid whooshed and dribbled out. Then the tube was withdrawn.

"You can get dressed now," said the woman. "You will feel some cramping, and then it will start. It might take a while. The hot water bottle will help, and make sure you have plenty of towels."

Josie got dressed and walked the few blocks to Haviland Street. Then she went upstairs to wait.

*****

Boston Daily *Globe*, January 14, 1917, page 1.

DEATH VICTIM A BEVERLY WOMAN
Vera J. Terrett's Body Identified by Half Sister
Succumbed in Back Bay Suite After Illegal Operation

The mystery which enshrouded the finding of the body of a well-dressed young woman in an apartment at 12 Haviland St, Back Bay, last Thursday night—a fact that was not brought to the attention of the police until yesterday morning—was partially solved late yesterday afternoon by the identification of the body as that of Miss Vera J. Terrett of Beverly, who for six months had roomed at 144 Huntington av. The police are on the hunt for the person or persons who were responsible for the young woman's condition and subsequent death as the result of an unsuccessful illegal operation.

Miss Terrett was the daughter of Mrs. Mary A. Terrett, of 10 Summer St Beverly, and last night the young woman's half-sister Mrs. George McGlynn, also of 10 Summer St, Beverly, came to Boston for the purpose of positively identifying the body and to be of whatever assistance she could in the police investigation.

Gave Name of Mrs. Nettleton

Miss Terrett, who introduced herself as Mrs. Nettleton, applied for a room of Mrs. Jeanette Sawyer who lets lodgings in suite 4, 12 Haviland St. In talking with the landlady, Miss Terrett said she had a child who would be 6 years old Monday, in whose honor she had planned a little celebration

When the young woman—she was 31 years old—applied for the room she had with her, besides a handbag, only a box with the name of a department store upon it. She said she intended to get the rest of her belongings the next day, Thursday. But she did not leave her room Thursday, and during the afternoon, she called for three cups of hot water, complaining she did not feel well. Mrs. Sawyer also gave her a cup of tea and an orange, and toward night she said she had a severe headache and shivered over a register. Finally she called the landlady and begged her to rub her heart, and after placing her upon a couch in the dining room, she was given whisky to stimulate her heart action.

Mrs. Sawyer suggested calling in her own family physician but the young woman insisted that Dr. John J. Hayes of 546 Columbus av be summoned. Upon the arrival of Dr. Hayes the woman was panting for breath, and she died soon after the physician had given her a pill.

Dr. Hayes, although he was unacquainted with the unfortunate victim, thought that she bore a strong resemblance to a young woman who came to him about 5½ years ago, and that at that time he placed her in a home in Jamaica Plain.

After her death the body of Miss Terrett was removed to the City Hospital Morgue, where Medical Examiner Timothy J. Leary performed an autopsy. He declared that death resulted from gases following an unsuccessful attempt at abortion.

When the young woman went to the Haviland st house, she carried a bag containing a nightgown and a pink and white kimono. She was well dressed, and wore a three-stone turquoise ring on the third finger of her right hand. The bag also contained two purses, a handkerchief, moccasins and green satin vanity bag.

Learned Name From Effects

It was from among these effects that the police learned of her identity. Miss Terrett roomed with Mrs. L. E. Crapser at suite 4, 144 Huntington av for about six months. Mrs. Crapser declared yesterday that she knew little about the young woman, as Miss Terrett was of a quiet, retiring disposition, worked all day in the millinery department of a downtown store, and retired early at night. Occasionally, according to Mrs. Crapser, her lodger went to motion picture shows, but always returned early.

Miss Terrett was accustomed to leave her room for weekends, said the landlady, but it was supposed she visited her sister. Mrs. Crapser added that she hardly ever saw the girl, except as she passed in and out from work, and Miss Terrett, in turn, never confided in her. She never entertained men callers, and lived, apparently, a lonely life. At Christmas time she was gone over the holiday and she stated that she was visiting with her sister.

If the young woman had a child she had not mentioned it during the time she lived in the Huntington av house. She had spoken, though, of having lived in Boston several years, always in the Back Bay.

Shortly before Christmas Miss Terrett went to hear Billy Sunday preach, procuring the ticket in the store where she was employed.

Last Wednesday Miss Terrett left her Huntington av room as usual, apparently to go to work. When she did not return that night Mrs. Crapser discovered that she had taken practically all her belongings with her—she did not have a trunk—and the effects were the ones found in the Haviland house.

When the woman applied for a room to Mrs. Sawyer at 12 Havilland st, she gave the name of a Mr. Brown, an employe in the women's shoe department of the store in which she worked, as reference. Mr. Brown, however, did not recognize the fictitious name, nor remember the girl, and Mr. Gilman, employment manager of the store, secured the identification through an employe of the millinery department.

*****

Josie was buried without a funeral service in Woburn's Calvary Cemetery, next to her father. Like her daughter's, her grave is unmarked.

Mary Terrett in 1906

Part Five

Mary Terrett McGlynn

Chapter 14

1901

Mary Terrett stood in the vestry of St. Charles's church, waiting for the May Procession to form. She kept calm by reminding herself that her dress of fine white lawn, tastefully trimmed in lace at the collar, was immaculate and beautifully ironed by her mother, and exhibited her own best needlework. She had to fight against vanity when it came to her needlework. She wore a crown of white roses and forget-me-nots, which she knew picked up the deep blue of her eyes, atop her blonde curls. A wispy net veil was attached to the crown, and the long white cape the Sodality had made for the May Procession trailed behind her. The crown on her head, and those of the six little girls who served as her attendants, matched the crown for the statue of the Blessed Virgin, which she held before her on a pillow covered with white silk. Mary knew that she looked the perfect May Queen, and she had rehearsed the procession and the crowning twice, so she was sure there would be no slip-ups.

At the last minute, Father Keegan appeared with the altar boys, a little rushed, but looking dignified and impressive as always. "You make a lovely May Queen, Mary," he said. "Your father and mother must be proud."

She lowered her eyes. "Oh, yes, father. It's a great honor."

He smiled. “Well, you must do your best to live up to it.”

She looked at him earnestly. “I’ll try, father.”

As if by magic, the procession formed itself out of the chaos in the yard. The altar boys and Father Keegan stepped out onto the stoop, and he gave a brief blessing to the marchers. Then Tommy Mahoney, holding the crucifix high, led the procession onto the street and around the block. He was followed by the Sodality girls in their white dresses with blue sashes, colors that honored their patron, the Blessed Virgin. Then the little seven-year-olds in the First Communion class, the girls in white dresses with veils and the boys in white shirts and white ties. Then came the young men of the Holy Name Society, the Ancient Order of Hibernians, and the Knights of Columbus. Following them were the four eighth-grade boys chosen to carry a small statue of the Blessed Virgin on a litter decorated with flowers by the Sodality, then the altar boys followed by Father Keegan, and then Mary, preceded by two little attendants dressed in blue, and followed by four attendants holding up the elegantly embroidered cape.

As the groups in front made their way around the block and then filed into their pews in the church, Mary walked slowly, with perfect posture, her eyes directly ahead, holding the pillow with its crown gracefully before her.

Once in the church vestibule, Father Keegan waited until the marchers were in their pews. Mary tried to think of the apparition of the Blessed Virgin to Bernadette Soubirous as the choir began singing the familiar strains of the Lourdes Hymn.

Immaculate Mary, thy praises we sing;
Thou reignest in splendor with Jesus our King.

As the second verse began, Father Keegan signaled to the altar boys, who preceded him slowly down the aisle, followed by the little girls and Mary. Although she could feel the eyes of a thousand people on her, she kept her head up and her gaze fixed on the altar ahead, following Father Keegan into the Sanctuary, and turning to the left where the altar of the Blessed Virgin stood below the fresco depicting the Annunciation. There she knelt with relief at the white prie-dieu set out for her while the little girls arranged the cape and then knelt by her side.

Father Keegan announced that they would pray the rosary together, meditating on the Five Joyful Mysteries. As the familiar incantation of "Hail Mary, full of grace, the Lord is with thee. Blessed art thou among women and blessed is the fruit of thy womb, Jesus" melted into the responses, "Holy Mary, Mother of God, pray for us sinners, now, and at the hour of our death, Amen," Mary tried to meditate on the Mysteries, but it was hard to concentrate. She felt that being chosen to crown the Blessed Virgin was the culmination of her spiritual life. For nearly four years, since she was fourteen years old, she had dedicated herself to the Blessed Virgin with the aim of becoming a nun. At that time, Sister Agnes had explained to the girls in the sophomore class that those of them who thought they had a religious vocation would be considered to enter the postulancy of the sisters of Notre Dame de Namur. Because they were a teaching Order, it would mean going to the mother house in Cincinnati to finish high school and normal school as postulants, and then at least three years as novices before they would take their vows.

Mary had wanted to join the Sisters of Notre Dame since she was in the fourth grade, and this step would take her to the heart of the Order. When she had talked to Sister Agnes about it, though, she was not as enthusiastic as Mary had expected.

"It's wonderful that you think you may have a vocation, Mary, but at fourteen you're younger than the girls we usually take. We discuss this possibility with the sophomore class because most of them are sixteen, or will be within the year. I know you could keep up with the school work, and I know you are devout, but fourteen is very young to make the decision."

"But I wouldn't be taking vows, would I, Sister?"

"No, you wouldn't, but you would be living a very different life. Postulants are subject to the discipline of the Order and live just as the Sisters do. You should probably take more time to experience the worldly life to make sure this is the choice you really want to make. Your calling now is to study hard and enjoy your girlhood. And of course, you would need the approval of your father and mother. Why don't you get advice from them first, and then we'll see."

This challenge simply made Mary more determined. She chose her moment for talking to her parents carefully, on Saturday evening after supper, when they were resting together in the parlor after the long week's work and she knew her father wasn't rushing out to a meeting. She put her case as she would have put it in the debating society, in what she thought was a rational and convincing way, stressing the fact that she would be receiving a free education as well as following her vocation for the religious life. Her father responded about as she expected.

"I don't know, Mary. Of course it would be an honor to give a child to the Church, but you're still so young to be leaving home. I think you could wait a year or two." Mary took his answer respectfully. She was pretty sure that she could bring him around on this, as she did on most things. But it was her mother, always agreeable, rarely even offering an opinion on family matters, who surprised her.

"No, Mary," she said. "You're too young to make a decision like this, and too young to leave home. I won't sign the papers."

"But Marm, you can think of it as going to boarding school. I won't be taking any vows, and I can come home if I find I'm not suited to it."

"No, Mary. My father was taken away from home by the Church like this, and no good came of it. If you go, it will not be with my permission. Time enough for you to make a decision like this when you've finished your education and you're an adult."

Richard Terrett, who did not want to lose his favorite child by any means, made a point of supporting his wife's unusual determination.

"Well, there you have it, Mary. We'll have to respect your mother's wishes."

Mary knew it was a rare thing for her father to respect her mother's wishes, but she could see that he was relieved to find this way out of something he was loathe to allow.

Mary would not concede the main point, but only the delay. She tried to sound reasonable. "How long will I have to wait to go?" she asked.

Richard considered. "Well, you have two years left of high school. You'll still be only seventeen when you graduate. I think you should do the post-graduate college prep year at St. Charles's, which will get you ready for normal school, and then when you're eighteen, if you still want to go into the convent, you'll be ready, or you can go on to normal school. What do you say, Maggie?"

"I have nothing against the extra year of high school if you want to be a teacher," said Maggie, and we can send you to normal school. As for the convent, I will tell you plainly, I don't think you're suited for it. I think you would regret going. I won't sign the papers as long as you're not of age."

Mary had been heart-broken, but had born her disappointment as well as she could, resolving to honor her father and mother in all circumstances. She finished high school and enjoyed it, particularly the Young Ladies Sodality activities, and she was recognized by the Sisters as a devout girl, but she didn't speak again of her determination to become a nun until one day when she was sixteen. Patsy O'Hare suddenly appeared at the fence as she was working in the flower beds her father had dug for her in the front yard. Mary had always liked Patsy, who lived four doors down from their house on Arlington Street. A tall, thin, red-headed fellow who seemed to have a perpetual grin on his face, he was one of Tom's friends who went out of his way to be nice to her.

"Good morning, Patsy," she said.

"Hello, Mary. What do you hear from Tom?"

"He's still on the *Solace* as far as we know. It's in Manila now. They sailed half way around the world."

"Yes, I read that in the *News*." He grinned. "Who would have thought that old Tom would really be seeing the world like this. It's what he always dreamed of."

"Yes, and we think he's safe on the transport ship. We miss him, though."

"I do too. Tom was always someone you could talk to if you needed advice, and I kind of need it now."

Mary sat back on her heels and looked up at him. "Why, Patsy?"

Patsy looked like a man about to plunge into the ocean on a January day. "Mary," he said. "I've something to ask you."

"Ask *me*? Well, go ahead, Patsy."

"Mary, I've been meaning to tell you for a long time now. I think you're the prettiest and the nicest girl I've ever seen, and I . . . I love you. I want to know if you could ever consider me as a husband. I know I'm young at twenty, but I've been in at McKay Machinery for four years now, and I'm almost through my apprenticeship. I could afford to give us a home, and there is no one in this world that I would want for a wife except you."

This was the last thing in the world Mary had expected to hear. She had never thought of Patsy O'Hare, or of any boy or man, in this light, and she had no answer prepared to soften the blow. She blurted out the first thing that came into her mind, which was the truth.

"I'm sorry, Patsy. I can't marry you. I'm going to be a nun."

It was Patsy's turn to be shocked. "A nun! *You*? I understand that you wouldn't want a big dope like me, maybe. But you couldn't ever be a nun, Mary."

"No, it's true, Patsy. I'll admit, I've never thought of you, or anyone, as a husband, but it's because all I've ever wanted was to be a nun."

Patsy shook his head. "Well, I'd never have guessed it. Never in a million." He was the picture of bewilderment. "I was prepared for a lot of different answers, but not this one. I guess I should be getting on, Mary. Thanks for listening."

"You're welcome, Patsy. I hope you know it's nothing personal. I've always liked you."

Patsy went off to his house and kept the conversation to himself. But just two days later, he came down with a fever, and after a few days of the best care his mother could give, he died. When the Terretts arrived at the wake, Mary found that Patsy had told his mother she was the girl he wanted to marry, but not that she had turned him down. In her grief, Mrs. O'Hare clung to Mary, introducing her to everyone as "the girl my Patsy was going to marry."

Mary never got over this traumatic event, nor was she able to convince her mother that there was not even a flirtation between her and Patsy. It just added to Maggie's conviction that Mary was not meant for the religious life. For her part, if she had been reserved around young men before, she became positively stand-offish, not wanting to be misunderstood as "interested." Since she was recognized as a beautiful girl, the young men took her attitude as arrogant and snobbish, and for the most part they left her alone.

Mary gave the automatic response, "Pray for us," as Father Keegan intoned the Litany of the Blessed Virgin.

Mother of Christ
Mother of the Church
Mother of divine grace
Mother most pure
Mother of chaste love
Mother and virgin
Sinless mother

Out of the corner of her eye, Mary glanced around the church. She saw Josie with the Sodality, a wave of white and blue in the front pews, and her father kneeling with the Hibernians behind them, beaming with pride. She didn't see the tiny figure of her mother in the congregation beyond, but she knew she was there, repeating the responses automatically as she examined the results of their combined handiwork on the dress with a critical eye. Mary looked down at her hands, holding the rosary, and tried to think of the Blessed Virgin.

When the litany came to a close, Mary straightened her back and prepared for the cue that came with the May hymn.

Bring flow'rs of the fairest,
Bring flow'rs of the rarest,
From garden and woodland
And hillside and vale;

At the beginning of the hymn, four little girls rose from their knees and, as they had been taught, neatly lifted the cape as Mary rose gracefully from the prie-dieu and turned toward the altar of the Blessed Virgin Mary. She took the crown of flowers from the pillow, then she mounted the temporary steps that had been placed before the altar.

With perfect timing, she placed the crown of flowers on the statue as the choir sang the chorus.

O Mary! We crown thee with blossoms today,
Queen of the angels, Queen of the May,

As the choir launched into the second verse, Mary bowed her head a moment in silent prayer. "Blessed Virgin Mary, I dedicate myself to your service," she prayed. "I will strive to live always according to your example." Many members of the congregation thought at that moment that they had never had a lovelier May Queen. As she took her place at the prie-dieu for the remainder of the hymn, Mary resolved to try again to convince her mother and father to let her join the Sisters of Notre Dame. She had no doubt that she was put on this earth to spend her life in devotion and service to the Blessed Virgin Mary.

The discussion with her parents on her eighteenth birthday, four days after the May Procession, did not go as well as Mary had hoped. She told them that she was absolutely sure now that she had a vocation for the convent, and that her heart's desire was to be a teaching Sister of Notre Dame de Namur. Her father said that, now that she was eighteen, he would consent to her going if her mother would. But Maggie Terrett was still unconvinced.

"Are you sure it's not all this May Procession fuss that's got into your head, Mary? You may be eighteen by the calendar, but you're still seventeen to me, and you've not had experience with the kind of discipline and hard work and lack of comfort that convent life means. You may think you want to make the sacrifice in your head, and in your heart, but that's a world of difference from sleeping in a cold cell, wearing drab uncomfortable clothes, and getting up at all hours to pray."

Despite herself, Mary bristled. "But, Marm, how will I know whether I can do it if I don't try? This is the life I feel called to live."

Maggie's face showed determination. "I'll be blunt, Mary. You've never had a young man you really cared for. You have no idea what you'd be giving up if you sacrificed marriage and a family."

"What about what I'd be giving up if I sacrificed the religious life to get married? You don't know the higher joy that is possible for me there."

Maggie shook her head. "That's true, Mary. But remember that the religious life is sacrifice by its very nature. I want to make sure that you know what you would be sacrificing before you make the decision."

Richard looked at Maggie with a new respect. "Your mother is right, Mary," he said. "And surely, there's no rush if you plan to be in the convent for the rest of your life. What if I make this offer. You do two years of normal school, which will be a preparation for teaching, no matter what you decide about the convent. When you turn twenty, the same age that Tom was when I let him make his decision about the Navy, we will let you decide for yourself about the convent. What do you say, Maggie?"

Maggie calculated quickly. Two years was a long time for a girl Mary's age, and she did believe that she would change her mind about all this if she met the right young man. "All right," she said. "Two more years of school, and then it's for you to decide."

Mary was not happy with this outcome, but she tried to use the situation to practice patience and resignation. After all, in comparison with the suffering many of the saints had to endure to dedicate their lives to serving God and the Church, this was nothing. She resolved to prepare herself as well as she could, both academically and spiritually, so she would be ready for the convent when the time came. She signed up to take the entrance exam at Salem Normal School, and started attending the 6:00 a.m. Mass at St. Charles's daily.

On the morning of June 28th, Mary had to skip Mass in order to take her exam. She was rushing out the door to catch the earliest train for Salem when her mother said, "Aren't you going to say good-bye to your father?"

Mary called out, "Goodbye, Pa."

Richard answered, "So you're off? Good luck!" At noon, her brother Tom, who had been out of the Navy just three months, came to the building where she was taking the exam. Someone had telephoned to his machine shop to tell him his father had died. He'd come to take Mary home to Woburn with him.

Richard Terrett's death changed everything for his daughter. Besides the emotional devastation of losing the father she so loved and revered, there was the financial impact. She and her mother and her sister Josie were well-provided for by a working family's standards. A house with no mortgage, a small savings account, and a thousand dollars in insurance from the Ancient Order of Hibernians was more than most families were left with. But a two-year course at the normal school was out of the question now. Mary had to start contributing to the household. She found a six-months' business course that, along with courses she had taken in the post-graduate year of high school, would fit her for a well-paying job in a Boston office. So Mary began commuting to Boston, but she made daily Mass, which had become a great comfort to her after her father's death, into her routine, and she began meeting her cousin Delia Gill for Mass and a quick breakfast before they began their work days.

Mary finished the business course with distinction, and, after a short stint keeping the books at a jewelry store, landed a dream job, secretary for the architectural firm of Cram, Goodhue, and Ferguson. Mary came to have the greatest respect for Ralph Adams Cram, a celebrated architect and major rival of Frank Lloyd Wright. While Wright put his stock in the modern, Cram championed a Gothic revival, particularly in church and academic architecture. He and his partner Bertram Goodhue were responsible for the Gothicism of Princeton University's campus and the Cathedral of St. John the Divine in New York.

When Mary worked for Mr. Cram, he was deeply involved in his study of everything medieval, an obsession that eventually resulted in his book *Walled Cities*, a plan to save civilization after World War I by reverting to the model of the medieval city. Mary knew nothing about architecture when she came to work for the firm, but she loved the Gothic architecture it produced, particularly the churches. She came to know Mr. Cram's mind a little as she worked with him on the manuscripts for his essays and lectures. He was the most learned man she had ever encountered, and although he was a High-Church Anglican rather than a Catholic, she developed a deep respect for his knowledge of Church history and doctrine and the sincerity of his faith.

Chapter 15

1906

When Josie introduced Mary to Felix O'Connor and his friend George McGlynn at St. Charles's annual church social, Mary didn't take much notice of George, who looked to be in his mid-thirties. She was aware that Felix and Josie were just looking for a convenient way to pair off. But George was pleasant and friendly, and she ended up enjoying the social on his arm for most of the afternoon. He was a nice-looking man of average height, a couple of inches taller than she, with a strong jaw, green eyes, dark hair and a somewhat receding hairline.

As the afternoon went on, Mary became aware of something about George's attention to her that was different from that of any man she had spent time with. She thought perhaps that it was because he was older, but besides buying her ice cream and supplying the usual jokes and pleasantries to make her smile, he listened intently to her whenever she talked, and she tended to talk a lot when she was slightly nervous as she was now. Never had a young man shown any interest in the sewing and art booths at the social, but George paid close attention, and asked questions that drew her out. She found herself explaining just what was good about one piece or where another had failed. Toward the end of the afternoon, he looked at her face in a searching way that made her vaguely uncomfortable.

George escorted Mary home and secured permission to visit the following Sunday before he went off to catch the trolley for Winchester. She didn't quite know what to make of him, but her interest was piqued. During the next few months, George courted Mary avidly. He visited every week, and as he got to know her and her interests, he devised outings to appeal to her. Their shared love of music was central to this. He played the cornet in a band, and he often took her to hear it. Sometimes on Saturdays when his own band wasn't playing, he would hurry into Boston after work to meet her and take her to hear some music or to a play or vaudeville show. On a few special occasions, they went to hear the Boston Pops or the Boston Symphony Orchestra. George told her that he had once auditioned for the orchestra, with favorable results, but had decided that his future as a musician was too uncertain for him to give up his good job as a skilled machinist.

During this time, Mary's sense of George's intense involvement in her never diminished. If anything it increased. As their conversations became more personal, he drew her out, and showed a genuine interest in her ideas and feelings. She told him about her deep religious faith, which he respected and shared in many ways. He looked at her with admiration, and often complimented her, which made her blush, but also gave her pleasure. Since her father's death, there had been no one who so admired her and valued her opinions. She found herself looking forward to his visits as the highlight of her week, and often stored up her ideas and opinions throughout the week to tell George. One Sunday in early September, George asked Mary to take a walk out into the country with him. It was a beautiful day, and Mary was enjoying the country air and the now familiar and comforting support of his arm when he said, "I have something to ask you, Mary. You must know what it is."

The image of Patsy O'Hare flashed into her mind, but Mary was much more prepared for the question this time. "You know how much I like and respect you, George, but I don't know if I want to marry. As you know, my dream was always to be a nun. My life hasn't worked out that way, but I still have a deep dedication to the Blessed Virgin. I don't know if I can reconcile that with marriage."

George was expecting something like this. "I understand, Mary, and you know how I admire your spiritual life and your dedication, but you know the Blessed Virgin was a mother too. Don't you think it's possible to follow her ideal in that vocation as well as in the convent? If you do neither of those things, you'll be depriving yourself of the opportunity for spiritual development. Not to mention depriving me of the most wonderful wife I could ever imagine." He smiled.

She couldn't help smiling back. "I'll think about it, George," she said, "and ask Father Keegan's advice."

Father Keegan agreed heartily with George. "It's your duty, Mary," he said, "to become a good Catholic wife and mother. What would you be otherwise? From what I've seen, George is an exemplary Catholic and a good, steady man. My advice is to marry him."

As Mary expected, Marm was overjoyed to hear of the proposal, and couldn't imagine why Mary would hesitate. "He's a good man, Mary, and so easy to get on with. He has a good steady job, and he's told me he has two thousand dollars to get married on. And anyone can see he worships the ground you walk on. It's not often you'll find a man like that."

Mary spent several sleepless nights over her decision. She felt it was her moment of truth, forever deciding between two lives. If she accepted George's proposal, she would be giving up the ideal that she had set for herself since she was old enough to think about such things. She knew that becoming a nun was out of the question at this point, but she had created for herself a sort of private religious rule, based on her devotions and her promise to emulate the Blessed Virgin. Father Keegan was right that the Blessed Virgin could be emulated as a mother as well as a virgin, but she had so long considered chastity as central to her devotion, had so firmly repressed any temptation to impurity in word, deed, or thought, that she could not imagine that part of marriage as anything but weakness and degradation. She, unfortunately, could not be Virgin and Mother. She would have to be an ordinary wife, with a wife's duties to her husband.

Still Father Keegan's words haunted her, "What would you be otherwise?" Just another twenty-four-year-old office girl, helping to support her mother. And when her mother died? A single woman living with her sister, or on her own in a boarding house? Mary had to agree with Marm that she was not likely to receive another marriage proposal from a man as suitable as George. And she did care a great deal for George. She knew that his calm and pleasant disposition, his tendency to see the humorous side of things, his friendly manner and ease with people, would be the perfect complement for her own intensity. She thought of a life filled with his love and support and admiration.

When George came up the steps at 19 Arlington Street the next Sunday, he had an uncharacteristically anxious look on his face. No one was in the parlor, so Mary led him in there, and placed both her hands in his. She looked up into his eyes, and then looked down and quietly said, "Yes."

George was so excited he nearly whooped. He threw his arms around her and kissed her, the first kiss they exchanged that wasn't a decorous good-night peck. Mary was a little shocked, but later, she had to admit to herself that she liked it, and she liked the gentler kisses that came later. From that afternoon on, Mary became progressively more excited about her wedding. She took pleasure in all of the preparations, from their announcement of the engagement to Marm and Josie that afternoon to the last stitch of sewing on her trousseau and her wedding dress. For an engagement ring, George asked Mary what kind of stone she would like most, and she told him she would prefer a plain gold band with an image of the Sacred Heart, as a symbol that their marriage would be a living out of their Catholic faith. He had a jeweler make it especially for her.

On November 18, 1906, Mary and George were married by Father Keegan at St. Charles's, and her new life began.

Chapter 16

1908

Mary had just put Edna into her cradle by the stove for her nap, and she and her mother were sitting down to a welcome cup of tea on this frigid February afternoon when there was a knock at the door. They looked at each other. Neither was expecting anyone. It was a cold day for visiting. Mary opened the door, and there stood Mrs. McClellan, a neighbor from a three-decker two houses down. Mary was a little mystified, since they had only a nodding acquaintance, but she was glad to see company nonetheless.

"Come in and have a cup of tea, Mrs. McClellan," she said. "You know my mother, Mrs. Terrett?"

"Oh yes, of course, I see you with the chickens, Mrs. Terrett. You're building a fine little flock."

"Why, thank you, Mrs. McClellan. I'll soon have enough hens to have eggs to spare, so let me know if you'd be wanting any."

"I would. There's no comparison between fresh eggs and what you get in the market."

Mary had poured a cup of tea and placed the chair nearest the stove for their guest. She took her coat and hung it over the back of another chair. "Will you have a bit of cake?" asked Maggie. "Mary made it this morning, and she's a fine hand at baking."

"Why, thank you," said Mrs. McClellan. She sat comfortably by the stove, and they ate and drank companionably for a few minutes.

"This is lovely," said Mrs. McClellan. "And how dear the little one looks there. Edna, isn't it? Let's see. You've been here several months, now, haven't you? Do you like Beverly?"

"Yes, we do," said Mary. "The air is much cleaner than Woburn's, and we're so conveniently situated here, close to my husband's work at the United Shoe, and not far from the shops at Gloucester Crossing. We like St. Mary's too. Such a beautiful new church, and Father Curran gives very inspiring sermons." Maggie simply nodded agreement. She was studying Mrs. McClellan's face.

"Oh, you came from Woburn," she said. "I have a cousin who was married at St. Charles's. Is that where you were married, Mrs. McGlynn?"

Mary nodded. "Oh yes. We were married by Father John Keegan, a dear friend of the family as well as the Pastor."

"That's lovely," said Mrs. McClellan. "I wonder, would you happen to have a picture, or your wedding announcement by? I'd love to see them."

Mary, who had only been married a little over a year, was happy to oblige. She jumped up and retrieved a little album from the table in the sitting room. "These are our wedding portraits," she said. "And the announcement."

Mrs. McClellan glanced at the announcement, and then looked closely at Mary's picture. "What a beautiful bodice and sleeve on that gown," she said. "All that ruching. Did you make it yourself?"

"Oh, yes," said Mary. Her cheeks flushed a bit. "It took hours and hours, but I thought the effect was worth it."

"I would certainly say so. It's a lovely effect on a girl as slim as you. Not something I could wear, though." She laughed good-naturedly, and finished her tea.

"Well, this has been grand," Mrs. McClellan said, "but I should be getting off home to start my husband's supper. I wonder if I could ask a favor. Would you mind if I borrowed your wedding announcement for a day or two?"

"My wedding announcement? Why, what for?"

"I think some of the neighbors would enjoy seeing it."

This was a custom Mary had never heard of, but she didn't see any harm in lending a wedding invitation. She had a few extras. She glanced at her mother, who nodded slightly. "Why, of course, if you think so, Mrs. McClellan." She took a wedding invitation in its envelope from the back of the album and handed it to her.

"Lovely. I'll make sure to return it to you." She got to her feet and put on her coat. "I'll be off, now. Thank you for the tea and cake. You must come to me soon, and bring little Edna."

Maggie shook hands with her. "It was very nice of you to come," she said, looking her full in the face.

As she closed the door behind Mrs. McClellan, Mary looked at her mother. "Did you think that was a little strange, Marm?" she asked.

Maggie looked her in the eye. "I wasn't sure at first, but that woman just did you a great kindness, Mary," she said. "Some of the looks I've gotten from the neighbors make sense to me now. I think some of them have been talking because Edna was born so soon after we moved in here. They probably think you were married just in the nick of time, so to speak. She's taken that announcement to show them that there's nothing wrong with your marriage or with Edna's birth."

Mary was shocked that anyone could think such a thing of her. It never occurred to her to think about what people might be saying. In Woburn, and at work, it was just assumed that her behavior was above reproach. But here was a whole neighborhood of women gossiping about her and speculating about her moral character. Her face burned, and she felt exposed, somehow, although there was nothing to expose. "I don't think I want to leave this house again," she said to Maggie. "I don't think I can face all those women, knowing what they were thinking and saying about me."

Maggie sighed. "Gossip is an awful thing," she said. "But that's why you should be grateful to Mrs. McClellan. She'll show that announcement to two women or three, and in two days time, every woman in the neighborhood will be saying they never doubted you for a minute. That's how these things go. Sometimes you're just too sensitive for this world, Lovie. This time you will have to hold your head high for a few weeks and pretend you never knew anything about it, and in a month it will be forgotten."

"I suppose you're right, Marm, but that doesn't mean *I* will forget it. It's a horrible feeling. We'd best not say anything about it to George."

"You're right there," said Maggie.

Chapter 17

1917–1918

There had been a few snowflakes in the morning, but George came home from the United Shoe at Saturday noon with the news that it was warming up to a real January thaw. It must be fifty degrees outside, a big change from the record cold temperatures just two days earlier. He and Mary started discussing whether to take advantage of the unseasonably warm weather to take a Saturday afternoon trip to Salem for shopping. It was evident that Edna, George, and Andrew were in favor, but Mary was dubious about taking them out in the car for a long ride. "We'll bundle up, Mama," said Edna. " And we'll put a blanket over us. We'll be plenty warm enough." Seeing how eager Edna and the boys were to go, Maggie offered to stay home with Evvie and Doris and baby Arthur. "We'll be grand here for the afternoon, Mary, and you and the children can certainly use an outing."

While Mary was thinking about it, or dithering, as Edna thought to herself, someone knocked on the door. George opened it to Mike McCarthy, a young man he knew slightly from the Holy Name Society. "Well, hello, Mike," he said, taking in his policeman's uniform. "Are you on patrol? I'll bet you're glad to have some warm weather at last."

"Hello, George," said Mike. "Might I have a word in private?"

George looked at him in surprise, but stepped out into the hall with him, closing the door behind him. "I have some bad news, George," said Mike. "We've just had a telephone call from one of the precincts in Boston. They have someone who's died. They think she's related to you."

"Who is it, Mike?" George asked, but he already knew.

"It's a young woman. From some papers found in her belongings, they think her name was Vera J. Terrett, and that she had a connection to your family."

"That's my wife's half-sister. She hasn't been sick that we know of. What happened to her?"

Mike looked past him. "It seems there was an illegal operation of some kind."

"I see."

"They will need her next of kin to go up to Boston to positively identify the body and give instructions for burial."

George was at a loss. "Would that be her stepmother, my mother-in-law, or her half sister?"

"You probably should bring them both, George. It's the morgue at City Hospital, on Harrison street in the South End. They'll tell you what you need to do."

George looked at him blankly. "I guess we should go right away. Should I drive, do you think?"

"No need for that, George. It would probably be best to take the train, under the circumstances. Give you time to collect yourselves."

"Yes. Thank you, Mike. You've been very kind."

Mary looked up in alarm when he came back in. "What's happened, George?" she asked. "You've gone pale."

"Take the boys upstairs, Edna," he said. "I need to talk to your mother and Marmsie for a few minutes."

From the look on his face, Edna knew not to ask if their trip to Salem was off. She led the boys up the stairs with a promise to play with them. As gently as he could, George explained to Mary and Maggie what the policeman had said to him. Maggie dropped to a chair, covered her face with her hands, and began a subdued rocking and keening. "Oh, Josie," she kept repeating to herself, "It's my fault, so. I knew I should never have let you go and live in Boston."

Mary's face registered shock, but she was able to function. "We'll have to go right away," she said. "I'll get Mrs. McClellan's daughter to watch the children. We probably won't be back until tonight."

On the train to Boston, Maggie and Mary sat across from George, looking numbly at each other. "Where will we bury her?" asked Maggie. "Sure, Father Curran will not say a funeral Mass for her here."

"She should be buried in Woburn," said Mary, "near Pa and her mother. I know there is room in the Kernan plot."

"She can have my plot, next to her father. I would rather be buried here in Beverly now anyway."

It did take all afternoon and most of the night to get to Boston and answer all the police's questions. Maggie made the official identification of the body. The police called the McKenna funeral home in Woburn, and they agreed to handle the burial. There would be no funeral Mass or wake, but at least she would be buried in sacred ground next to her father.

Josie's secret burial in an unmarked grave would become an enduring cause of shame and regret for both Mary and her mother. Maggie's sense of shame went back to the Great Hunger, when an unmarked "pauper's grave" was the final ignominy that ended the slow starvation of the destitute in the workhouses. Neither of them would recover from the bewildering circumstances of the death and the shame they felt about the burial. The one personal item of Josie's that Mary took with her was the ring that Tom and Mary had given her when she served as bridesmaid at their wedding. She thought the family should keep it.

As if the experience were not enough of a nightmare, a reporter for the Boston *Globe* who had been hanging around the Boylston Street police station on Saturday morning when the death was first reported got wind of the story and set out to investigate. The result was the Sunday paper's front page story detailing the events of Josie's death and clearly identifying the McGlynn family at 10 Summer Street in Beverly as her relatives. With her horror of gossip and scandal, opening the paper to this story the day after her ordeal in Boston was traumatic for Mary. It was followed on Monday by a front-page story in the Beverly *Times*, much shorter, but likely to reach everyone they knew with the report of Josie's death from an "illegal operation." Mary realized later that if she had not had four-week-old Arthur to care for, she would have collapsed. But Maggie, resilient as always after her first heavy grieving, managed to steady her daughter and keep the household going for those first weeks.

With this beginning, 1917 proved to be a very hard year for Mary. A pacifist who had absorbed her parents' antipathy for Great Britain as a heartless, imperialistic country, she ardently supported Woodrow Wilson on the ground that he had maintained U. S. neutrality on the Great War. When Wilson requested a declaration of war from Congress on April second, she felt personally betrayed. And immediately following came the wartime shortages in flour, sugar, butter, and coal, which affected her family directly. Cooking food that her children would eat became a daily challenge.

In the winter, it was especially hard to heat the Summer Street apartment, with its two third-story bedrooms. With the coal shortage, they often could only have the fire in the kitchen stove, which was barely adequate to heat the second-floor rooms. Everyone had colds that winter, and for Arthur, only a few weeks old, the cold turned into pneumonia. For weeks in January and February, Mary sat with him through the night, nursing him and praying, while Maggie did her best to keep the rest of the household going. George, who was on overtime hours Tuesday through Friday and idle Saturday through Monday because of the shortage of fuel at the United Shoe, tried to amuse the children on the weekends. With the spring weather, Arthur's health slowly returned, and Mary made a novena to give thanks to the Blessed Virgin for the life of her youngest child.

In the spring, partly to get Mary out of the apartment, George started taking her to look for a house that would be easier to heat and more comfortable for their family of nine. Mary had shrunk from meeting her Summer Street neighbors since the story about Josie had been in the *Globe*. She left the house as little as possible, and never visited with the other women in the neighborhood. After a few trips to look at houses, she embraced George's idea, and was eager to move to a new neighborhood.

They finally found a house for rent at 88 McKay Street, in a new subdivision owned by the United Shoe on the other side of the huge factory complex from Summer Street, where they knew no one, and better, no one knew them. The house was a two-story just two years old, and had a modern coal furnace and the latest in plumbing, including an upstairs bathroom. It was on the market, but the Shoe's agent was willing to rent to them on a short lease on the condition that they allow the house to be shown. They moved in, and within two months, George went to the agent and told him not to show the house anymore because they were buying it. He paid the thirty-five hundred dollars in cash. It took all their savings, but he wanted no part of a mortgage. He had been taken out of school at the age of twelve in order to help meet the balloon payment on a mortgage that had bedeviled his parents. There would be no burden like that for his children.

Mary was happy in the new house. She liked the neighbors, the Eastmans and the Jorgensens, who had children near the ages of hers, and she formed a habit of having tea most afternoons with Mrs. Guilford and Mrs. Lund. George walked home for his dinner at noon, and the children could easily walk to the McKay elementary school at the end of the block. The children loved the new house, with the big yard all their own, as well as the "back field" behind where all the neighborhood children played. And there was the Shoe Pond, just across the street, which was cleared for skating in the winter, and where they fished, with persistence despite their lack of success, in the summer.

Gradually, Mary began to enjoy life again. The children were healthy, and doing well in school. She and George started the habit of going to the movies whenever the picture changed, which was three times a week. George was always thinking up some "expedition" for the family to take on the weekends.

After they had owned the car for a couple of years, Mary persuaded George to teach her to drive. It took a while for her to master the controls—operating the spark and throttle levers on the steering wheel at the same time that she managed the three pedals for high and low speed, reverse, and braking. After a while, though, she began to see George's point that it was not so much different than playing the piano, with the bass and treble and pedals all working together. Once she got the hang of it, Mary was delighted with the new freedom she had, and proud to be the first woman of their acquaintance who could drive a car. After the Armistice in November of 1918, food and fuel again became abundant. It was a good time for the McGlynns.

In the Ford, about 1914, (from left) Mary, Everett, Edna, George L., George H., and Andrew McGlynn

Chapter 18

1922

Mary rinsed the cloth in the cold water and wrung it out, carefully placing it back on Everett's forehead. He had seemed to be a little better today. With the unusually warm weather for April, they'd been able to open the windows, and his breathing seemed less labored. But the fever had spiked again at midnight, and now he was struggling for breath, although he was finally asleep, a respite from the awful pain in his throat. Images flashed into her mind of the many sleepless nights she had spent nursing her children. It had been weeks when Edna had rheumatic fever when she was six, and months when Arthur had pneumonia when he was just a year old.

It had been a miracle that Arthur lived, a gift from God, a golden child. That had made it so much worse when he was taken from her so suddenly in 1919. She could still hear Haynes Jorgensen at the front door screaming, "It's Arthur. He was hit by a car!" Before she could take it in, a strange man appeared at the door with the smashed little body in his arms. "Run and tell your mother to call Dr. Stickney," George yelled to Haynes. "Hurry!" The Jorgensens had the only telephone in the neighborhood, and they lived all the way at the end of the street. George carried Arthur into the house and up the stairs and laid him on his bed. At the sight of him lying there, Mary knew he was dead. The beautiful little boy that God had given back to her had been taken away again.

She had had no idea what she said or did, but George told her afterwards that she had knelt sobbing by the bed and kept saying "Why this one? Not this one!" Four-year-old Doris, who had been playing with Arthur in front of the house when he ran into the street, slipped into the room and stood against the wall, looking at the still form of her brother and her mother sobbing and screaming. Mary had turned on her and said, "How could you let this happen? You should have been watching him!" Doris ran out of the room. The doctor came quickly and pronounced Arthur dead. The police and the funeral director followed soon after.

Mary had been inconsolable after Arthur's death. She could not stop weeping. She could not think about anything else. She felt that God had purposely taken away this greatest of gifts, and she could not understand why. She spent as much of her time as she could in prayer. She developed a routine of leaving the house in the middle of the day, walking the mile-and-a-half to St. Mary's, where she would pray the rosary, meditating on the Sorrowful Mysteries, and then walking up Brimble Avenue to the cemetery, where she would stay a long time before she would walk the three-and-a-half miles along Herrick and Balch Streets home. She came to believe that the death was a punishment for breaking the vow she had made so many years before to consecrate her life to the Blessed Virgin. She should never have married. She should never have brought little children into the world to suffer.

At a loss to deal with his wife's grief, George had consulted both Dr. Hayes and Father Curran, who had given him the same advice. Mary needed another child to demand her attention and take her mind off her grief. When he explained what they had told him, Mary reluctantly agreed that it was her duty to try to overcome her grief. Since her life had taken this path, she must devote herself to motherhood as completely as she could. So Anita was born in May of 1920, just ten months after Arthur's death.

George and the priest and the doctor turned out to be right, to some extent. Demanding her full attention, the new baby did take her mind off her grief for periods of time, and she was a cheerful, healthy baby. George doted on her, and Mary came to think of her as a special child, sent by God as recompense for the loss of Arthur. When Priscilla came along in 1922, Mary was almost too busy to grieve. At the age of thirty-eight, she now had seven children, including two in diapers. Her mother was in her late seventies or eighties, and not able to do nearly as much around the house as she used to. At fourteen, Edna was of some help, but now that she was in high school, her studies took a lot of her time. So the major burden of child care, cooking, and cleaning fell on Mary. She was very busy, and tired most of the time. There certainly was no time for walks to the church or the cemetery, although she continued to say the rosary every day, and Father Curran gave her a tablet depicting the stations of the cross so she could perform this devotion without having to walk to St. Mary's.

When Everett had felt sick a week ago, it had seemed just a sore throat at first, but his throat became so discolored that they'd called in Dr. Hayes, and he had seen immediately that it was diphtheria. "It's very painful," he said, but he should pull through if you keep him warm and quiet. He shouldn't have a high fever, but bring it down if he does. I'll look in every couple of days to see how he's doing."

When he had come earlier today, Dr. Hayes had been concerned. Everett was very pale and listless, his pulse was rapid, and he hadn't been able to eat for several days now. "Give him as much liquid as you can get him to take," he said.

"Keep his fever down. If he loses consciousness, be sure to call me right away."

Mary looked at the boy on the bed. His breathing was very shallow and his face was paler than the sheet. She suddenly felt a wave of fear. She touched his shoulder, and then shook him gently. "Evvie," she said. "Wake up."

When she couldn't rouse him, she went to get George, who also tried and failed. "We should get Dr. Hayes," she said. "He said to get him right away if he lost consciousness."

Without a word, George dressed and left the house. She heard the car start up and looked at the clock. It was after 3:00. Within half an hour, George was back with Dr. Hayes, who examined the boy. "I must tell you," he said. "It doesn't look good for him. He's in a coma. Sometimes people come out of this, and sometimes they don't. Try to keep his fever down, and keep getting moisture into his mouth, a tiny bit at a time with an eyedropper. You have to be careful he doesn't choke. I'll be back in the morning, but come and get me if there is a change for the worse."

Everett died in the morning. Exhausted and emotionally spent, Mary grieved much more quietly this time, but again she was bewildered. Why had he been taken from her? What had she done, or failed to do? She could only go back to her failure to live up to her promise to the Blessed Virgin. After a few weeks, she went to see Father Curran and explained things to him, asking if there was anything she could do to mend her broken vow to consecrate herself to the service of the Blessed Virgin.

"Mary, you haven't done anything wrong," he said. "There are many ways to serve the Blessed Virgin. Being a nun is one, but so is being a devoted wife and mother, just as she was. You must find your path to salvation in the life God has called you to live."

"But I feel I have to do more. I want to live a life of special devotion."

"Well, you can never be a nun now. But there are other options for lay people. Have you ever been part of a Sodality?"

"Yes, when I was a girl, I was in the Young Ladies Sodality, and it meant a good deal to me."

"Why don't you join St. Mary's Guild? They take care of the sanctuary and the vestments and altar linens. I think you would find it a good deal like the Sodality. And if you feel called to deepen your spiritual life, you can set aside as much time as you can spare each day to make a novena or read the Bible. Start by praying the rosary every day. Eventually, you might think of joining something like the Third Order of St. Francis. It's a way for lay people to follow a religious rule while they live their normal lives."

Mary took Father Curran's suggestions to heart. She joined the Guild, and she began praying the rosary and making her way through the Bible from Old Testament to New. When Andrew came down with scarlet fever, she feared the worst, but she immediately started a novena for him and kept up her devotions, saying the rosary over and over while she sat at his bedside.

When Andrew's symptoms worsened, Dr. Hayes told them about a new experimental serum that had been developed by a Dr. Place at Harvard, and suggested that they try it. George, who had read about it in the newspaper, immediately agreed, and Mary was eager to try anything to save her boy. When Dr. Place administered the serum, Andrew began to get better almost immediately. Within a couple of hours, there was no trace of the fever. George was ecstatic, and kept talking about the wonders of modern science. Mary thought that science might have been the immediate cause of the cure, but she still considered it a miracle in response to her prayers. In thanksgiving, she intensified her prayers to the Blessed Virgin, and she took the Guild's care of the altar linen as her special devotion.

From this time on, Mary took less and less interest in keeping house. She continued to put meals on the table, including the delicious pies that George ate at breakfast, lunch, and dinner, and to see to it that the children were clean and had good instruction in manners and morals, but the things that she had been proud of, like her sewing and baking, were no longer of much importance to her. She was more interested in getting her housework done quickly than in doing praiseworthy work, which she came to see as a species of vanity. George and Mary had one more child, Walter, in 1924, when George was fifty-three and Mary was forty. They decided that he should be their last child. After that, they slept apart, Mary in the big bedroom with Edna, Doris, Anita, and Priscilla, and George on a couch in the dining room.

George McGlynn, about 1939

Chapter 19

1939

George McGlynn missed only two days of work before he died at the age of sixty-seven, but Mary was more prepared for his loss than she had been for those of her father, her sister, and her two sons. In the fall, George had been having abdominal pain, which he put down to the hernia he had had for years. He began to have a lot of trouble getting around, walking more and more slowly to and from the United Shoe. He ate at the cafeteria rather than coming home for lunch, and finally asked Mary to meet him at the factory gate with the car in the evenings. He carried a paper bag of aspirin in his pocket, and chewed it as if it were candy. Mary told him to take some time off and rest, or at least to see Dr. Murphy at the Shoe, but George said he couldn't. He had been on short hours for most of the time since the Depression had begun. If he took time off, or if Dr. Murphy put him on sick leave, he was pretty sure Management would not let him return, since they were doing their best to get rid of the "old fellows." George was trying hard to make them think he was still a dependable worker, in the pink of health.

Finally, on January eighth, George couldn't get out of bed, and Mary called Dr. Murphy, who came right away, and after a quick examination, called an ambulance to rush him to Beverly Hospital. The children gathered immediately when they were notified. Edna, now teaching at Salem State College, was living with the family, along with the younger children, Anita, Priscilla, and Walter, who were still in school. Andrew came from New York, George from Springfield, Massachusetts and Doris from Kansas City, Missouri. It was a comfort to George, whose family was everything to him, that all of his living children were in his hospital room with him when the last rites were administered. The next day, George died

Having the children at her side helped Mary to get through the days of the funeral and burial. As time passed, she still missed George terribly. She knew she had lost a great deal in his love for her and the children and in his unwavering stability. But she was not prostrated with grief as she had been with the boys. She knew now that her solace was in prayer and religious devotion, and she put all of the time and energy she could spare from her household duties into it. For years now, since the younger children had started school at St. Mary's, she had made a habit of going to daily Mass after driving them to school in the morning. She had become Secretary of the Guild, and managed many of their fund-raising activities as well as taking her turn at cleaning the sanctuary and washing and ironing the altar linens and the albs and surplices for the priests and altar boys.

After George died, Mary made the decision to join the Third Order of St. Francis, coming as close to becoming a nun as was possible in her circumstances. Her cousin and best friend, Delia Gill, was already a member, and she helped Mary to negotiate the process. The local Fraternity she would be joining was in Boston, but she had to get a letter from her parish to certify her spiritual fitness to join. Father Leahy, with whom she had worked for years in Guild activities, was very happy to write it. For the three months of her postulancy, Mary attended both the monthly meetings of the Fraternity and the monthly instructional sessions which informed the postulants about St. Francis and about the Rule of the Order.

The Order stressed the Franciscan virtue of simplicity, which included plainness in dress, abstention from dances and public spectacles, and moderation in food and drink. Members were required to perform particular devotions—daily Mass when possible, monthly Confession and Communion, and daily recitation of either the Little Office of the Blessed Virgin Mary or twelve repetitions of several prayers. They also strove to set a good example of piety in their families, to reconcile discord, and to curb the reading of books "from which destruction comes to virtue" as well as "foul speech" and "scurrilous jokes." The members of the Fraternity visited other members who were sick and recited the Rosary together at their funerals.

Since Mary was doing most of the things the Order prescribed already, she did not find the discipline at all difficult. She enjoyed the Little Office of the Blessed Virgin, which extended the devotion to the Blessed Virgin she had carried on since her teenage years. She was excited on the day that her novitiate began, with the reception of the Third Order habit, a large brown scapular to be worn around her neck and a small knotted cord like those of the nuns to be tied around her waist, both of which were to be worn under her clothing and taken off when she undressed. On this day, she also chose her religious name, Clare, in honor of St. Clare of Assisi. Her novitiate consisted of a full year, during which the novices attended instructional meetings and tested their ability to follow the Rule. Mary followed both the letter and the spirit of the Rule, as fully as she could, insisting that her children respect its standards for decency and purity.

At this time, there were six of her children living in the house on McKay Street. Chances for employment during the Depression were slim, but they had been able to draw on the cash settlement the family had been awarded after Arthur's death to continue their education beyond high school. After teaching for a few years in the normal school at Keene, New Hampshire, Edna had gotten the job at Salem Teachers College and moved back to Beverly, helping to support the household while George was on short hours during the terrible decade of the thirties. Young George had received his degree from Boston University and moved to Springfield, but Andrew, who had recently earned his MBA and gotten a job as an accountant, was now living at home and contributing to the household. Doris was at home in the summers while teaching at St. Teresa's College in Kansas City. Anita was in nurses' training, and Priscilla and Walter were still in high school. Now that she was getting older and the girls were grown, Mary was able to parcel out most of the housekeeping duties to them, which gave her more time to devote to the Guild and the Third Order.

When Edna was a child, Mary had taken pleasure in sewing her daughter's clothes as she always had her own. She had been proud in 1913 when she'd sent her to school in a red plaid dress trimmed with a lace collar and little bows of red ribbon, and Edna reported that the second grade teacher had taken her by the hand to the third grade teacher, and said, "do you want to see a real, live doll?" Mary made beautiful clothes for Edna and for all the babies until Josie's death in 1917, which had brought such a great shadow into their lives.

Among other things, her sister's death made Mary think differently about clothing and sewing. Josie had never been very interested in her clothes until she started working at Filene's, and she had to dress stylishly. Because she was also trying to look younger than she was at that time, Josie paid a lot of attention to her appearance and became quite attractive. Mary was convinced that Josie's newfound attractiveness to men was what had led to her downfall. Determined that her daughters would not go down that path, she warned them often about the dangers of vanity, and talked to them about the importance of a woman's modesty. After 1917, the dresses she made for Edna, and for Doris, Anita, and Priscilla as they grew older, were simple, plain, and modest. If she saw one of her daughters primping, or studying herself in the mirror, she voiced her disapproval. She insisted that they wear their hair simply, and of course they were not allowed to use cosmetics. The girls grew up believing that their minds were something to be proud of, but their bodies should be ignored as much as possible.

In 1939, her senior year, Priscilla was an officer in the St. Mary's High School Sodality. They began to plan the group's annual Spring Formal, which was going to be held at the United Shoe Country Club, just up McKay Street from their house. At seventeen, Priscilla was not allowed to date boys or to go to dances, and Mary told her she couldn't go to this one.

"But I have to go. I'm an officer," she said.

"You can help to plan the dance, but you can't go."

"But why not, Mama? There's nothing wrong with dancing. Don't you trust my morals?"

"It's not *your* morals I don't trust. You're too young to be out with men by yourself."

Try as she might, Priscilla could not budge her mother on this. It was one of the times she missed her father. He would probably have seen how unreasonable her mother was being and gotten her to agree to let her go. But her mother had gotten even more prudish and closed-minded since his death. She went to Edna for advice, but she wasn't much help.

"She's just not going to let you go while you're still in high school."

"But didn't you go to your high school prom? And you were younger than I am."

Edna thought a minute, and then laughed. "That's true, I did go. But she insisted that Georgie had to go with me. So there I was at the senior prom with my fifteen-year-old brother who did nothing but sulk because it was the last place in the world he wanted to be."

"Can't you do anything? Maybe you could talk her into it."

"I'll try. But I doubt it."

Edna was right. Mary's newfound devotion to the Rule of the Third Order only made her more determined that her daughters would avoid any occasion that would place their moral purity in danger. Disappointed and embarrassed in front of the other girls, Priscilla ignored her mother to a point that just skirted disrespect for the next few weeks as they planned the dance. About a week before the dance, she came down with a bad cold. As she lay on the dining room couch feeling miserable, her mother started hovering over her, asking if she wanted a cup of tea or a blanket. "Oh, just leave me alone for once, would you," she burst out. "I can't stand you!"

Mary was shocked. Her quiet youngest daughter had never spoken like this to her before. There was no way to respond. She just turned and left the room, and tried to take solace in reading the Little Office. When Edna got home, she sat down at the kitchen table and told her what had happened, finally breaking down in tears. Priscilla, still in the dining room, heard part of the conversation, Edna telling her mother that she was just upset and disappointed and sick, and wasn't thinking what she was saying. Priscilla said nothing about it, and neither did Mary.

On the night of the dance, Priscilla, depressed and still not completely over her cold, went up to her room right after supper. At about nine o'clock, she heard the front door close, and then her mother's step on the stairs. She pulled up the covers and turned her face away from the door, and, as she expected, her mother came and stood at the door of the girls' bedroom, looking at her for a few moments, then she went down the hall to the little room where she now slept.

Mary had walked up the street to the Country Club hall. She had been surprised at what she saw. Priscilla's classmates, in elegant dresses, came and went, some on the arms of young men wearing their Sunday best. As she walked by, she saw in the big, well-lighted and fancifully decorated rooms that the dance was well-supplied with chaperones, and the young people looked elegant dancing. She was taken back to her own youth, and the Sodality dances that she and Josie had gone to, escorted by their brother Tom, or another friend of the family. It was innocent fun, and they had loved it.

One day when she was talking to Father Leahy about Guild business, she asked him if he thought it was proper for her daughter Priscilla to go the senior prom.

"Well, why not? She's a senior. How old is she, seventeen? That's old enough to go out to dances."

When it came time for the senior prom, Mary told Priscilla she could go. Priscilla was excited, but of course she had nothing suitable to wear, and buying a dress was out of the question. She was talking to her friend Junie about making a dress when Junie said there was no need to do that. “You can wear my dress from last year’s dance at Beverly High. There won’t be many people at the Catholic dance who were there.”

Priscilla was thrilled. Junie had such nice clothes. When she brought the dress home, Mary and Edna were sitting in the kitchen. “You’ll look very pretty in that,” said Edna.

Priscilla beamed. “Junie’s going to help me do my hair, too.”

Two days later, Priscilla came home from school to find her mother cutting some material on the dining-room table. It was black velvet for an evening cape. “It might get chilly walking home,” she said.

Priscilla McGlynn in 1939

Chapter 20

1959

After World War II, Priscilla married Dr. Murphy's son Phil, and they bought the McKay Street house from Mary. Edna bought a three-decker house on Prospect Street, and Mary lived on the second floor with Edna, who was still teaching at what was now Salem State College, Doris, who had returned home and was working for an insurance company in Boston, and Anita, who was nursing at Beverly Hospital. None of them ever married.

After serving in the Army, Andrew earned his CPA, married Geri Linehan from Beverly Farms, and moved to California, where they adopted two sons. Back from the Navy, Walter married Ginny Davis, whom he'd met in art school, and started working as a commercial artist. They lived on the third floor of the Prospect Street house until they bought a house in the Beverly Cove, where they eventually raised seven daughters and a son. George lived in Springfield, where he and his wife Pearl were active in the Socialist Labor Party, both running for statewide office. Their relationship with the family was strained, but they came to Beverly on holidays and avoided talking politics or religion.

In 1957, Phil Murphy's job demanded that he and Priscilla move their five children to Indiana. They made annual trips back to Beverly in the summers, but in April, 1959, a new daughter was born, and Edna, Doris, and Anita decided to take the three-day car trip that summer and bring their mother to visit Indiana instead. Mary was now blinded by glaucoma and not able to get around very well. While she still did what housework she could, her day revolved around her religious devotions. She could no longer drive, of course, and she wasn't able to attend daily Mass, but in the late mornings, she always knelt in the kitchen and said the rosary along with Cardinal Cushing on the radio, although she had to race through the responses to keep up with him. In any spare moment, she generally sat with her rosary beads in her hands and her lips moving in silent prayer.

At her daughter's house in Indiana, Mary enjoyed sitting in the shade on the front porch and saying the rosary. As a grandchild came up to her, she would put her hands on the little head, and, depending on the length of the hair, ask "Which little girl is this?" or "Which little boy is this?" One afternoon, her nine-year-old granddaughter Brenda was coming out the back door when Ronnie from next door came running up. "Gamma's on the porch,"' he said. "Get her to tell us some stories." They ran around to the front and Brenda went through the recognition ritual. "Tell us about the olden days when you were a little girl," she said.

Mary leaned back in her chair and closed her eyes. "Well, back in those days, there weren't any cars, and you had to walk to most of the places you wanted to go. One Sunday afternoon," she started, "my sister Josie and I decided to take a long walk along the river to visit our Aunt Mag in Arlington." Not only her grandchildren, but many of the kids in the neighborhood, all from somewhere else and cut off from extended family in this brand new subdivision, drifted over to the porch and sat on the floor or the steps, whiling away the hot afternoon as they listened to her stories from a time they could hardly imagine.

Afterword

This book began with Josie's ring, a Victorian piece, three unpolished turquoise stones surrounded by tiny seed pearls in a fussy rose gold setting. Inside the slim band, in script that can be read only with a magnifying glass, are the initials JVT, for Josie Veronica Terrett, and a date, "Nov. 27 1901." I was glad to be given this material connection to my great-aunt, a figure who had always been enveloped in mystery for me, and wondered about the date, not her birthday, and the occasion for the ring. She was twenty-one in 1901. A love affair or broken engagement?

When we were small children, my grandmother would tell us stories about her childhood that often included Josie, but as I grew older, any questions about Josie's life as an adult always brought evasions. "She never married and died young." "She worked at Filene's, and one day she collapsed in the store and died." That was about it. Even my Aunt Edna McGlynn, a historian by profession and keenly interested in her family's story, had little to add. She had been nine years old when Josie died in 1917, and remembered her as a kind and generous aunt, but professed to know little else. When Edna wrote a pamphlet about the family for her nieces and nephews in the 1980s, she repeated the story that Josie had worked at Filene's and died after collapsing in a Boston department store.

My active quest to find out more about Josie started with an offhand comment by my mother, Priscilla McGlynn Murphy, then in her nineties. We were talking about the house in Beverly, Massachusetts where we had both spent our early childhoods, and I asked why her parents had moved from

Summer Street, on one side of the gigantic United Shoe Machinery complex, to McKay Street, on the other, which was so much further from the downtown, the train station, and the church. "I think they wanted to move because of the scandal when Josie died," she said. "It was all over the Boston papers." News to me. I searched the Boston *Globe* and found the story that appears in Chapter 13. This story, with its details, humanized Josie for me, but it also raised more profound questions about who she was and the life that she lived. As I dug deeper, I uncovered the events in Josie's life that form the basis for the story I finally wrote.

My initial motive for writing was to give voice to Josie's life. It had been sealed by silence, and I wanted to open it up. This led me to the rest of her family. Edna had recorded the family lore, and what facts she knew, about Josie's stepmother and father, who were my great-grandparents, and her half-sister, my grandmother. But Edna recorded almost nothing about Josie's brother Tom, except that after serving in the Navy during the Spanish-American and Philippine-American Wars, he had married and moved from Massachusetts to California. The political and labor activism that had been central to my great-grandfather Richard's life was also a blank. My search for facts yielded two fascinating characters whom I've tried to understand by imagining their lives.

This book is a combination of fact and fiction. With the exception of a couple of characters that Henry James would call "ficelles," Tim Malloy and Manny Almeida, and two characters who had to be invented, Jimmy Boyle and Terry Burns, everyone who acts a significant part in this narrative was a real person, although I had to supply Leonard Brown with a first name. Public events such as births, marriages, deaths, employment, residences, etc., as well as the names and whereabouts of Tom's various ships in the Navy, the events of the Woburn tannery strike, and the description of life in the House of the Good Shepherd, are a matter of public record. The newspaper stories, including Tom's and Richard's letters to the editor, are all real. David Moreland's speech about the Knights of Labor and Sister Mary of St. Genevieve's description of the House of the Good Shepherd are based on contemporary newspaper accounts. Private events are sometimes drawn from family lore but mostly invented. Likewise, characterizations are informed by memory, family lore and other sources, but they are to a large degree a matter of imagined construction. The conversations and personal letters are all imagined, as are the characters' thoughts, but I have tried to include quotations from various people that have survived in the collective family memory. This is particularly true of Maggie Qualter Terrett, who had a distinctive way with words.

Acknowledgements

In the course of writing this book, I have accumulated a great many debts that I most happily acknowledge. The book would not exist if my friend and colleague of twenty-five years, Gina Barreca, had not read the first twenty pages I wrote in 2012 and made me believe there was a book to be written. The generosity with which she has shared her precious time and her more precious commentary on the work as it took shape has been both extraordinary and characteristic. Throughout the three years I was writing, my mother, Priscilla McGlynn Murphy, shared hours of family lore with me, suggested stories to pursue, and, like her sister Edna, is present in the whole narrative. My cousin, Jean McGlynn Dabbs, has not only contributed in very material ways with documents, pictures, research, and suggestions, but has kept me going by sharing my enthusiasm for the project. I am grateful to the family members who have read the manuscript at various stages and provided valuable suggestions, material, information, and help: John McGlynn, Patricia Murphy, Richard Murphy, Bill Murphy, Claire Murphy, Beverly McGlynn Hobbs, and Jennifer Douglas. Kate Monteiro and Mary Burke supplied key information at crucial times. The staffs of the University of Connecticut Libraries and the Woburn Public Library have helped to make research a joy, and I would be nowhere without Ancestry.com.

Finally, I am most indebted to my husband, George Monteiro, whose enthusiastic support and material help was with me every step of the way on this project, as it always is.

Further Reading

There are a great many books, as well as articles in periodicals and newspapers, that figure in the background of this story. This is a list of some of the books I found particularly useful or interesting for readers who would like to learn more about various topics that the story touches. There are many excellent books on the Great Hunger, but Cecil Woodham-Smith's *The Great Hunger: Ireland: 1845–1849* is still the authoritative work. Some powerful fictional accounts are Anthony Trollope, *Castle Richmond*, William Carleton, *The Black Prophet*, Michael Grant, *In the Time of Famine*, Harolyn Enis, *When Ireland Fell Silent,* and Joseph O'Connor, *Star of the Sea.* Maria Edgeworth's *The Absentee* is a revealing fictional treatment of life among the Irish landlords.

On Irish maids and their lives, Margaret Lynch-Brennan, *The Irish Bridget: Irish Immigrant Women in Domestic Service in America, 1840–1930* sheds a good deal of light. On the Knights of Labor, *Knights of Labor Illustrated, "Adelphon Kruptos," The Full, Illustrated Ritual* gives the details of their principles and activities, and Leon Fink, *Workingmen's Democracy: The Knights of Labor and American Politics* is a good historical account.

On the Spanish-American War, Brad K. Berner, *The Spanish-American War: A Documentary History with Commentaries* provides vivid historical accounts and Russell Doubleday's *A Gunner Aboard the "Yankee," From the Diary of Number Five of the After Port Gun* is a fascinating first-hand account of the life aboard a naval vessel during the war.

On the department store, George E. Berkley, *The Filenes* tells the interesting story of the Filene family's store and their influential ideas. Two absorbing novels about the life of department store workers are Émile Zola, *The Ladies' Paradise* and C. N. and A. M. Williamson, *Winnie Childs the Shop Girl.* Sinclair Lewis's novel, *The Job,* about young women office workers in the early twentieth century, should be better known.

About the Author

Brenda Murphy lives with her husband George Monteiro in Windham, Connecticut. She is the author of twenty books, centered mainly on American drama and theater, and taught for more than thirty years at The University of Connecticut and St. Lawrence University.

www.ingramcontent.com/pod-product-compliance
Lightning Source LLC
LaVergne TN
LVHW091107080826
845145LV00008B/1840